WILLIAM LIGHTFOOT

JON D. ANTHONY

WILLIAM LIGHTFOOT
Copyright © 2017 by JFI and Jon D. Anthony

For information contact:
JFI Publications
www.LightfootBook.com

Book and Cover design by Farhat

ISBN: 978-0692884508

First Edition: May 2017

10 9 8 7 6 5 4 3 2 1

For Stephanie

ONE

"The Great Lakes"

Neither the boiling hot surface of primordial ooze, nor the earthquakes that tear the landmasses apart, bear any clue that this could be Earth. Long before cellular organisms begin exhaling oxygen to form an atmosphere and long before the birth of oceanic soups of life, there is only this angry stew of geology. Stormy winds of carbon dioxide and ash dispatch from the west and whip a migration of tumbling rocks across the surface. The little boulders roll effortlessly, their rough edges long worn down from years of travel over each other. Across the horizon, blisters of spasmodic lava and soot explode into the sky. Ejected boulders return to the surface as ballistic cluster bombs, further sculpting the terrain and forming red-hot lakes of molten rock, just as it has for thousands of years. But today, this violent monotony is broken by something unusual. For in the sky, behind a thick screen of greyish particulate, a white-hot light quickly

1

expands in size and brilliance. What little atmosphere exists around the infant planet becomes seared in a jet stream behind this comet of ice, gas and heavy metals from somewhere in time. With the force of a thousand nuclear bombs, this raging space traveler explodes into the Earth's surface, scattering ejecta and debris over five hundred square miles and digging a series of craters into the area that will someday be known as the Great Lakes of North America.

A dim gloom follows, sparsely lit by the occasional re-entry of flaming debris. The air begins to thicken with smoldering grit and ash, blocking all sunlight from reaching the surface. Total darkness quickly spreads across the entire continent, and will remain that way for many years to come.

TWO

"Two billion years later"

The old horse stops at the edge of the ridge, just as she has for years. She needn't a command from her rider to know that this outlook was the destination they climbed the mountain to reach. This was a ritual. The pony plants her hooves at the cliff's edge into well-worn groves, waiting for her like a pair of favorite slippers. The mare snorts two warm jets of steam into the freezing air, signaling their arrival. If she could speak to the rider on her back, she wouldn't bother. They are too close, too familiar with what this spot meant to each other. The old friends watch as the coots peck at the shoreline below while Canvasback ducks and Widgeons paddle through the reeds of the wild rice that extend the entire length of the water's edge. The old man turns to the call of a single loon who pipes a timeless note across the water. A sound that as a child he was certain was the voice of a shy lake that would only sing when humans weren't looking.

Not much has changed, Papa Leo considers, since he began making this morning ramble up the mountain so many winters ago. The old man adjusts, pressing into his stirrups and straightening his back, recalling those early years, when he sat so firm in the saddle. He expands his chest while memories of the past fills his spirit like the chilly air entering his lungs.

The mare seems to follow his gaze, as the old man looks further down, past the shoreline. This is where the majesty of the raw land stops cold. Porch lights are beginning to flicker off across the few rundown houses scattered along the shore, as the sun's rays begin to light the little village from across the lake. He sits perfectly still, tracking the long shadow's movement across the ground while the sun pulls above the horizon's edge. Papa Leo cherishes this time of day. Noon was his least favorite time, because the shadows were short and nipped at his heels. Papa Leo sits quietly, like a conductor cuing a sunrise orchestra from a well-worn page of sheet music.

Right on time, that old red hound begins to chase the same roosters to their pulpits, just as it did the day before, and the day before that. Belligerent ravens ride the morning thermals and challenge the slow moving blades of the large wind generator spinning above the tree line. Not much else is moving though. Most of the humans were still sleeping off the warming spirits that prepared them for another cold night.

Papa Leo expels all the air from his lungs as he eyes the canker of modern reservation life. That damn casino, a pathetic attempt at enterprise that drew few outsiders, and fooled most of the younger tribe members into believing they were independent. Papa Leo knew what independence meant. After all, he was old enough to remember losing it.

❖   ❖   ❖

A thousand miles to the east, another community is beginning its day. Bright down jackets and printed sweatshirts emerge from the low fog, trapped between towering buildings and wet asphalt. This too was a morning ritual, gradually populated with the faces of young students and eccentric intellectuals as they make their way to the same watering holes they've frequented all winter long. William Lightfoot stands out among the foot traffic, looking more suited to nature's elements in his oiled cloth jacket and long black hair, than to the hardscaping that surrounds him. Or is he standing out as the only one not fixated on a mobile device as he walks?

He arrives at Café Luna in Central Square, a favorite morning spot of students and faculty of the Massachusetts Institute of Technology.

5

The front door swings outward just as he reaches for the knob. He uses his boot to hold it open further, as two coeds exit, their annoyed babble silenced when the icy air slaps their precious faces.

"Oh-my-gawwd. It's like living on Neptune," the lead girl cries out. They pull their overcoats up and over their noses like children hiding under the covers, then trod into the harsh wind. Lightfoot shivers in amazement as he watches them babble their way into the fog. He enters the café.

"Over here!" Tyler shouts from one of the small tables in the back. Lightfoot peels off his jacket and squeezes past the crowded line at the coffee counter to find Tyler Penrose, camped out and surrounded by glowing mobile devices and sections of newspaper.

"Sorry, I missed the bus," Lightfoot says, while pulling up a chair. He motions to a server at the counter who returns a nod and heads his way.

"No problem. Just got here myself. And I took the bus," Tyler says while scanning the headlines of a newspaper, iPhone and laptop simultaneously. "Check it out, the 'live breaking news' is already printed in this morning's paper. What's that tell you about news cycles?"

A young crimson-haired woman skids to a stop before the table, and sets Lightfoot's usual coffee down in front of him.

"Morning William," she says while pretending it's no big deal to lay eyes on him.

"Thanks Kate," he says with that adorable grin she tries not to focus on for too long. She busily pivots back toward the counter, before her smile becomes too obvious.

"Of course," Kate states, tossing the matter-of-fact reply over her shoulder as she heads back to the front. Tyler mimes 'of course' and bats his eyelashes at Lightfoot who is now reaching in his pocket for a flask. Tyler watches him pour an ounce of brown spirits into his coffee.

"Figure you'd be used to this kind of weather where you come from, being an 'immigrant' and all," Tyler says.

"We were here first," Lightfoot groans.

"Oh, didn't you hear, all brown people are immigrants," Tyler says while returning to his newspaper. Lightfoot doesn't reply, except to grunt into his cup as he savors the first sip of *brew*.

Tyler scoffs at the sight of another sensational morning headline. He folds his newsprint to highlight the article and flips the paper around to present it to Lightfoot, but notices him looking in the direction of Kate at the counter. Tyler starts to read aloud.

"So, check it out. Senator got called out for trying to start 'White History Month,'" he says as he wags his head. "Says he doesn't understand what all the flap's about. What a tool!"

"My grandfather used to say, 'you can't wake a person who's pretending to be asleep'," Lightfoot says, while watching Kate charm the patrons at the bar.

"Your grandpa, he's like a chief or something, right?" Tyler asks. Lightfoot glances over the rim of his cup. "No really, I think that's so cool," Tyler says. "Hell, my grandfather was a pimp. Not that I'm ashamed of that, but you... You come from nobility."

"If you say so," Lightfoot mumbles into his mug. Tyler checks his watch.

"Shit!" he yelps, grabbing his coat and gathering his debris. "It's after eight." Both men empty their mugs with a gulp, and rise to head out. Lightfoot looks over to the counter, catching Kate's glance just as her attention is called back to another demanding patron. Tyler snickers as he spies Lightfoot slip a ten-dollar bill under his saucer.

❖ ❖ ❖

The lecture hall is packed with first term students awaiting their Professor's arrival. Lightfoot enters the arena while carrying a red plastic bucket. He impatiently grins when he notices all heads bowed and buried in their mobile phones. Professor Lightfoot stands before the class with the bucket at his side, considering the room of *busy* millennials. He releases the bucket from his grip, allowing it to fall to the polished concrete floor with a hollow thud.

The students lift their heads to give the impression of acknowledgement, but their eyes slowly struggle to disengage from the devices in their hands. Eventually the last punctuations and send buttons are keyed and the class turns its full attention to the head of the room. Lightfoot walks to the front wall and pulls down a sliding chalkboard.

"My name is Professor William Lightfoot," he announces while following along with the chalk. "Welcome," he says, turning to the room and dusting the chalk from his hands. "This is a two-year course and is presented from the point of view that you all are going to be physicists. Of course, this may not be the case for some of you but this is what every professor of every subject at MIT must assume about the courses they teach." He grabs the red bucket and paces the front row from one end to the other. "And if you are going to be a physicist, you have a lot of work to do." Lightfoot approaches a tall lanky student at one end of the front row, and drops the bucket in his lap.

The kid quickly ditches the phone in his hand just in time to receive the pail. "First, we need to make something clear," Lightfoot asserts. "And for most of you I'm afraid – painfully clear."

Lanky boy is frozen, staring over the edge of the large pail that eclipses half his face. He looks inside.

"In this bucket you will find an envelope," Lightfoot says, while heading back to the front of the class. "Take one out, and pass it to the left until you all have one." Lanky Boy looks at the bucket for a moment like he's never seen one before. "C'mon," the professor prompts. Soon the bucket is making its way down the front row.

"In each envelope, you will find a pad of paper and a pencil. These may be alien objects to you. Remove them now, then use the pencil to write your name on the front of the envelope." He follows the bucket as it travels along. "Once your name is clearly marked, I want you to turn your phone off, place it in the envelope and seal it." A rather expressive girl sitting a couple rows back raises her hand. Lightfoot smiles knowingly. "You're going to tell me that you use the phone to record the lecture and to photograph the chalkboard, correct?"

"Uh... yeah," she admits.

"Exactly," states the professor. "Not in my class. Many of you have had a device in your hand since you were four years old, some even earlier. Most of you are not able to remember anything unless you play back what you've recorded, two or three times. A lot of you consider this to be 'studying'. However, in this class you will use a pencil to record your notes on something we call paper."

The young faces, illuminated by the morbid blue haze of a mobile screen, begin switching to normal skin tones, as the students shut down their devices.

"I am here to help you learn, but those devices in your hand are not. Nor are they helping you to form relationships or to interact with others who are becoming physicists, but that's beyond the scope of this subject," he explains. Lightfoot notices the bucket has nearly made it to the back row. "Now, pass the bucket back down the way it came and drop your envelope with your phone back into it. And while that's happening, I'd like to tell you a story." Lightfoot takes his place at the podium while the red bucket makes the return trip to the front. "We have a need to understand nearly two hundred years of the most rapidly developing field of knowledge," he says. "No way you're going to learn it all in four years, if you make it that far." The red bucket is about to complete its round trip, arriving back at Lanky Boy in the front row. Lightfoot abandons the podium and meets it there.

"Let me start by outlining what this course entails. So why can't we teach physics simply by giving the basic laws and then showing how this all works in all situations?" he asks, looking across the gallery to emphasize that this was not a rhetorical question. "Anyone?" Eagerly, the same girl from the mid row raises her hand. "Yes!" he says pointing at her with the flair of a conductor's wand.

"Like... that's how it's done in mathematics. We have axioms then we like, make deductions that prove the axioms," she states proudly.

"Ah, looks *like* we have a spark in this pile of firewood," Lightfoot says as he retrieves the bucket from Lanky Boy and walks back to the center of the stage. "You're right about math. So why can't we do this in physics?" He looks around the room again, but the students simply stare back. "By the way," Lightfoot notes, "you can start using your wooden recording device and paper now." *Oh right*, they realize and begin taking notes.

Lightfoot watches the class record their thoughts, as he quietly holds the bucket at his side. "Now, anyone know why we don't line the laws of physics up and start the process of proving them?" he asks of a dumbfounded crowd. "Okay, for two reasons," he continues. "First, we don't know all the basic laws of physics yet. Our ignorance of the physical world exceeds our understanding of it. Second, to correctly state the laws that we do know requires an advanced level of mathematics that frankly, most of you are not familiar with yet. So, we have to begin, piece by piece." Lightfoot firmly plants the bucket on the floor in front of them, for all to see. "You can retrieve those at the end of the lecture," the professor says before spinning back to the board.

"Every piece of the total sum of knowledge can only be an approximation of the complete truth," Lightfoot explains while drawing a puzzle piece on the board, then another adjacent piece, and so on. "As far as we know it," he says. He circles the sum of the pieces with the chalk and next to it he writes the word TRUTH. "The only truth we know for certain is that we don't know the sum of all truth. There are still many things to learn, only to be unlearned, or better... *corrected* over time."

He writes the next word, *EXPERIMENTATION* and turns back to the class. "Experimentation is the process we use to do this! This is the definition of science. Sounds basic I know, but we must understand this truth fully before we can proceed. Physics is NOT a collection of laws, but rather a process of discovery. And my job, and yours for that matter, is learning to work through that process." He drops the chalk back in the trough and turns back to face the class.

Standing still before them, "Getting all this?"

Lightfoot asks, as his eyes scan the room for any sign of life. Taking the cue, pencils begin to dance again.

❖   ❖   ❖

In the Staff Lounge, Tyler is unsuccessfully trying to extract a coffee from the single-cup brewing robot. Falling back on his socially sensitive critique of all things that don't go his way, he holds up the little vacuum-packed canister and snarls at it.

"Oh c'mon! What a scam," he gripes to the machine. "A dollar per hit, and you know it cost five cents to make," Tyler states.

Behind him, a handsome grey-haired academic in her sixties takes the canister from him.

"Let me try," she insists, expertly inserting it without a fuss. "Cream?" she asks, mockingly.

"Yeah, sure," Tyler says, while stepping backwards, in case the damn thing explodes.

To drive the point home, she extends a single finger and looks him in the eye as it makes contact with the bright red button. She smiles smugly as she finishes her magic trick and hands him a perfect cappuccino. Tyler takes the cup and stares at the brew.

"Thanks Lilly," Tyler says before adding, "smart ass!" She walks off, flipping him the finger.

Lightfoot enters the lounge, still toting his red bucket.

"Ah look, fresh cream," Tyler exclaims, motioning to the milking pail. "Figured you'd have moved on to cave paintings by now."

Lightfoot glances under his brow.

"Sorry that was a bit insensitive," Tyler confesses.

"It's all good. How's day one going?"

"Yeah, about that," Tyler launches into commentary. "Out of seventy-six students in the first group, only four of them were born in the U.S. Can you believe that? My Chinese students are rocking it." Tyler burns his mouth on the first swig. "Crap!" he gurgles while letting the scalding coffee dribble back into the cup from his gaping mouth. Lightfoot laughs his way to the coffee machine. Within seconds, he expertly produces a coffee and walks into the lounge.

JON D. ANTHONY

THREE

"The Tremor"

Papa Leo rides along the shoreline and into the village. Just ahead and standing side-by-side, the three old Loon sisters are already passing their usual morning cigar among them.

"Those things will kill you," Papa Leo says with that lack of urgency derived from years of repetition. And just as certain, the old women reply as a single organism, always beginning with the tallest of them, an alpha dame named 'Keezheknoi', the Chippewa word for Burning Fire.

"I'm eighty-four!" Keezheknoi claims, challenging his logic. Second in line and the slighter of the three, is 'Small Duck'.

"You're eighty-four?" Small Duck asks in a way that makes you wonder if she knows how old she is herself.

"She's older than that," the third sister explains in a huff. This is 'Meoquanee', a more down to earth spirit, usually the one to punctuate the end of every thought with a disclaimer or endorsement. She wears red exclusively.

"Who'd lie about being eighty-four?" Keezheknoi asks incredulously.

"Someone who's ninety-four," Meoquanee says, while billowing a cloud of smoke. Keezheknoi grunts and reaches for the stogie. Small Duck in the middle pulls the cigar from the Meoquanee and passes it to the head of the line.

"Do you ladies ever sleep?" Papa Leo asks.

"No," they croak in unison.

Papa Leo gently nudges his mare along toward the shore. He passes a simple house where an adorable child sweeps the porch. She waves cheerfully to the old man and he tips his well-worn hat toward her, when a gust of wind kicks up and blows it from his hand. The gust rips a bingo flyer off the casino wall, blowing it back down the road. Papa Leo turns to see the three old ladies try to catch the flyer, then chase it across the ground like a loose hen.

Papa Leo stops before a mountain of a man in his mid fifties wearing a black round-rimmed hat. He's currently on his knees in the patchy grass and bent at the waist to touch the soil with his palms.

"Harvey Bearheart, what are you up to now my brother?" Papa Leo inquires. For some reason that no one can recall, it's always customary to use his full name when addressing Mr. Bearheart. He's a mechanical genius who with Papa Leo, engineered the inner-workings of the reservation with minimal resources except what they could gather, or order on Amazon.

"Something's amiss," Harvey Bearheart reveals, while still feeling the ground for vibrations. Papa Leo isn't surprised to hear the news.

"Birds and foxes are taking cover," Papa Leo notes. "I suspect you're right brother."

"There's a rumble, you can feel it," Bearheart says, with his hands still flat against the soil. Papa Leo dismounts as the young girl hands him the hat she fetched from the wind.

"Thank you Anna," he says while heading over to kneel next to the big fellow on the ground. He places both palms on the ground and closes his eyes when Mary Bearheart, a lovely young girl in her twenties steps up to them. She wears an MIT sweatshirt and a wool cap over her long ivory black hair. Mary plants her work boots firmly in the soil and folds her arms in a dubious sort of stance.

"You better not let the goats see you like that," she declares. Papa Leo opens a single eye, humored by what they must look like from her viewpoint.

"Morning Mary," Papa Leo says, greeting her as if all is normal.

"Come here, feel this," Harvey Bearheart says. Mary Bearheart steps over and kneels next to her father, then curiously places her palms on the ground as they have.

Back down the road, near the first house, the three old women stand fixated, watching the ritual of the prostrate elders and Mary on their knees. They continue passing the stogie back and forth. Little Duck sucks on the cigar but can't drag a puff.

"You let it go out," she complains, holding out her hand to the lady in red, while never taking her eyes off the grounded trio up the path.

"No, you let it go out," Meoquanee retorts as she hands the lighter over.

Back on the ground, Mary's face changes to concern.

"I feel it," she says, looking up to her father. What is it?" Mary asks. No sooner do those words leave her lips when the ground begins to rumble, slowly at first, then followed by a violent jolt that sends the three of them springing to their feet.

The Loon sisters do the opposite, crumbling at the knees and dropping their arms towards the ground, bracing for a fall. And then it happens – a sustained earthquake, unheard of for these parts. The quake relentlessly shakes the ground beneath them as cinder block houses and simple wooden structures sway and crack violently.

❖   ❖   ❖

Back at Café Luna, Kate walks a lunch order to Lightfoot's table.

"I'm going on break," she says. "Tim will take over for me."

"Where are you going?" he asks.

"Anywhere really. A walk, maybe grab a coffee."

"I hear they have good coffee here," he says while motioning to the empty chair. "Join me?" Kate thinks it over for a microsecond, then quickly nods and pulls off the apron. Lightfoot motions toward Tim at the front counter.

"Another coffee please," he calls to the counter, as Kate settles into her seat.

"You're a Professor aren't you?" she asks, already knowing the answer.

"Yeah, for the time being," he admits, tossing his head from side to side indefinitely.

"For the time being? she asks. What's next then?" Lightfoot offers an indifferent shrug, a gesture that usually indicates when someone is in an unfulfilling job but not concerned enough to elaborate.

"What about you?" he asks.

"What's next? For me? Well, I'm just getting started.

Settling into town now, hoping to start classes in the spring. Sloan Law School," she says with anticipation before focusing the conversation back his way. "So, I've heard about you actually," Kate admits, having actually researched his background and hoping not to sound like a stalker. "You're pretty famous for a physics prof. I read the article about you in the *The Tech*. Native American genius, full scholarship to MIT, very impressive." Kate notices he's looking uncomfortable. "I'm sorry, I don't mean to put you on the spot. It's just that I hope to practice land law and, well... I've studied Tribal Sovereignty and I thought it was cool when I heard your story." Kate is starting to doubt her first impression. "I mean... I hope you don't think I'm being too intrusive?"

"No, not at all. I think it's really cool," Lightfoot says, followed by an awkward silence. "So, um... You want to grab a drink, maybe an early dinner? Tonight maybe?" he asks.

"Yes," Kate says much too quickly.

"Okay great. You heard of Anna's Taqueria?" he says but notices her pause. It figures he'd pick the place she works a second job.

"I, uh... work there on Fridays," she confesses.

"Yeah, that might be awkward, I get that. How about..." while considering an alternative.

"How about *The Automatic* in Kendall Square?" Kate offers, slightly jumping up in her seat at the thought.

"Perfect!" Lightfoot confirms. "I'm done with my last class at four, so I can meet you back here, say between five and six?"

"Sure, let's say six," Kate agrees. "We can walk there from here." She catches herself again fixating on those brown eyes of his and decides to leave the rest until later. "Well, I suppose my break's up soon and I have to make a call so, I should go. See you tonight. I mean you know, I'll be over there," she says, pointing to the counter.

"Tim never did bring your coffee," Lightfoot notes while watching her slip back into her apron.

"Yeah the service sucks here," she snickers or rather *snorts!* Kate abashedly covers her mouth with a weak hand before leaving the table.

On her way to the counter, she passes Tim who is finally delivering the coffee to the table. *There she goes, over thinking things again,* Kate realizes, wondering if she should have just stayed to enjoy the coffee rather than hurry off to avoid appearing too interested. She turns back to catch Lightfoot's eye as Tim sets the coffee down in front of him. They share a wry look when his phone begins to ring.

Lightfoot searches the pockets of his jacket that's draped over the chair, but by the time he fishes it out,

23

the ringing has stopped. He checks the screen to see a missed call from his grandfather and quickly dials the number.

❖ ❖ ❖

The reservation is decimated. Most of the wood structures and brick houses have cracked and tumbled into piles around their foundations. Young boys and their fathers chase down the spooked horses while the smaller children try to round up the goats and foul.

The Loon sisters are chain smoking, grabbing the stogie from each other before anyone can pass it. They examine a fallen blade from the wind generator, which struck the exact spot they last stood before running from its path.

Mary Bearheart helps her dad up, noticing he has a gash on his head from a flying piece of aluminum that lay at his feet. She and her father survey the extensive damage across the village. Lake water still sloshes over the levy road. The entire top half of the wind generator tower has snapped in two and hangs from sparking wires. The casino windows have all blown out and the main road is now split across its center.

Near the shoreline, Papa Leo approaches his spooked horse who broke free from the hitching post which now lies on the ground in pieces. He takes the reins and carefully strokes her neck, trying to calm her when his phone rings, startling them both all over again. He carefully fishes for his phone with one hand while petting the pony's head with the other.

"Billy!" he calls out, relieved to hear his grandson's voice. "We just had an earthquake up here, a big one."

At Café Luna, Kate watches Lightfoot on the phone, who looks distressed from what he's hearing on the other end. He rises to his feet and places his hand over his face while slowly moving to the back of the café. He stops just short of the back wall and turns back, frozen and listening intently.

"How are you, Granddad? Is mom okay?" Lightfoot asks, while catching the concern in Kate's eyes from across the café. But there is no answer, at least not quick enough to dispel his consideration of the worst.

On the reservation, Papa Leo leads his horse back towards the commotion with the phone to his ear and fixated on a gathering near a certain damaged house.

"*Granddad?*" Lightfoot begs into his ear as the old man continues up the road. "*Have you seen mom?*" he asks, swallowing the knot in his throat.

"That's exactly where I'm headed now son," Papa Leo says, arriving near the growing crowd.

Back at the café, Lightfoot begins to pace near the back wall. Kate leaves her post and approaches tentatively. She slows, beginning to hear the dread in his voice.

"You're too quiet Granddad, what's going on there?" he begs, worried about his reluctance to answer.

Papa Leo catches sight of the three old women, now somber, their heads bowed in grief. He ices over when he sees Harvey Bearheart exit the crumbled building, ducking through a shattered doorframe, with a woman draped and motionless in his arms. Papa Leo steps closer as Harvey Bearheart looks up from the woman in his arms, catching sight of the stoic old man who freezes again. Harvey Bearheart shakes his head negatively.

"I'll call you back Billy," Papa Leo says in a tone he hopes will prepare his grandson for the time he can bear to confirm the worst. "I have to go." He hangs up, dropping the horse's reins to the ground and approaches his daughter's lifeless body in Bearheart's arms.

A young boy lifts the leads from the ground and holds the patriarch's horse steady as Papa Leo moves the thick black hair that covers his daughter's face.

Harvey Bearheart plants himself firmly, presenting her body before her father. Papa Leo calmly removes his broad floppy hat, internalizing all signs of emotion within a stone cold stare that packages his grief in a way tears never could. Papa Leo brushes the hair from her sleeping eyes, and kisses her forehead.

Mary covers her mouth, stricken in that way when youth is faced with the raw truth of mortality.

At the café, Kate hasn't taken her eyes off Lightfoot this entire time. He turns, still holding the phone in front of him, looking puzzled and unresolved. He lifts his eyes over the crowd and beyond the front windows, avoiding any possible eye contact. Kate decides to approach.

"Is everything okay?" she asks carefully.

"I don't know yet," he says, still looking off into the distance at nothing in particular. Finally he focuses across the room, to the monitor above the counter. "Can you turn on the news?" he asks.

"Sure, no problem," Kate says, while hurrying toward the counter to grab the remote.

Lightfoot steps under the TV as Kate flips through the channels. Soon, it appears on screen. *'MAJOR EARTHQUAKE HITS GREAT LAKES REGION'.*

❖   ❖   ❖

The Saturday morning flight to Minnesota from Boston arrives early into this small regional airport. Lightfoot gathers his bag from the simple carousel in this terminal the size of a mini-mart. He wheels it to the parking lot out front, as Mary Bearheart pulls up in a white Ford Bronco. She jumps out, and hurries to him. Mary tries to smile through sad eyes when

27

she faces him. Lightfoot can't believe his eyes as he takes in the sight of little Mary Bearheart, having transformed into a woman within the three years he's been gone. She spreads her arms wide and embraces him as her eyes begin to moisten.

"I'm sorry, Billy," she says, at a loss for any further words, at least until something more appropriate can come to her. Lightfoot folds himself into her warm jacket, wrapping his arms completely around her for a while, before placing his hands on each of her shoulders and leans back just far enough to get a good look at her.

"You're all grow'd up," he quips, trying to lighten the tone.

"I'm twenty-four now," Mary declares, her eyes instead telling the story of a much older soul. Lightfoot marvels at the person she's become, standing before him with the confidence and radiant fitness of a wise and earthly spirit.

"C'mon, we need to get you back," she says as she lifts his bag with ease.

"No, no, I got it," Lightfoot protests, trying to grab for the handle.

"Nope," Mary insists, already opening the passenger door for him. "Don't be silly, you've traveled a long way. I've got this."

❖   ❖   ❖

Mary swings the Ford Bronco onto the rural highway with the skill of a truck driver. A fresh layer of light Minnesota snow spirals behind the SUV as they travel northbound to the reservation.

Lightfoot watches the terrain fly past. He focuses on nothing really, if anything it's the blur of motion he fixates on, which seems the perfect metaphor while he considers how quickly life has passed to this point. The streaked lines on the road flow by in soft animation, pulsing endlessly beside him. Mary glances across the cab.

"Your mother was so proud of you Billy," she says quietly. "She was such a happy woman - made everyone laugh." Mary turns back to the road. "I loved her very much."

"She called me the day before, when I was in class," he says while trying to shake that shame one feels from being too busy for a last chance to connect with a departed soul. "I can't stop thinking about that. I was so..." but he stops, at a loss to continue. The blaring silence continues for an eternity except for the throbbing rhythm of the road reverberating in the cab. Mary continues to glance over, starting to get concerned for him but knowing better than to assume anything she could say would help. They travel a mile or two until he can bring himself to speak again.

"Did she suffer?" he asks, fully aware that any thoughtful answer might not convince him otherwise.

"I don't think so," Mary replies assuredly. "She was sleeping when it hit. It all happened quickly," Mary says, looking to check him again. "The damage is devastating, Billy." Lightfoot turns toward his side window, fixing his eyes on the familiar tree line that separates the road from the Red Rock reservation.

❖ ❖ ❖

Mary's Bronco turns off the main highway and travels down the gravel road, under the welded sign of the Red Rock Chippewa tribe. The sun is low in the sky now and the snow flurries have stopped. They pass a Tribal Police vehicle, a white pickup truck filled with broken debris, leaving the reservation. Mary simply lifts a couple fingers from her steering wheel, motioning a greeting to the passing truck. The other driver does the same.

When they pull into the village center, Lightfoot sees that Papa Leo and Harvey Bearheart are already waiting for them in the center of the road. Scattered across the village, at least a hundred members are working together to clear the damage and begin repairs.

Mary's truck stops in front of the small community center, just short of her father and Papa Leo. Lightfoot doesn't wait for the truck to stop completely before jumping out and heading toward his grandfather. Harvey Bearheart opens the door for his daughter. They watch as Papa Leo holds an arm out to Lightfoot, who instead wraps himself around his grandfather. Lightfoot releases his hold and looks into the old man's eyes.

"Can I see her?" he asks.

Papa Leo nods silently and walks him toward the remains of his mother's home, the first of the damaged buildings to be cleared and cleaned in her honor. As they get closer, Lightfoot notices the flowers and tokens that surround the front of the house.

"We waited for the burial, so you could be here when she moves on," his grandfather says.

"When?" Lightfoot asks.

"Tonight," Papa Leo says, motioning to the sunset over the lake. "It'll be dark soon and everything is prepared up the shore."

❖ ❖ ❖

Lightfoot sits alone facing his mother's funeral pyre, now a smoldering of ash and smoke. He can feel the warmth of the morning sun against his back as it rises behind him and over the lake. He's wrapped from the shoulders down in a traditional wool blanket, the fur-lined hood of his winter coat covering much of his face. A light snow has fallen around him, erasing all footprints and any sign of mourners from the night before. He hasn't moved since. Snowflakes hit the charred remains and sizzle like the whispers of delicate sprites. He focuses on the long, crisp shadow he casts across his mother's ashes as it shortens, slowly pulling away from shading her ashes as the sun rises higher in the sky.

Soon, another shaded form appears behind his and joins the penumbra he casts forward. He recognizes the shape of the rider on horseback when another shadow appears, this time of a riderless horse, stopping a few steps back. Lightfoot looks over his shoulder, squinting into the distant fireball, which rim-lights the old man's silhouette.

"She's in a good place now, son," Papa Leo says in a hoarse and compassionate timber, hoping also to find some comfort in the thought. Lightfoot smiles back then turns to watch the last wisps rise from the pyre.

"I know. She just left," he says. He pulls himself to his feet, stretching the blood back into his limbs. "There's never been a quake like this up here."

"We've been having small tremors over the last couple years. Harvey Bearheart thinks it's from the fracking," Papa Leo says. But Lightfoot isn't so sure.

"Fracking screws up the water quality, but it really doesn't cause earthquakes like most people think,"

Lightfoot says. "It doesn't add to the pressure, they're just pumping fluids back into the voids where they removed oil. No, if I were to bet, I'd say it's more from all the wastewater injection they've been doing up here." Lightfoot turns back to the pyre. "It really doesn't matter," he says. "I missed her. I still do."

The young palomino scrapes the soil nervously with his hoof. Lightfoot smiles and approaches the pony, stroking his nose.

"Mount up, Son. I need to show you something," Papa Leo says quietly as he swings the reins, guiding his pony back toward the base of his mountain.

FOUR

"The Elements"

Lightfoot and Papa Leo ride along the top of the ridge. The sunrise has transformed into a full burning sphere, mirrored in a streak across the great lake.

"When I was a child, I thought the sun was a god," Lightfoot says as he turns to feel its warmth on his face. Papa Leo isn't surprised by the concept, just surprised to hear it to be a feeling of the past.

"And now?" his grandfather asks.

"Now, well… it's just a flaming ball of hydrogen," stating the obvious as any professor of physics would tell you. Papa Leo considers and nods upward as if to catch his grandson's attention from across the room.

"I think you had it right the first time," the old man says. Lightfoot laughs at the charming thought, but Papa Leo patiently eyes him as someone who knows better. "Can I ask you a question, Billy?" Papa Leo says.

"Sure, go ahead," Lightfoot replies, as he follows him up the trail.

"You have no problem comprehending that the three pounds of electric meat inside your skull can reason and feel or even talk to itself, right?" Papa Leo asks rhetorically.

"That's one way of looking at it. Sure," Lightfoot says cautiously, having been at the opposite end of his grandfather's reasoning before.

"I think you call that, consciousness," Papa Leo adds.

"Fair enough," Lightfoot replies with a grin, wondering where this is going.

"Yet, you're unwilling to believe that the sun, the center of all life on this planet, cannot be conscious?" Papa Leo asks. "Yet a simple glob of grey meat in your head can." *Whoa*, once again Lightfoot is trounced his grandfather's natural debating skill. With his young spirit cracked wide open, Papa Leo proceeds to drive the final wedge into his reality. "Here we are, able to step away from ourselves and think about what our brain is thinking about," Papa Leo continues. "Doesn't that open the possibility that maybe our minds aren't really centered in that handful of meat in our head? How else could we observe our own thoughts without being more than our own reality?"

"I never thought of it like that before, Granddad," Lightfoot confesses.

"If something as insignificant as our brain can

observe the world around itself..." Papa Leo postulates, "...then why doesn't the Earth it came from or that 'ball of hydrogen' as you call it, deserve the right to feel the same way?" With that, the old man taps his mare's side and gallops to the top of the ridge, leaving his grandson to ponder below. Where does he get this stuff? Lightfoot wonders silently. He gallops to catch up with the old man.

Meeting Papa Leo at the top of the ridge, Lightfoot stops alongside just as his grandfather points into the valley below. To his amazement, the valley basin has split in two, separated by a deep chasm nearly a hundred feet wide. Lightfoot closes his eyes while raising his brow in disbelief. He opens them again as wide as he can to try and focus on the impossible sight below.

"The earthquake did this?" he asks, knowing full well that's exactly what happened. Papa Leo dismounts and ties his mare off to a freshly fallen tree, no doubt toppled as a result of the tremor.

"We need to walk it from here," the old man says, starting into the valley with the ease of a mountain goat. "It gets better!" Papa Leo calls out on his way down the hill. Lightfoot follows his lead, tying off his horse and then making his way down the slope, trying to keep pace with the nearly century old man.

In the base of the valley, the magnitude of the gorge

is hard enough to believe, but is soon upstaged by an even more impossible sight. Over the edge of the huge crack in the earth and along the chasm's walls, millions of shattered orange rocks float just below the edges. Literally floating in mid air! Lightfoot's mind struggles to explain the event with mere physics. *Are those rocks floating in water?* His mind struggles to reason with his lying eyes. *Wait a minute*, he realizes that there aren't any water ripples or reflections to indicate a flooded gorge. Instead, the orange metallic rocks are *really* floating in the air! A slight wind blows into the valley and stirs the levitating rocks within the dark fissure, like a sort of terrestrial asteroid belt, all while they maintain a constant altitude in the vast abyss.

"I don't get it," Lightfoot mutters.

"I'm with you on that," Papa Leo says in a resigned tone. After all, being nearly a hundred years old, there's not much that surprises him any longer. Lightfoot carefully steps to the edge of the crevice. He braces himself between the steep ridge and a slight shelf that lies about a meter below the edge. "Careful," his grandfather warns firmly. Lightfoot reaches out and snatches one of the orange metal shards that waft past him. He stuffs the stone in his pocket and then climbs back out. Papa Leo grabs hold of his arm to steady his climb. Together they closely examine the small metallic shard. Tossing it in his hand, Lightfoot quickly notices that up here, the rock doesn't float. He lets it fall to their feet but when it hits the ground it does so with a thud and stays put, right where it hit. Papa Leo shrugs.

"Okay, that didn't really happen, did it?" Lightfoot says. He picks it up and throws it back into the gorge where it drops a bit lower than the others, but floats right back up to a consistent level with the rest of them. He finds another 'normal' rock on the surface and tosses it into the pit, but unlike the others, it falls straight down, completely out of sight and with no indication it even hit bottom.

"Okay, so it has to do with the rock itself then," Lightfoot concludes. "It's like whatever kind of magnetic field emanates from these things, isn't enough on its own," he reasons aloud. "It needs the others, like some kind of cumulative force."

"Whatever you say," his grandfather says plainly. Papa Leo leans over the edge and considers the floating rocks with a sort of unimpassioned acceptance of the oddity.

"Yeah, but why only here?" Lightfoot asks, before returning to the edge and climbing back into the chasm. "There has to be an easy explanation for this," he says affirmatively. The old man blows a satirical burst of air. Of course his grandson would say that.

Lightfoot braces his arm against the ridge and inserts himself onto the ledge just below the surface. He starts grabbing rocks as they meander by and tosses them up and over the edge.

Papa Leo watches the rocks fly up and over, landing motionless at his feet. He catches one in mid-air and examines it curiously while his grandson continues tossing samples from below.

❖ ❖ ❖

The interior of the community center has become a refuge for the displaced. Mary finishes dropping off blankets and provisions on cots lined up along the long wall. With the last blanket distributed, she stops for a moment to look across the large hall. Her eyes follow the string of bare and flickering light bulbs hung from one end of the room to the other, powered by the throbbing diesel generator which bangs on outside. She then weaves through a band of running children on her way to join the elders who gather around the open fire pit. The kids romp from one end of the center to the other, laughing as they torment their dogs with a laser pointer. The dogs chase the spot across the floor and the children chase the dogs, like an armada blowing into their own sails.

Harvey Bearheart impatiently clocks the crazed

pack across the room while warming his hands over the fire.

"They're just letting off steam," Mary says, noticing that her dad is moments away from shutting the ruckus down.

"Yeah, when the kettle lets off steam, I turn it off," he grumbles.

Mary thinks better of talking him out of it and instead returns to the conversation in progress. Papa Leo and Lightfoot study a sample of the mysterious orange material.

"It's definitely a metal. Not like anything I've seen though," Lightfoot claims. He grabs one of the rocks with a pair of tongs and holds it in the fire, turning it so the flame heats its surface evenly. Everyone watches as the flame bends around the metal without melting or blackening it. He pulls it back out and examines the shard, carefully touching it with his finger. "It's not hot", he says while shooting a puzzled look to the others. He drops the rock into Papa Leo's palm.

"It's cold!" Papa Leo affirms.

"I just don't get it," Lightfoot says. "It's defying gravity when combined in large quantities, but alone..." Just then, the laser dot races across their feet as the pack of dogs barrel into the team, knocking some of the rocks onto the floor. The kids skid to a stop and hold their distance.

"Okay, time's up, hand it over," Harvey Bearheart commands. Mary fails to suppress a laugh, as the leader of the pack, an adorable ten-year-old girl steps over and plops the laser pointer into the big guy's hand.

"Sorry Papa," little Anna Bearheart says contritely. She's a spitfire of a child and tall for her age. Except for the black-framed glasses, she resembles a miniature version of Mary. Lightfoot gets an idea.

"Can I see that?" he asks.

"Oh, don't you start now," Harvey Bearheart groans.

"No, I have an idea." Lightfoot takes the laser and aims it at the wall across the hall. Of course the dogs go on the attack toward the distant spot. Everyone watches curiously, as Lightfoot places the pointer firmly on the top of a beer can while still focused on the distant wall. Even the children come closer to watch curiously as the professor fiddles with the installation in the center of the table. Across the room, the dogs stop and sit motionless, staring at the stationary dot on the wall. Lightfoot places one of the larger copper colored rocks just under the source of the beam. Papa Leo tilts his head to the side, remembering how he'd watch this intensity develop in his grandson as a child.

"What are you doing?" Mary asks.

"Maybe they aren't defying gravity at all. Maybe they're emitting gravity," Lightfoot hypothesizes. As he places the rock close to the source of the beam, *the laser dot shifts down,* on the opposite wall about six inches. The dogs jump to their feet, ready to chase the strange red bug again. But when Lightfoot lowers the rock away from the beam, the laser dot returns to its original spot. He grins widely and checks the others to make sure they're seeing it as well. Lightfoot repeats the experiment, over and over. Each time, as soon as the rock is within a couple millimeters from the business end of the laser pointer, the beam is deflected downward about six inches. The dogs bark excitedly, as the dot dances up and down the far wall.

"I don't get it," Mary says. "Why's it doing that?" Lightfoot looks at them, so deep in thought he actually appears to look through everyone staring at him.

"Gravity bends light," he says. "Safe to say, these rocks are emitting gravity." He reaches for his phone, but in the course of the day, it's gone dead. "Mary, can I use your phone?" he asks. She happily hands it over, before thinking better of it, when he notices the home screen image is of the two of them from a couple years back. Mary would blush if she were that type, but instead she just looks away quickly when he glances over. Harvey Bearheart presses his lips together wittingly, checking Papa Leo and wondering if he's just imagining the ardor between the two. Moving on, Lightfoot keys a query into the online search.

"I've heard about this before," Lightfoot says, while scanning the search results. "Ah right, here it is," he says, stopping to read the results while the others wait patiently. "I didn't believe his story when I first heard it, but seeing it happen, it has to be true."

"What's he talking about?" Anna asks, nudging Mary's arm.

"Shhhh, I'm not sure either," Mary replies, more for Lightfoot's benefit.

"Back in the late eighties, there was this guy – Bob Lazar," Lightfoot explains while continuing to scan the articles. "He was a scientist that apparently worked in a secret program for the U.S. government, at *Area 51*. He said they were reverse-engineering alien flying saucers that they got from an extra-terrestrial race."

"Cooool!" the jaunty young Anna exclaims.

"Oh, here we go," Harvey Bearheart bemoans again.

"I know, I know," Lightfoot empathizes. "But the point is, he claimed the spacecraft used a fuel that was merely a super heavy element, one that doesn't occur naturally on Earth, but if it did, it would fit just perfectly on our periodic table, in the one-fifteen, one-sixteen range. And it was supposed to be stable."

"What's that have to do with this stuff?" Papa Leo asks, still not following the thread of his thinking.

"The idea behind it is that the strong nuclear force within matter behaves a lot like gravity." Lightfoot explains. "When a raw element is so heavy, meaning it is so dense with particles, the cumulative strong nuclear force which some believe is just a form of gravity anyway - that force extends beyond the perimeter of the atom and it then can be accessed and amplified to be used as gravity propulsion." He looks up to find everyone staring at him as if he were painted green. "They discovered what it was, when they used a laser and it bent light, just like this!" he says, mesmerized as he rotates the orange rock, then once again sticks it under the laser source, grinning widely as the beam moves one last time. Everyone, even the kids seem engrossed and bewildered. "That's why the more of it you have together, the combined force causes it to float, like in the gorge," he concludes. Papa Leo is never surprised by his grandson's genius. Lightfoot begins to pace the room, the walking motion seeming to turn the cranks in his head.

"But, how did it get here? I mean if it's not from Earth?" Mary wonders. Little Anna looks up with a spark of obviousness.

"Miss Achambo said the Great Lakes were made by a giant meteor," Anna proudly explains.

"Exactly!" Lightfoot lauds the little Bearheart. "A comet actually, but you're right. Almost two billion years ago. Miss Achambo told us that when I was in school. The comet formed the second largest impact crater on the planet. Not far from here in the Sudbury Basin in Ontario, Canada. Something that big would easily throw ejecta and debris this far away with enormous earthquakes and fissures. The earthquake we just had probably ripped open a huge deposit that's been there all this time."

"And we're sitting on top of it?" Harvey Bearheart realizes in amazement.

"This could possibly be the most valuable resource on the planet if it is what I think," Lightfoot proposes. "Bigger than oil, nuclear fuel, you name it." As sensibility sets in, Lightfoot starts pacing again, while tossing the rock over and over. "We can't tell anyone about this yet."

"You got that right," Harvey Bearheart nods effusively. "The feds will just screw us out of it like they did the oil rights," he laments. "Hell, look at what we went through just to get the casino!"

"I'd take grizzly claws over the Indian Commerce Clause any day," Papa Leo jokes.

"Very clever," Harvey Bearheart says. Papa Leo takes a bow.

"We need time to research this properly and make a plan," Lightfoot asserts, while punctuating his thought with a toss of the rock in the air and then snatching it abruptly.

"This means you're staying for a while?" Papa Leo asks, raising a brow to confirm.

"Leave now?" Lightfoot says. "And miss all this fun?"

Mary beams for a fraction of a second, then gathers her expression before anyone notices, except Anna of course, who picks up on everything her big sister does.

❖ ❖ ❖

Empty paper cups line up along Café Luna's counter like little soldiers waiting for inspection. The familiar sound of morning commuters, and the occasional rush of chilled air filter in each time the front door opens with a clang of the hanging doorbell.

Kate expertly pilots the espresso machine with one hand while trashing the spent grounds onto a hole with the other. She cringes every time the door clobbers the bell. It's an unusually charged morning and the line is stacking up much longer than her fuse. Again with that annoying bell, constantly reminding her of how behind she is. Then it happens, that one last clang tips her scale and she spins away from the coffee machine and abandons her post. Kate rounds the corner, stomps to the door and grabs the bell clean off its hook without losing a step. The customers clear a path as she passes. She tosses the bell into a basket of individually wrapped biscotti and returns to the screaming gurgle of steaming milk.

"I'd stay out of her way this morning," says a familiar customer, maybe just a bit too loud to escape her wrath.

"You're already in my way, Todd" Kate snaps, "and your chai latte with a dash of foam and two pumps of caramel syrup is busting my balls right now!" Kate wipes the rim then snaps a styrene cap on the concoction, plopping it down on the counter so hard it spurts out the suck-hole. Todd gently takes the cup and leaves the area, quietly backing away from the counter as if discovering a bear in the woods. The café phone blares.

"Can you get that?" Kate calls over her shoulder. A very popular barista wearing a slinky tank-top, leans over the counter to the joy of girls and boys alike. She cautiously extracts the phone from Kate's vicinity.

"Café Luna - let's hope you don't have an order to go - can I help you?" Barista says. Kate produces another perfect cup and delivers it to the waiting shelf.

"Sanji, decaf-double-cap, bone dry!" Another plop, another geyser of foam. Kate can't help but overhear the junior barista on the phone.

"I'm sorry the manager's helping us make coffees right now," she says. "We're short handed this morning, can I take a message?"

"Who is it?" Kate calls over the jet stream.

"One second," the junior barista pauses, holding

the receiver to her ample chest. "Someone called Lightfoot?" Suddenly Kate's Monday morning shitstorm just got a power wash.

"Cover me!" she says, grabbing the handset and flying to the back of the room. "William Lightfoot? How are you?" she asks while subconsciously fixing her hair and tamping her tone into a gentle morning breeze. The sudden transformation plays inanely among the staff and regulars. "How's your, tribe? Your family, I mean." She smacks her forehead in an attempt to knock aside the awkwardness. "Oh hell, I'm just glad to hear from you," she says. "How are you?"

❖   ❖   ❖

Lightfoot sits high in the saddle, atop the palomino and overlooking the village below. His long black hair is no longer tied back, hanging freely now and whipping his face from the breeze rising up the cliff. Papa Leo rides up to meet him.

"The damage is bad Kate," Lightfoot says, turning to see his grandfather join him at the precipice. "I'm going to be here a while." Papa Leo turns to the sunrise, pretending not to listen. "No, she didn't make it," Lightfoot continues. He drops his head slightly lower as he hears those words leave his lips. "We had her ceremony the night I arrived." Papa Leo looks back to see his head slung low, nearly whispering into the phone. "Thank you," he replies before summoning himself to move the conversation forward. "Look, I was wondering if you could help me with something," he asks, all the while questioning his motives for enlisting her help.

Kate slaps a hand over her exposed ear, trying to filter out the ambient static of the café.

"Sure one second, let me get to where I can hear." She pushes through the herd and out onto the sidewalk. It's not much quieter outside, except this is a less familiar dissonance, and thus much less demanding of her attention. "Okay, go ahead," Kate continues, planting her feet at the curb.

Lightfoot dismounts and leads his horse back from the ridge. He finds a rock to lean against while overlooking the village below.

"You mentioned you've got some experience in tribal law," he says, while sharing a quick glance with his granddad in the saddle. "I think we may have a resource issue, one that will need some very sharp teeth, legally speaking." The palomino nudges him as he talks. Papa Leo watches him stroke the palomino's nose as he listens, seemingly pleased with the response on the other end. "Good, that's great! It has to do with mineral rights, sovereignty, and the Bureau of Indian Affairs. Historically, three very opposing forces."

❖ ❖ ❖

In the village below, Mary catches sight of Lightfoot and Papa Leo on the distant ridge. Mary's little sister quietly steps to her side, her eyes also focused on the overlook above.

"You like him don't you?" Anna asks.

"Of course I do," Mary replies obviously.

"You know what I mean," Anna insists. Mary smiles choosing not to insult Anna's intuition by denying it. Instead, Mary continues to admire Lightfoot's silhouette against the royal sky. "He belongs here, you know," Anna says innocently.

"Do you think he knows that?" Mary asks, still focused on the ridge above.

"When the snow melts away from a man's footprints, the path home becomes visible again," Anna states, speaking eloquently as if she were an elderly sage.

"Are you for real?" Mary asks, staring in awe at the little seer. "That's brilliant!"

"I know," Anna replies as she removes her glasses and cleans them with her shirt.

"Did you learn that from Papa Leo?" Mary asks, still shaking her head in wonder.

"No. Miss Achambo again," says the little Bearheart, while casually placing her over-sized glasses back on that adorable face. Mary melts at the sight of her.

"Speaking of which," Mary remembers. "Let's get you off to school." They walk towards the village center, past a cleanup crew in the process of reconstruction. Anna waves to the workers as they pass. "I still can't believe you just said that," Mary says while mussing the little girl's thick head of ebony hair.

FIVE

"Native Affairs"

The large bonfire is ferocious and splendid. Long crackling shafts of flame shoot with such force into the sky that they produce a deep thumping rhythm as the fire gulps the oxygen in the air. Encircled at the fire's base is an extended family, the influential members of the clan, elders and observers all gathering at what they will all remember some day as a pivotal moment for their people. Flickering orange reflections animate across silent faces as they watch their patriarch Papa Leo, take his place before them under the watchful eyes of a million stars.

"This fire symbolizes what we now face together," Papa Leo explains. "Just as she protects us with her warmth and power, we are here to supply her fuel. The fire lives only as we tend to it, while our brothers and sisters sleep near its warmth. If any member fails to feed her, the fire recedes to smoldering embers and our family is exposed." The members nod in agreement. "By now, many of you have traveled to the gorge that split the valley in two. This very same tremor that toppled our buildings also lifted out of the Earth, a resource with unimaginable potential." Papa Leo holds a couple of the orange rocks up to the council. "These stones promise to improve our lives, but if we fail to protect our secret, they will be taken from us and we'll be left again with nothing but another meaningless treaty." Harvey Bearheart rises and nods to Papa Leo. "Yes brother?" Papa Leo says, welcoming his friend's thoughts.

"We remember how the oil companies used the Bureau of Indian Affairs to corrupt our cousins at Dakota-three," Harvey Bearheart declares. "They believed they were being protected by the BIA," he says as his tone becomes increasingly acrid. "But as the oil companies fracked more oil from under their feet than they paid for, they slept unaware." He sits as quietly as he stood.

"Harvey Bearheart speaks the truth," Papa Leo continues. "White men's government is run by schizophrenic beavers and their laws change for the highest bidder. No one will protect our rights better than ourselves." Again the old patriarch pauses for effect, convinced of the need to sink the next point home. "And we do that by hiding our hand," he concludes. Papa Leo turns to Lightfoot. "You all know our brother, Billy Lightfoot. A scientist now and one of the youngest professors at such a respected school," Papa Leo proudly exclaims. "He has offered to help us protect and secure our rights."

Mary beams and pats Lightfoot's hand. Papa Leo holds his hand out, welcoming him to the front. Lightfoot stands and looks across the gathering, his senses stripped of all the urgencies of city life. He catches Mary's dark eyes, fully reflecting the kinetic orange flickers of the bonfire. Lightfoot takes his place in front of the group as his grandfather steps back against the fire and folds his arms.

"When I was little, Grandfather used to tell me that we don't inherit the earth from our ancestors, we borrow it from our children," Lightfoot says. He glances back at his grandfather noticing the slightest smile break through his stoic exterior. "Back then, I thought I knew what he meant. Maybe back then I even thought it was merely a quaint thing to say." The raging fire rim lights Lightfoot's form, as he speaks to the heart of the members. "But now, those words make complete sense to me. He knew back then that I wouldn't understand fully until much later. I just needed to remember it for when that time came. As with many of his stories... stories that worked just fine for the ears of a child, they would some day grow 'like seeds of meaning', as he put it, 'when watered with the tears of an adult.' " While tossing one of the orange rocks up and down in his hand, Lightfoot walks along the semicircle. "In physics we've learned that there are vast amounts of truth we have yet to discover. We know for sure, that we know very little. But, those truths are out there and in the future they will reveal themselves. For now, we must assume that our children are already there, already looking back at us from their future and in their spirit, reaching into our time and loaning us their adult years to craft and prepare for them now." The members observe before them, the birth of a new leader, even as he remains totally unaware of it himself. He stops at the other side of the fire, looking through its flames back to Papa Leo. "That's the seed my grandfather dropped in my brain when I was only nine years old." Lightfoot holds up the amber stone with two fingers for all the members to see. "It's my belief that this is a very rare element, like gold, platinum or uranium, except that it didn't come from earth. Everything we touch, everything we are, is made up of atoms." Lightfoot points to an old woman in the crowd with stunning white hair and a kind and wrinkled face. "Our teacher Miss Achambo, taught us this in school. But some atoms, like the ones that make up this stone, are more complex. We call those atoms 'heavier' because they have more protons and neutrons spinning around their centers, like planets around the sun." Lightfoot continues, as he walks the perimeter of enraptured listeners. "But, there's a limit when elements get very heavy, because sometimes all you have to do is shoot just one more particle, one more proton into it, and suddenly the whole thing breaks apart producing a lot of heat. Heat we can use to power other things. And that is what I think this is. And now, we need to prove it." Sitting next to Mary, little Anna Bearheart raises her hand. "Yes Miss Bearheart," Lightfoot yields, pointing to the charming girl.

"That's called a hypothesis!" Anna says, happy to be of service.

"Very good!" Lightfoot exclaims, nearly cheering with delight.

"See, I totally get it," Anna quietly tells Mary while nudging her in the side.

"So why is it on our land and no where else on the planet?" Lightfoot asks rhetorically while walking to Miss Achambo. He takes her hand, gently leading her to the front to stand next to him by the fire. "Miss Achambo and I did a little homework last night. It turns out that, well – I'll let our teacher tell us." Lightfoot motions for miss Achambo to continue the story.

"Thank you, Billy," her small voice still resonating with the kindness and firm commitment to teaching that inspired many of this tribe's children. "We live in a center of life on Earth," she continues, as images of Proterozoic Earth seem to appear over the fire while the group listens to her narration. "Almost two billion years ago, a comet smashed into this land where we sit." Almost on cue, the fire pops and sparks when a large log falls further into the bed of embers, startling those in the front row. Miss Achambo continues as if she willed the event. "This comet was made of ice, living organisms, exotic metals and apparently, lots of this." She removes the stone from Lightfoot's hand and holds it up as she continues. "The whole planet felt its force. Earthquakes hundreds of times more powerful than the one we are cleaning up from now, rattled the entire planet and broke the Earth apart. The comet broke apart, throwing its pieces back into the air, eventually crashing back to the ground hundreds of miles away. Much of the smaller bits floated around the earth's atmosphere for thousands of years before slowly settling back into the soil."

For many of the adults around the fire, this was like being back in Miss Achambo's humble classroom again. Lightfoot fondly recalls how this little woman sparked his interest in science and nature with her compelling, over-dramatic tales. "But as time went on," the teacher continues, "the land healed itself, burying much of these alien metals deep below the surface. Until this week, when the earthquake split the valley open again and gave us this resource." In the crowd, a small unassuming man raises his hand. "Yes Little Deer, my dear," she says, barely missing a beat from when he sat in her class, nearly thirty-five years ago.

"So, what can we do with it? Or, what can it do for us?" Little Deer inquires.

"Billy, you're up again!" Miss Achambo says, tossing the rock into the air as she leaves the front. Lightfoot reaches out just in time to catch it. The listeners erupt with laughter, quite familiar with her spry humor. Lightfoot takes the cue to answer Little Deer's question as the old woman creaks her way back to her place in the semi-circle.

"Think of it as fuel," Lightfoot explains. "More powerful than a nuclear reactor and more valuable than oil. It's possible that we are sitting on the only major deposit of this element on the planet. It's ironic isn't it? The government forced us to this land, away from our original land, rich with oil, water and resources, and said we could exercise our sovereignty over all the worthless rocks and dirt under our feet." Lightfoot chuckles, "Not so worthless now, is it?" The three Loon sisters confer among themselves. Keezheknoi raises her hand.

"If the feds control the sale of souvenirs to tourists,

surely they'd try to control something like this," Keezheknoi says.

"They'll just take it from us the minute we start selling it," Small Duck laments.

"Ah, but that's it. We don't sell it. Not just yet anyway." Lightfoot explains. "We give just enough of it away to other countries around the world who support indigenous rights, and let them confirm to the world what we're sitting on. We use them to fight for our right to share it with them. The last thing they will want is for the U.S. to control it. Ultimately, we only sell it to the U.S. Government, once they've been held to task on the world stage. Much of what America has done to the original tribes only happened when we were silenced and no one else was watching." Stoic faces across the circle silently mime a collective realization that can only be described as "Whoa!" "In the meantime we will build a case," Lightfoot concludes. "One built on legal precedent and lots of research." He welcomes Papa Leo back to the front to address the members.

"Let me repeat," Papa Leo summates. "That for now, our edge is only preserved only by our silence. No one can hear about this yet, not until we weave a plan. If a man is as wise as a serpent, he can afford to be as harmless as a dove."

❖ ❖ ❖

The three Loon sisters work together along an assembly line of trinkets with the same handoff of effort they use to utter a single sentence. Their workshop warehouse is sectioned off accordingly, starting with construction and making its way across tables of processes, to end at the shipping station. Today, they're making leather moccasins. As is customary, Keezheknoi opens the dialogue.

"I can't believe people actually wear this shit," she says as she hands a stack of shoes down the line.

"We could get more for these you know," Small Duck adds, while meticulously stuffing boxes with leather shoes and trinkets. At the end of the line, Meoquanee holds a handful of shipping labels in one hand while tapping her fingers on the table with the other. She watches impatiently as her sister fusses with the packaging.

"We may need to, at the speed you're working," Meoquanee grumbles. Small Duck abruptly slides a stack of boxes to the side, motioning with a brush of the hand to label them up. Mary and Lightfoot enter the crowded trading post, carefully stepping around boxes and years of clutter. Lightfoot looks around the familiar space. Except for a new computer workstation and a coffee maker, the clock stopped on this place twenty-five years ago.

"Just as I remember it," Lightfoot says, breathing in the familiar air. "I miss the scent of leather and sage."

"That's the stench of quaint you're smelling," Keezheknoi says, never missing an opportunity to find the dung pile in a field of flowers.

"Nothing wrong with tradition, Sister," Small Duck says, trying to burnish the sharp edges off her sister's constant complaining.

"Speaking of tradition, you remember working here after school, Billy?" Meoquanee asks.

"Yeah," Lightfoot chuckles. "You ladies worked my fingers to the bone."

"You lasted a day," Keezheknoi states. "Maybe two." The other two ladies try to move it along, beyond their older sister's cranky disposition.

"What brings you here children?" Small Duck asks with a welcoming smile.

"A fine couple, I must say," Meoquanee observes rather artlessly. Mary quickly hijacks the conversation, steering the old bird's interest to the issue at hand. She pulls the canvas sack from Lightfoot's shoulder and empties its contents onto the main worktable in the center of the room.

"We want to package these up," she says. "And include them with some of your…"

"Junk?" Keezheknoi interjects acerbically. The

other two ladies quickly throw impatient looks over their shoulders.

"I was going to say products," Mary states politely. Normally in charge of packaging, Small Duck examines one of the stones before passing it on to Meoquanee at the end of the line.

"Certainly child," Small Duck says while motioning Mary past Keezheknoi, who has never stopped lacing moccasins during the conversation.

"Where are we sending these?" Meoquanee asks, as she smells the rock. Lightfoot unfolds a note and lays it on the table. He begins pointing down the list of names.

"Head of Physics, Oxford University in London," he says, while moving his finger down the list. "Lab for Heavy Ion Research in Darmstadt, Germany. United Nations Science Committee, care of Dr. Louis Ambrose. And lastly, this one," pointing to a name on the list. "Head of the Physics Department, University of Tokyo." Lightfoot motions to some of the trinkets scattered along the assembly line. "I'll let them know what to expect so we need to make sure it looks like a normal Internet order of - "

"Products?" Keezheknoi confirms.

"Exactly," Mary replies for him.

"Fine couple, indeed," Meoquanee gushes. Mary is abashed, turning to Lightfoot with a thin smile.

"We should get back. Papa Leo's getting ready to head to the valley," Mary recovers.

"Yep, good idea," Lightfoot agrees, slightly sharing her fluster. "I'll come back to get the tracking numbers. Thank you ladies." The couple exits the small trinket factory so quickly they nearly stumble over each other on the way out the door. Small Duck wastes no time beginning to package the samples. She tilts her head at Meoquanee.

"You had to put them on the spot, didn't you?" Small Duck says, while continuing to fiddle with the art of packaging.

"Oh, like you couldn't see how they looked at each other?" Meoquanee responds.

"He won't be here long," Keezheknoi predicts while firing up another cigar.

❖ ❖ ❖

Papa Leo rides out of the stable as Mary and Lightfoot arrive. He's leading the palomino by the reins, as well as a glorious black stallion that glistens when it steps into the afternoon sun.

Mary hurries to the black horse and nuzzles her boy, nose to nose.

"Batman! Hello baby," Mary exclaims affectionately, while stroking his nose. The grand pony is happy to see her and nuzzles her neck.

"Batman?" Lightfoot says, tossing his head back in disbelief. Papa Leo shrugs out a grimace.

"He looks like Batman," Mary says, seeming more content to explain it to the stallion than to the boys who'd never understand anyway. Lightfoot snickers through that portent expression we see men do to mask their infatuation. Papa Leo considers his grandson's growing appreciation of her, and possibly the bearing of his own heritage.

❖　❖　❖

The three riders have been experts in the saddle since childhood. Mary's horse leads Papa Leo and Lightfoot as they march up the green ramp of mountain slope, towards the chasm just over the ridge. Lightfoot turns his gaze to the swell and valleys three hundred feet below, dotted with clumps of pines and the decimated remnants of clustered homes in the process of being rebuilt. He absorbs the trailing voices and engines of the yellow skip loaders, which clear debris from the buildings and roads.

❖　❖　❖

From the ridgeline above, the massive slice into the floor of the valley looks like a giant grin in the earth, even more dramatic now as the low rays of sunset periodically illuminate the highest terrain of fallen trees and rock slides produced by the quake. The three riders rest a moment, silently considering the impossible sight below. Both Lightfoot and Mary's long jet-black hair whip their traditional faces, a sight reminiscent of those Smithsonian photos from a hundred years earlier. Papa Leo is the first to dismount, looking up for a moment at his two favorite people sitting high in their saddles. He continues to tie off his mare to a fallen tree. Nearly in unison, Mary and Lightfoot swing their legs over their saddles and drop down to do the same. Papa Leo leads the way in a sure-footed descent to the crevice below.

Upon arriving at the edge of the fissure, Mary peers into the dark chasm for the first time. Lightfoot stands back with Papa Leo, allowing her to discover the weight of the event for herself. They seem to relish the feeling of realization all over again, this time through her eyes. Mary kneels at its edge, looking deep into the darkness that continues on with no floor in sight. And then it hits her, the rocks - the river of floating orange shards of metal of all sizes, gently bumping into each other as slight gusts stir the pot. Mary looks up, spurning what her own eyes tell her as Lightfoot kneels to her side.

"I thought it was full of water at first," Mary confesses, "I don't know what's harder to believe, rocks floating in air, or rocks floating in water."

"I know the feeling," he says of the optical illusion before them. Another disturbance which grows around them, an unnatural thumping sound that arrests their interest. Lightfoot's brow wrinkles at the familiar resonance of chopping air. Papa Leo and Mary look puzzled though, while turning to pinpoint the sound's direction from over the peak. And then they appear. Just over the ridge, two massive Blackhawk helicopters flare to a hover!

"Get to the tree line!" Lightfoot calls out. He leads Mary by the arm as they hurry from the crevice, taking cover below some foliage up the valley wall. The helicopters begin their descent into the valley, hovering over the anomaly in the earth. "Blackhawks," Lightfoot claims, not entirely surprised to see them. Papa Leo's jaw tightens.

"How dare they use that name," the old man chides.

Inside the lead helicopter, the Pilot-In-Command announces their arrival while descending slowly into the bowl and positioning for a better look of the damage.

"Superior six-one - arrived coordinate zero six niner," the PIC confirms. He clocks his sister ship, settling into view just behind and to the side.

"Superior six-two, got your four o'clock at zero six niner," the second chopper announces itself over the comm. *"That's one hell of a crack!"* the sister ship continues.

"Where have I heard that before?" the PIC retorts. "Okay, Let's make quick work of this. Get those poindexters on the move."

"Wilco six-one, the science-types are all over it," the other ship calls back.

Papa Leo ducks back deeper into the cover of some fallen timbers motioning for Mary and Lightfoot to follow. Together the three of them watch a side panel door slide open on the second Blackhawk. Two men in plain clothes slide a strange looking device on rails over the edge. The civilian engineers aim the nose of the device deep into the fissure below.

"Okay, perfect! Let's hold it there," says the lead engineer, a young ruddy type with longish red hair. He motions the technician toward a workstation behind them. "Start recording before I fire it up," the engineer orders. The technician prepares the computer with a few keystrokes before sending back a thumbs-up.

"Speed!" the guy at the computer yells. The engineer at the edge engages the device.

"Sixty seconds is all we need, anything else is gravy!" the engineer says, panning the nose of the strange sensor along the crack in the earth.

Below the chopper, Mary and Lightfoot shield their eyes from the flying debris, whipped up by the rotor wash. Papa Leo looks up apathetically, perhaps even bored with white men's antics. Mary has never seen a sight the likes of these beasts.

"How'd they find out?" she asks.

"Let's hope it's just the earthquake that they're interested in," Lightfoot says, but that was before he leans out and catches sight of the device that is now aimed into the crevice. "Nope, scratch that," Lightfoot says. "They know what they're looking for. No doubt a gravity anomaly registered on a satellite somewhere." Lightfoot pats every pocket he's got before he finds his mobile phone. He starts shooting video of the raid from their camouflaged position. The machinery mounted to the Blackhawk whines and clicks for nearly thirty seconds before the operator pans to another spot along the line of the chasm.

Inside Blackhawk two, the science team continues to gather and log the data. Redhead at the door notices the small floating stones, now starting to bounce into each other and off the walls from the rotor wash. He leans forward, not quite trusting his eyes.

"Hey, you got those field glasses back there?" the engineer shouts over the whining scanner and thumping of rotor blades. The technician locates a pair of binoculars and passes them forward to the engineer, who uses them to look back into the crater. He quickly lowers them in disbelief, not sure of what he's seeing. Redhead adjusts the focus one more time and once again spies into the crater. "No way!" he exclaims, totally bewildered by the sight. He motions for the technician to join him at the door. The technician confirms that the computer is still recording data, and then grabs the binoculars to peer into the crevice himself.

"Well slap my grandma. They're flying!" the mind-blown technician exclaims. "What are those?" he asks, handing the field glasses back. The engineer can only offer a clueless shrug, entirely lost for words.

From the cockpit, the pilot notices the three horses tied off on the nearby ridge. With two fingers, he thrusts a pointing motion to the sister ship pilot and then to the horses.

At the device, Redhead and the technician are still trying to make sense of the impossible sight below.

"How much more time you two need back there?" the pilot calls over the comm. *We're drawing too much attention as it is, we need to wrap it up."* Redhead touches his earpiece, receiving the call from the front.

"We got what we need!" the engineer calls back into the mic on his collar. He motions a slicing finger across his throat, indicating for the technician to cut the recording.

Mary sees the horses panicking, spooked by the hovering predators. Her black stallion, the youngest of the team is exceptionally freaked out, pulling at his reins in a frenzy. Mary breaks out of the blind, and runs back up hill to calm them, but the black beauty breaks free and wastes no time galloping off.

"Mary!" Lightfoot calls out, leaving the cover to follow her up the hill. He stops briefly to catch the sight of the choppers lifting out of the valley and sees his grandfather moving into the open, appearing to challenge the Blackhawks.

"Shit!" the pilot of the science ship yells when he notices Mary and Lightfoot bolting up the valley wall. "Lock it down, we got to go!" he calls back to the engineers who are just beginning to pull the device along its tracks and back into the hold.

"Superior six-one, we got a couple Indians in the valley," the pilot announces over the radio.

"*Copy that six-two, we're pulling up now,*" the PIC responds as the lead ship clears the way above.

"*Superior six-one on the go!*" the PIC announces as the first Blackhawk rotates and flies off over the ridge.

Lightfoot stops momentarily from running after Mary to find his grandfather stepping into the center of the rotor wash near the crevice.

The old man removes his hat, allowing the engineers to catch his steely glare as they finally manage to stow the device and slide the door shut. Lightfoot watches the final chopper clear the tree line and fly off over the ridge. He turns to chase after Mary.

❖ ❖ ❖

Papa Leo rides back down the ridge toward the village, followed by his grandson and Mary, who ride together on the palomino. The young palomino steps into a bit of shale loosened from the quake, and buckles a knee to quickly recover. Mary throws her arms around Lightfoot's waist.

"Sorry," she says, balancing herself again with one hand against the saddle, and the other returning to her thigh. Lightfoot reaches back and places a hand on her leg.

"You okay!" he asks.

"Of course," she replies while eyeing his hand. Lightfoot feels a deep vibration in his pocket, followed shortly by a ringtone that reminds him and everyone else on the trail of his second life. He manages to locate his phone, and answers it on the last ring.

"Hey Kate, how's it going?" he asks excitedly. Papa Leo looks back, catching sight of Mary who wastes no time furrowing a brow. Grandfather turns back to the trail, deliberately pursing his lips at the awkwardness on the hill.

Back in Boston, Kate rummages through research papers strewn across a law library desk.

"I just wanted to check in, let you know what I'm finding on this end," Kate begins. "There's actually some good news," she says, while flipping through the sheets of a dog-eared legal pad. "So, we know that reservation lands are still held in trust by the U.S. government," she prefaces. "And as a trustee, the Department of Interior has full responsibility for overseeing the development of oil and gas on tribal lands, and ensuring that any sales by the tribes are made in 'the best interest' of the Native Americans. At least that was the idea."

"Yeah, like using a wolf as a sheepdog," Lightfoot says. Mary cranes her head around to catch his eye. She mimes a question by alternating between a thumb up and then down. "You said something about good news?" Lightfoot follows.

Kate leans back in her chair and tosses the legal pad on the pile of books in front of her.

"The good news is what they don't say. Federal policy is clear that unless a treaty or Congressional statute specifically removes a power over a resource, than the tribe is assumed to possess it," she reveals, rather excitedly. "The point is, all they talk about is oil, lumber, mineral rights - as in natural resources. There's nothing about an *unnatural resource*, or in your case, a raw element that didn't originate on Earth. Meaning, if we can prove it originated from, you know... outer space, then I think we just might have a case." Kate leans back over the research sprawled out across the desk and forages for another reference when – ah, there it is. "Also, your idea of a sovereign nation gifting the element to another nation isn't prohibited by the Indian Commerce Clause, as long as you don't *sell* it to them," Kate confirms.

Lightfoot leans back to Mary, replying to her earlier query with a thumb up! Papa Leo turns back just as Mary happily relays the thumbs-up to him as well. Of course that's until she hears Lightfoot continue to gush over the lady on the other end of the line.

"Kate, you are so amazing, thank you!" Mary looks up, pretending to be distracted by a screeching hawk passing overhead, but Papa Leo knows better and turns back to the front again.

"I really appreciate you doing this Kate," Lightfoot says. "Look, I'm going to be here for a while so if you can, it would be great if you could make the trip out here." Mary's eyes widen as she continues to track the fleeting bird across the sky and pretending not to be listening. What was she thinking anyway? she asks of herself. He's an east coast creature now, how could he ever be satisfied going backward?

Kate stands to walk down an aisle of the library.

"Yeah I'd like that," Kate beams. "Let me put some more ideas together, maybe by the end of next week. But I'm sure I'll talk to you before then." She arrives at a window overlooking the snow flurries in the street below. "Yeah, you too, bye for now." She hangs up allowing herself a moment to daydream, then snaps herself out of it, and returns to the books with even more resolve.

Lightfoot hangs up and continues riding down the path to the village.

"We might just have the perfect legal argument to fight back," Lightfoot says.

"Those helicopters didn't look too interested in the law," Mary states, rather profoundly.

"Then there's that," Lightfoot agrees.

❖　❖　❖

The sun has nearly settled below the horizon by the time the team enters the village. Harvey Bearheart is waiting in the road, holding the reins of Mary's horse. She jumps off the palomino mid trot, and runs to her boy.

"Batman!" she exclaims, taking the reins and profusely stroking his side.

"We worried when he showed up without you," Harvey Bearheart confesses.

"I'm okay," Mary replies. "He got spooked by the helicopters." Papa Leo extends a hand to greet his friend.

"Harvey Bearheart, I think we're about to have some visitors if those choppers are any indication," the old man predicts confidently.

"We saw them from down here too," Harvey Bearheart says, pointing across the lake. "They left the same way they came – from the west." Lightfoot dismounts and walks to Mary. He joins her in stroking Batman's forehead.

"Will you come with me later, back up the hill? I have an idea," Lightfoot asks. Mary isn't quite sure where this is going, but nods anyway.

"Sure" she says, still focusing on her stallion. He turns to Papa Leo.

"Granddad, you remember those motion sensitive cameras we used with the wolves?"

"I never throw anything away," the old man replies.

"Perfect," Lightfoot says before turning back to Mary. "I just need a couple hours to get some things together before we ride back up there," Lightfoot explains.

"I have to cool him down and get him fed anyway," Mary says. "What are you thinking?" He looks at her in a way she hasn't seen before. And as such, in a way she has no way of interpreting.

"Honestly, I'm thinking of a lot of things right now. I'm not sure they all make sense," Lightfoot says elusively. Mary nods unaffectedly and offers a puzzled smile. She turns and leads Batman back to the stable. Harvey Bearheart helps Papa Leo down from the horse when he catches sight of the approaching Loon sisters, each holding a small package.

"Look, it's the three wise men, and they're bearing gifts," he wisecracks.

"Not for you, Brutus," Keezheknoi croaks. Small Duck hands Lightfoot a UPS delivery and Meoquanee places a foil-wrapped plate on top of that.

"Came for you this morning," Small Duck says of the shipment, followed by handing over a printed sheet of paper. "And your tracking numbers," she explains. With no free hand to receive it, Lightfoot balances the box and plate in one hand while he takes the sheet from her.

"Thanks, what's in the foil?" Lightfoot asks.

"Cookies!" Meoquanee proudly exclaims. Made them myself. Harvey Bearheart lifts an edge of foil and peeks inside.

"Not for you," Meoquanee reminds.

"If I saw those on the ground, I'd pick them up with a shovel," the big Bearheart sniggles.

"Thank you ladies," Lightfoot says. "That's very sweet."

"They better be," Keezheknoi says while trying in vain to pull a drag on the cigar. "She put enough sugar in them to kill a swarm of bees." The old ladies turn and shuffle away as quickly as they appeared.

"You let it go out again," Keezheknoi complains.

"You were the last one to have it," Small Duck retorts, not in any mood to take her older sister's shit this evening.

"Ah there they go, with the charm of flying glass," Harvey Bearheart notes, as he watches the old birds bicker their way into the night.

"Old age is not as honorable as death," Papa Leo expounds, dropping a large weathered paw on his friend's shoulder. "But most people want it." He turns to retire for the night. "I'll bet the sun rises in the morning," he says while walking off and waving a hand over his shoulder.

"Good night brother" Harvey Bearheart replies, as he too heads off in the opposite direction. Lightfoot stands alone near the shoreline, holding his packages and watching everyone vector off in separate directions. He sniffs the foil-covered plate, then peeks inside and grimaces. Resting the plate of cookies on the ground for moment, he opens the UPS package. He pulls out a large flashlight-type object and fires off an intense green laser dot into the distant tree line. This is a much higher-powered device than the laser pointer used before. Suddenly chomping sounds appear rapidly turning to growls, as two dogs begin to devour the plate of cookies at his feet.

"Get out of there," he scolds the hounds, trying to chase them away from the dish. But the two dogs take turns circling back to snap at the cookies while Lightfoot chases the other one away. That is until he realizes the potential of the new toy in his hand. He fires off a powerful green dot on the ground between the dogs and the plate of cookies. They pounce on the glowing spot, which he directs further and further into the woods. He manages to lead the maniacal hounds far enough away, to snatch the plate off the ground. But for a few crumbs, it's been entirely demolished.

❖   ❖   ❖

Looking up through the crevice at night, the floating stones are but black asteroids, eclipsing the nearly waxing moon. Soft voices echo slightly off the fissure's walls when moments later, Mary peers over the sharp ridgeline above.

On the surface, Lightfoot steps to the edge alongside her, taking her hand and gently motioning her back to a safer distance.

"What were you hoping to see at night?" Mary asks as she watches him reach into his shoulder pack. Lightfoot pulls out the large laser and fires it into the chasm. Instantly, the single line of vibrant green light splits into a thousand strands, deflecting and intersecting in all directions as the stones bend the light within the shear walls. Lightfoot shoots a certain grin, turning to Mary with the realization that his hypothesis stood the test.

"Gravity bends light. A lot of gravity bends a lot of light," he says logically. Mary needn't fully understand the laws of physics to appreciate the magnificent light show in front of her. "We may be sitting on the most powerful source of energy this world has ever seen," he continues. "Of all the technologies and modes of propulsion we've achieved by burning oil, none of them can compare to what this promises."

"Do you think they know it? The people in the helicopters?" Mary asks.

"I'm sure they know it. In fact, I'll bet they were testing it the same way, except they were using an infrared laser that only their sensors would pick up," he explains. "This stuff is not only a fuel source, it's possibly the answer to field propulsion if we can amplify its gravity." He fetches an old canvas bag from the ground and pulls out a couple camouflaged field cameras. He tosses one of them to Mary.

"Granddad and I used to put these old film cameras in the woods to track the wolves. They're motion activated" he says.

"Ah, smart," Mary says while examining the old technology.

"You can be sure our new pack of wolves will be back, especially after that fly over today," he says while scanning the nearby trees for best view of the site. He runs to a choice spot and straps one of the cameras to a birch tree and aims it towards the gorge.

"Go ahead and pick a tree over there and strap that one just like this," he says. "I'll set it up."

"Oooh, I like it," Mary says as she trots to another perfect viewpoint. "This is starting to feel like a spy novel," she says while bounding effortlessly over the rough terrain. Lightfoot smiles, watching her identify a tree and tie the strap around its base. "Okay, got it," she calls over, standing back to follow its viewing angle. When she turns to point the lens toward the fissure, she notices Lightfoot standing still and studying her. "What?" Mary asks. Lightfoot snaps out of his daze, hikes over to her and begins winding the camera's spring. Mary watches him, nearly giddy with adventure as he clips on the battery. The sight of him brings back memories of when he would set up experiments or build contraptions when he was younger, always hoping to be a scientist and grow beyond the reservation. Billy was always a beacon, an example for all the young Chippewa in the tribe of what you could become when you work hard and insist on your rights. How he must view his heritage now, she wonders? Does he simply consider his heritage in some laughable way, a quaint acceptance seen through his modern perspective? Mary listens

81

to the sound of the tensioning spring, as he winds the mechanism tighter. Lightfoot engages the camera and stands back to behold their setup.

"We're using infrared film too, so we'll see at night," he grins. Mary smiles at the geeky charm that counters his strong, handsome stature. Maybe this is a good time to broach the question that's been consuming her all day, she wonders.

"That lady who called you, how is she helping?" she asks, more matter-of-fact than tentative, but still, he knew the question would arise.

"Kate?" he replies, without removing his eyes from the camera setup. "She's got some experience in Tribal Law," he says plainly. "We could use her help building a case." He turns to focus on Mary, knowing full well where this is going. Oh hell, Mary thinks. Why keep beating around this bush?

"Are you and she, you know... close?" she asks tentatively, and for the first time showing a hint of vulnerability. He steps closer and moves Mary's hair from her eyes, pulling a last wisp from the edge of her lips. Mary stops breathing.

"I was just wondering," she explains factually.

Lightfoot leans forward, touching his forehead to hers, just as she's fond of doing with her horse. Mary doesn't wait, instead she starts kissing him carefully at first, then again - until they both form a single silhouette on the edge of the chasm.

❖   ❖   ❖

Lightfoot's eyes open as the rooster's call signals another impending sunrise. He wasn't really sleeping anyway. Instead he lies there, his thoughts meandering in no real direction as he wonders why roosters feel the need to wake everything up? He strokes a small but thick lock of Mary's hair between his thumb and fingers, obsessing on its texture and length. Mary's breath rakes across his chest as she sleeps. He moves his hand slowly so as not to wake her. His eyes move across the room where the quake's power is clearly evident from the cracks along the walls. He considers his bags lying in the corner, still unpacked and lying open, ready to zip back up and head to the airport if need be. Or, was it his way of putting off any acceptance of the reservation actually becoming home again. He can't just leave his position at the university he rationalizes, an achievement for which he worked so hard. Then again, it's not as if it ever felt like home there either. He focuses again on Mary, watching her sleep while his right arm rests across her muscular back. How naturally stunning and boldly sure she is of herself. And that hair, that perfect mane of black hair, released from the ponytail and flowing across both of their bodies like some kind of perfect ebony silk. The rooster crows again, possibly intended to give him head start? he considers. Was it trying to wake him soon enough to prepare an explanation for all this, before they would face each other in the daylight? He watches her sleep, her eyes darting under their lids as the sounds of waking animals ramp up outside. It's been a long time since he woke to these sounds. The rampages of the village hounds who chase the shorebirds and the lake water slapping into the reeds of wild rice. Surely these noises are narrating her dreams and working their way into the images playing out in her head. How could she not be hearing this?

"How long have you been awake?" she asks quietly, her eyes still closed and her body content not to move a muscle. How did she know, he thought? How long was she alert and reading his mind? Lightfoot starts to laugh, but realizing that Mary probably wouldn't get the point, he changes the chuckle into a comforting sort of breathing sound that matches the stroke of his hand across her back.

"Not long," he replies, noticing her eyes are still closed. "I'm not used to the roosters anymore. I remember when I first moved to the city, I couldn't sleep through the night without waking just before sunrise and wondering where they were. Funny though, they never woke me up when I was a kid. I only started missing them when they weren't there any longer. It took me a long time to get used to it. Being away I mean."

"And now?" she asks quietly, almost in a dream state. He has to wonder about this for a moment before he's able to answer.

"And now? I feel like I'm floating no matter where I am, if that makes sense." Mary opens her eyes and lifts her head off his chest to focus on him with an intensity that seems to pull his feelings out further. "When I grew up here, I saw my life through my intellect. I thought that would make me better than my past I guess. Rather than always looking at life through a collection of traditional sayings, like the one-liners we grew up hearing from our elders. I couldn't see how the physical world, with all its laws and mysteries could simply be explained by Papa Leo's proverbs. I mean, I loved them and they made me feel good, like having a dad. But I wanted to do better. Look where our poetic pacifism got us. Shoved to the edges of some lake in a land the government didn't really want, while they convinced us they were doing us some big favor while we pretended to be sovereign. I guess I never could understand how to succeed in a white man's world with sticks and stones. I guess..." he pauses for a moment, saying the next thing in his head first before committing it to speech. "I guess I sort of understand now." Mary uses her strong sienna arms to lift herself over him.

"And what is it that you understand, Billy Lightfoot?" she asks, tauntingly exposing her bare body above him. Lightfoot smiles and kisses her abs, moving his face and forehead upwards across her warm skin. Mary slides her torso down, following his upward travel, savoring his touch. He buries his lips into the small of her neck, fitting perfectly in that little spot above her clavicle.

"I understand now, what it means when the past and present exist at the same time," Lightfoot chuckles as a thought overtakes him.

"What?" Mary asks.

"Just that, speaking of proverbs," he says. "Granddad used to say, when a man moves away from nature, his heart becomes hard." Mary can't help herself.

"I don't think that's your heart I'm feeling right now," she quips. She settles her body gently over his, her train of black hair shading both of them from the beam of sunlight starting to filter across the bed. Together they move slowly, raking their bodies across one another and eventually entwining into a sensual and synchronized motion.

SIX

"Federal Assistance"

Like trading caravans forging across native lands generations ago, three black SUVs navigate the main highway leading to the Red Rock reservation.

The lead car transports the brain trust, a generous term for these heavyweights on a mission disguised behind a veil of benevolence. In the front seat, a puffy man inside and out, named Edward Drummond, or Doctor Edward Drummond, as he'll quickly remind you. Assuming anyone would engage him beyond his pompous exterior, he'd also share how he earned that prefix with much hard work and years of experience in the field of high-energy systems. He looks at his watch and scowls.

"When we get there, let me do the talking," he says, mastering the art of the yelling at people in a low volume of indifference. Bristling at the *command*, another ego-laden white man from the Bureau of

Indian Affairs, Superintendent Hank Poysen, chooses to differ.

"Uh, I'll cue you on that, if you don't mind," Hank promptly corrects the doctor. "First we take the pulse, then after that I'll defer to you," Hank explains. "Then you can start your pitch." Drummond's face drops in weary impatience and a total disregard for protocol. "We'll meet the Tribal Police at the main gate and they'll escort us in," Hank says in a tone that seems to sympathize with the inconvenient protocol, but tempered with first-hand experience of the blow back from ignoring it. "We can't appear to disrespect their independence or I'll have Washington up my ass," Hank confesses. Drummond tweaks his meaty face into a 'yeah, yeah' type of scoff.

"Whatever," Drummond mumbles while letting his eyes retreat up into his skull in disgust.

❖   ❖   ❖

Sleeping and entangled, the couple rests peacefully where last they've exhausted themselves. Mary opens her eyes with a peculiar awareness. She furls her brow, her eyes darting side-to-side, until she senses a presence behind her. Mary turns over her shoulder to see Papa Leo standing at the foot of the bed. His arms are folded in a statuesque pose that can only be settled into over time. Slowly, she rotates her shoulders back to Lightfoot and nudges him in the ribs. He smiles when he sees her face, realizing he wasn't just dreaming. Except she returns a frozen and awkward grin, twitching a look over her shoulder for him to follow.

"What?" he asks, while slightly lifting his head until his eyes appear beyond the curve of her neck. There stands Papa Leo, motionless and staring back. Papa Leo unfolds his arms and inserts them into the pockets of his jacket and without a hint of judgment, the old man turns matter-of-factly to the door.

"Tribal Police are escorting some visitors in," he says exiting the room and closing the door gently behind him. They grin excruciatingly at each other and quickly climb out of bed.

❖ ❖ ❖

Papa Leo joins Harvey Bearheart who is already standing in the middle of the road, ready to receive the caravan. The Tribal Police Bronco leads the way into the village center. Lightfoot and Mary join them just as the SUVs coil to a stop nearby.

"Morning Pop," Mary says, not quite making eye contact and hoping Papa Leo remained silent before they arrived. Her father nods back kindly.

"Morning Son," Harvey Bearheart says, placing an affectionate arm on Lightfoot's shoulder. Mary cranes her eyes away, humorously pained by the man-to-man gesture. She agonizingly tries to move on, inhaling so profoundly it lifts her head toward the approaching delegation. The Tribal Police hop out and strike sentry positions, flanking the assembly as the delegation climbs from the vehicles. Drummond of course assumes it's all about him and steps to the front, about to present his hand when Hank quickly upstages any attempt to usurp protocol. According to plan, Hank is the first to greet the elders, motioning with outstretched hand.

"Leo, Harvey – good morning gentlemen," Hank Poysen says while motioning towards a rustic sort with a fifties crew cut and work boots. "This is Casper Elliot, Army Corps of Engineers," Hank introduces.

"I believe we met, few years back," Casper says, in a refined delivery. "How are you this morning, gentlemen?" The two elders remain silent and merely nod politely. Having taken that pulse, so to speak, Hank continues with the niceties.

"Also, I'd like you to meet Ed Drummond, with…"

"Doctor Edward Drummond, pleasure to meet you both," the brash doctor interjects without wasting any of his precious time. Lightfoot raises an eyebrow.

"As in, Doctor Drummond, from Los Alamos?" he asks, while being the first to extend his hand in return.

"This is my Grand..." Papa Leo begins an introduction that Drummond drives right over.

"Yes, Professor William Lightfoot," the Doctor huffs. "You're a long way from home, professor!"

"Actually I am home, Sir," Lightfoot affirms. They shake hands tightly, but Drummond tries to hold on much longer than Lightfoot prefers.

"And this is Mister Bearheart," Hank declares.

"Harvey P. Bearheart actually," he says in a timbre already flavored by his instinct to despise this bombastic ass. Harvey Bearheart looks Drummond in the eye while pretending not to see him offer his hand. In an effort to counter the not-so-subtle slight, Drummond blurts another inflated opinion.

"Harvey P. Bearheart, I like a man with a full name!" Mary suppresses a grin at the penis-fest playing out in the middle of the road.

"Mary Bearheart," she announces, firmly extending her hand on behalf of her dad. "Pleasure to meet you," she says warmly.

"That would be my pleasure Miss," Drummond says, shaking her hand with a buttery creepiness, all while sizing her up in the process. Again, Hank tries to keep it moving accordingly.

"Let me offer our condolences on the damage caused by the quake," Hank says quickly.

"And loss of life, or hadn't you heard?" Papa Leo

says to set a level of priority that speaks volumes to all dealings with the Bureau over the years.

"Of course Sir, of course," Hank emotes in faux empathy. "We'd like to offer Red Rock any assistance in your rebuilding efforts. In fact, we've asked the Corps of Engineers to join us for that reason, possibly survey the damage, that's if you'd like to take us up on the offer?" Hank says with a toothy grin. "Up to you of course," Poysen adds.

"Of course," Papa Leo states.

"So, as we've heard, the earth opened up quite a trench," Elliot says.

"You mean, as you've seen," Lightfoot corrects. Drummond has had enough of the subtleties.

"Professor Lightfoot, I won't pretend to insult your intelligence. Let me just get to the point," Drummond blurts.

"That's a good start," Lightfoot replies.

"Yes, you're right," Drummond continues. "We've observed an anomaly emanating from the opening created by the quake. One that frankly has us a bit concerned," he explains, while pulling a data plot from his pocket. He unfurls the sheet and lays it out on the hood of the Police Bronco and turns the sheet primarily in Lightfoot's direction. "As you can see, this is from one of our seismic analysis satellites. We're getting fluctuation readings that are off the charts and beginning shortly after the quake."

"What kind of fluctuations?" Lightfoot asks, playing dumb for the moment.

"Radiation to be exact," Drummond follows, knowing full well he's speaking to a peer in the field but hoping his many years of calling the shots will prevail. "We were hoping to spend some time studying the source of the anomaly. Should only be a few days for our engineers to fully examine the area," Drummond says while folding the readout back up and inserting it in his pocket.

"Well, to begin with, your engineers have already performed spectral analysis and waveform readings from the air, as well as laser measurements if that device in the Blackhawk is what I think it was. But then you know that, don't you," Lightfoot states. "Secondly, I've personally surveyed the area for gamma radiation and again, as you know there are no *unstable* sources of radiation at the location," Lightfoot asserts, done with this guy's bullshit. "Then there's the fact that the 'anomaly' as you're calling it, emanates from Tribal Land. Sovereign Tribal land," he affirms, turning now to Casper Elliot. "Isn't that right... *Casper?*" Lightfoot asks, in conclusion.

"Uh yes, you are correct," Casper Elliot replies. "Please understand, we're only here to inquire. Our survey can only proceed with your permission of course," he confirms in the most respectful of tones. Lightfoot looks to Papa Leo, knowing exactly what the official response will be.

"I'm sorry to disappoint you gentlemen," Papa Leo says. "But we have our hands full now cleaning up and rebuilding from the quake. Maybe another time." Harvey Bearheart extends a hand for the first time, albeit a disingenuous one.

"Thank you for your concern though," the big guy says, offering a satiated grin. With the commanding nod of a ship's captain, Papa Leo motions to the Tribal officers. The patriarch extends a polite arm, gesturing toward the road leading out of the reservation. Hank Poysen picks up on the thick and pointed cue.

"Yes, thank you for your time," Poysen says while nodding to the elders. Leo, Mister Bearheart, I trust you'll let us know if we can help. We're standing by," Poysen says, trying to chum his way off the reservation.

"I'm sure you are Hank," Papa Leo states conservatively. Drummond glances side to side along the gathering, then motions to Hank as if to say, 'that's it?' But Hank and Casper know the protocol well, and certainly when a tribe shows you the door. The delegation returns to the vehicles as the Tribal Police fire up the Bronco and pull around to *follow* the caravan off the grounds. Within less than a minute, the procession turns the vehicles around and retreats up the small road to the main highway. Lightfoot, Mary and the elders, watch as the 'concerned citizens' disappear around the bend in a trail of dust.

"That was subtle," Mary claims.

"As subtle as a rattlesnake's tail," Papa Leo says. Harvey Bearheart just smacks his lips from the bad taste in his mouth.

"I need something to wash this down," Harvey Bearheart declares. "Let's eat something," he says while walking off. The rest shrug and follow him to the Bearheart house.

❖　❖　❖

Harvey Bearheart swigs from a bottle of Moosehead, while flipping fish and small game on the outdoor grill. Lightfoot, Mary and Papa Leo are seated along a nearby table.

"It's so great to see you, Billy!" says Mama Bearheart, who arrives at the table with a platter of Ojibwe wild rice and coffees. She's a slender woman with an alert eye and a ticklish smile. She turns impatiently to the grill. "Are you grilling lunch or dinner over there?" she chides her burly man child.

"Good things take time, woman. I'm an expert!" Harvey Bearheart calls from behind a massive cloud of smoke that occludes any sight of him and seems to dispel the expert claim.

"Mister 'expert' over there actually lit his ponytail on fire last summer," she confides to Lightfoot as he admires the platters.

"You're an artist Misses B", Lightfoot says, breathing in the aroma.

"You should remember this," she says. "Your mother taught me this recipe…" but then she catches herself about the same time Mary's eyes burgeon. "I'm sorry Billy, I wasn't thinking," she confesses.

"It's okay," Lightfoot says patiently. "In fact it's perfect, thank you."

"She was my friend," rocking her head in utter disbelief. "Always will live near our hearts."

"Momma, please sit. You've done enough," Mary says, trying to redirect her mother's train of thought.

"No, no," she asserts. "I have to save the fish from your father's claws." She rushes off to hurry her husband along. Lightfoot and Mary find themselves facing Papa Leo for the first time since the awkward sunrise.

"So…" Lightfoot stammers, but Papa Leo is already on top of it.

"My lips are shut. It's up to you two," he remarks, pretending to busy himself by cleaning his fork on his shirt. "Gossip is the stuff of old ladies and young boys," he says. "I am neither." Then, Papa Leo sniffs the air. "Speaking of old ladies," he says. Mary and Lightfoot look up to notice the three Loon sisters approaching over his shoulder.

"They're behind me aren't they?" Papa Leo laments.

"Yep," Lightfoot confirms while Papa Leo turns to the grill master.

"Harvey Bearheart, scavengers have landed to pick at the bones," he says for the benefit of the approaching sisters. Mary buries her face in her palms then abashedly lifts a finger from over an eye to peer at Lightfoot. Surely the theater of this aging tribe represents all the reasons he left the reservation in the first place. Right on cue, her mother and father return to the table.

"Manny, Mo and Jack, right on time," Harvey Bearheart roars as his wife nudges him in the side and instead welcomes the trio.

"Ladies, will you join us, there's plenty?" she offers graciously.

"Between the three of you there might be enough teeth to form a bite," Harvey Bearheart snorts.

"Oh we couldn't," Keezheknoi replies while shooting a shit-eating grin at the burly guy.

"How lovely," Small Duck shrills as she claps her hands together like a seal.

"You sure there's enough?" Meoquanee asks,

knowing full well there always is. Harvey Bearheart motions to the stogie hanging from the lips of the kingpin.

"You'll have to snuff that turd out if you sit at this table," he blurts. Misses Bearheart pulls the platter away from her husband in a gruff.

"See what you've missed?" Mary tells Lightfoot while smiling painfully.

"I'll have you know that this is a Bolivar, Royal Corona," Keezheknoi mentions.

"From Cuba," Small Duck says.

"Actually, I think it's counterfeit, from Dominican Republic!" Meoquanee adds.

"I don't care where that donkey dick comes from," Harvey Bearheart declares. "It's time to eat and the smell of it is making me throw up in my mouth."

"Dad!" Mary exclaims but Lightfoot laughs fondly, sincerely appreciating the honesty of this maturing Chippewa community. Keezheknoi walks the cigar to a nearby log and sets is down gently, saving its glory for after the meal.

"How long you staying, Billy?" Misses Bearheart asks innocently. By this time, Mary has given up worrying about whether he's uncomfortable or not and continues to pass the plates with a resigned expression.

"I've got someone covering for me for the rest of

the semester if need be," Lightfoot reveals for the first time.

"So, *Doctor Evil*, who showed up with Hank this morning?" his grandfather prompts.

"Last I recall, he ran the Particle Physics Department at the Neutron Science facility in New Mexico," Lightfoot replies, while examining a badly charred fillet on the platter before passing it on to Mary. "He knows exactly what we have. And you can be sure they want in."

"How much is all that stuff worth, anyway?" Harvey Bearheart asks. Everyone at the table looks up in anticipation of the answer.

"I'll know for sure when I hear back from the labs we sent samples to," Lightfoot says. "But if I were to guess, billions I suspect." Now, if the diners were trying not to appear too interested in the question, they certainly look gobsmacked by the answer. In fact, they just stare uncontrollably. Even Mary gulps, nearly choking on her beer. She's been so caught up with the idea of Billy's return home, she never really bothered to understand the implications of the find, until just now.

"Billions, as in… dollars?" she asks while trying to maintain a sort of hard-boiled manner.

"Yeah," Lightfoot says simply, focusing on his plate of food. He takes a bite and looks up to receive the shocked faces at the table. He stops chewing at the sight of everyone's surprise, and then reiterates, "Billions of dollars. Maybe more," he says before returning to cut his fish, fully aware that everyone is staring at him in shock.

"If that's the case, we're going to have a big fight on our hands," Harvey Bearheart realizes.

"We already do," Papa Leo notes.

"Exactly. That visit today is just the beginning," Lightfoot says. "Things are going to change very quickly now." It's at this exact point, with the precision of watchful spirits, that Lightfoot's phone rings. He locates the device and looks at the number. "Ah, Germany. I have to take this," he says while rising from the table. He heads toward the shoreline, while everyone continues to stare.

"You make a mean fillet, Harvey Bearheart," Misses Bearheart says, trying to pull focus back to the table.

"Florian! Thanks for calling back," Lightfoot says. "I take it you got the package. So what did you find?" Lightfoot asks, while glancing back to find everyone still gawking his way. They all return to their meal, forcing their best appearance of preoccupation.

❖   ❖   ❖

On the other end of the line, Florian Mayer leans over a speakerphone, surrounded by other scientists from the Lab for Heavy Ion Research in Darmstadt, Germany, world renown for theorizing how super heavy elements, ones that we haven't yet discovered, will act.

"First, can I ask where you got this?" Florian asks. A chunk of the orange element rests on the table in front of him. The small team of extremely interested scientists and lab technicians listen intently, anxiously awaiting Lightfoot's response.

"*I'll get to that, but first, let's start with what your conclusions are,*" Lightfoot suggests over the speaker. "*Specifically, what about the hypothesis I wrote?*" he asks. Florian bobs his head in compliance, as he receives a sheet of stats from a coworker.

"Okay, sure enough Professor. As you know, we've theorized about an island of stability for a super heavy element in the one fifteen, one sixteen range," Florian says. "I guess that's why you sent this to us," he says. Florian looks across the table to the eager faces. "Um, I'll just say it, Professor. We think this is element one-fifteen on the periodic chart, as you suspected." Florian receives a second sheet from another coworker, who points to a certain line of text. "And yes, as you asked, we bombarded it with a narrow beam of protons. And again, as you suspected, when it transmuted to element one-sixteen, it became highly unstable. Meaning, it radiated a small amount of antimatter."

"*And?*" Lightfoot asks. Florian gulps, while the rest of his coworkers cringe and jerk upon remembering what happened next.

"It blew up. Totally! Totally, as in a total annihilation reaction, one hundred percent efficient man!" Florian exclaims excitedly.

Back on the shore, Lightfoot stops pacing, wondering if he missed that last bit.

"One hundred percent?" Lightfoot confirms the unimaginable. He places his free hand over his eyes while he listens.

"*Yeah Professor, one hundred percent of the matter converted to energy. So now can I ask... where did you get this?*" Florian asks over the phone.

"I'd like to show you," Lightfoot responds without moving an inch while gazing out across the lake.

In the lab, Florian scans the data lying on the table before him.

"*Can you come here?*" Then without a beat of consideration...

"YES!" Florian exclaims, as he leans clumsily into the speakerphone. "Yes, when? Now? Because now is good for me." His teammates nod enthusiastically.

❖   ❖   ❖

Back at the dining table, the gang watches Lightfoot hang up and take a moment to look out over the lake.

102

Even from the table's point of view, he's clearly feeling the impact of the call. When he turns back toward the table, the diners dive back into acting like they've been feasting all this time.

Eventually he finds his seat at the table and looks for a moment at all the foretelling faces, eating much too quietly to appear believably matter-of-fact about the last few minutes.

"Billions," he says while calmly taking another bite. Savoring the taste, he looks up at the stunned clan and smiles. "This is really great, Misses Bearheart."

SEVEN

"Rattlesnake's Tail"

Gogebic-Iron County Airport is a mere bald spot among the timbers in the Upper Peninsula of Michigan, near the Minnesota border. Once a day, a twelve-passenger shuttle flight, rarely filled to capacity, arrives here from Chicago, a common hub for East Coast travelers to the Great Lakes region.

No sooner does the small plane taxi to a stop, than the door tilts down into flight stairs. Kate quickly appears in the doorway with bags in hand. The look on her face betrays a long day of layovers and lines, and it's still only ten-thirty in the morning. She wobbles down the steps, finally planting her feet on solid ground. It's an unusually cold and blustery spring morning and by the look of her, there's no doubt the winds have ravaged the small aircraft en route. Kate wraps her stylish jacket tighter than the buttons allow, flips her hood over her head and follows the single painted line to the terminal building, as it's generously referred to.

Lightfoot waits inside the small wood and aluminum structure. When Kate sees him, she wonders if a hug would be appropriate, maybe a kiss on the cheek? After all, even good friends and some close business associates do that. Or should she shake hands, since she is acting as his attorney and maybe that's all he has in mind? 'Oh stop', she says to herself, thinking about how much she's over thinking.

In front of the terminal, Mary keeps the engine running at the curb. Only thirty feet and a paned glass entrance separate her from the center of the building where Lightfoot stands waiting. She catches sight of a city girl, supposedly Kate, walking from the plane to the sliding door of the lobby. Mary admires Kate's stylish urban look and heels, as she struggles to wheel her bags across the rocky tarmac. She sure has brought a lot of luggage, Mary considers. Lightfoot extends his arms in one of those come-to-papa greetings that men are so fond of.

Kate looks comfortable giving him a friendly bear hug, as Mary watches closely, ready to turn away and observe the weather the moment they rotate her way. How far will this greeting between the two of them go, Mary wonders? Then without even a peck on the cheek, Lightfoot grabs Kate's bags and leads her to the door. Mary pivots just in time.

"Watch your step", he warns, considering her lack of weather-appropriate footwear. "The ground is still pretty slick." He opens the door to the back seat and lets Kate in while he circles to load her bags in the back. Feigning surprise, Mary turns around from examining the moving clouds. She greets Kate as she plops into the seat. The first thing Kate notices is how little Mary wears in this cold.

"Kate, I've heard so much about you!" she says, offering her hand. "Mary Bearheart." Mary smiles graciously as they shake hands.

"Wow... Bearheart! That's a super-cool name," Kate proclaims. Lightfoot watches carefully from the back, as he pulls the hatch down and hurries around to the front. He jumps into the passenger seat.

"I see you two have met," Lightfoot says, turning to the back with that killer grin. "Kate is our lawyer. Our champion actually," he says. Kate blushes.

"Well I haven't passed the bar yet, but have some experience in Tribal Law," she explains, still wondering if this is as far as his interest goes.

"Buckle up, this tank's moving," Mary announces while throwing it into drive and swinging the back end around slightly on the slick pavement. Kate watches Mary pilot the Bronco, studying her confidence and strength. How could they not be a couple? Kate wonders. She's a strong, stunning, exotic beauty, who looks like she could wrestle a wolf to the ground. Kate admires her long perfectly straight hair, tucked adorably under that wool cap.

"So, are you two, related?" Kate asks, suddenly wishing she could call those words back. Holy hell, did she just say that out loud? Lightfoot thinks. He struggles to respond, but it's Mary who throws the best explanation over her shoulder as she forges down the road.

"I guess you could say that," she says, focusing on the road ahead. She turns to Lightfoot. "We *are* from the same tribe."

"Mary's father and my grandfather are best friends, and also serve as senior elders of the tribe," he adds. "We've known each other since we were kids."

"You mean since I was a kid," Mary corrects. "Billy was never a kid," Mary offers. Lightfoot tilts his head in mock reaction.

"Billy? I never knew you as a 'Billy.'" Kate says, knowing better than to just leave it hang in the air like that. "At MIT, we know him as Professor Lightfoot." Ah, that sounds professional enough, she thinks. And certainly on par with Mary's still undefined familiarity. Lightfoot looks straight ahead, considering how this week promises to be a long one. Lightfoot tries to direct the energy in the truck to a safer topic.

"We had a visit from the feds already," Lightfoot reveals. "They've shown their hand and are acting as if they're playing with a stacked deck."

"And you, what do you think?" Kate asks.

"Well, I got the reports back from three labs now, and they all confirm what I thought," he says. "We're sitting on a type of a fuel, a stable nuclear fuel that reacts with zero waste and fallout, there's nothing like it on the planet," he says, but lacking the excitement that usually accompanies his explanation. Kate can't help but feel a sense of defeat in him, a resignation entirely out of character.

"You don't sound too, I don't know... happy about it," Kate confesses, before trying to walk it back. "I mean..."

"No, it's okay – I know what you're saying," Lightfoot admits. "You're right, it's just that there is absolutely no precedent for any tribe exploiting a resource without the United States moving in and rewriting the rules. Not with oil, not with water or land, hell... it's just never happened before and this proves to be something much more valuable than any of that." Lightfoot looks out the window for a moment. Mary looks over, also unfamiliar with this level of doubt in his voice. "When we push back, Red

Rock has no future left unless we win," he attests. The pang in Lightfoot's tone strikes Mary in an almost tactile way. Not only from the urgent appreciation of the odds, but also from the conflicted vulnerability that Kate just brought out in him. Kate reaches in her bag and pulls out her yellow legal pad, now even more worn and full of inserts.

"Okay, what do we know so far?" Kate asks rhetorically. "On the subject of Tribal Sovereignty, we all know that the Bureau of Indian Affairs has wielded jurisdiction over commerce with the tribes. Even though it's been argued that since tribes are sovereign nations, tribal matters should be handled through the United States Secretary of State, the official responsible for foreign policy." Kate tosses past a few more sheets, "The idea that tribes have an inherent right to govern themselves is at the foundation of their constitutional status. Congress doesn't delegate their power, sure, but Congress can limit tribal sovereignty. Except like I said on the phone, unless some sort of law or statute removes a power, the tribe is assumed to possess that power or right." Kate leans forward towards the front seat. "If what you've discovered is so far, undefined and *unprecedented...* then there is NO precedent. You see where I'm going with this?" Kate turns from him to Mary and back again. "If this were oil, or water or even gold then yeah, you'd be screwed, just like you mentioned." Kate tosses her head back and forth as she shrugs a sort of 'tie it up' gesture. "Frankly, there's even more precedent of intentionally vague definitions being defined by the party with the most power, or the most money I should say. We know very well who's held the cards up to this point." Kate flops back in her seat, and for the first time takes in the passing scenery as she delivers the final point. "We can use their same tricks against them in the same way. We just have to be clear on what we want, make as many friends as we can on the international stage, and certainly exploit the *unprecedented* nature of the material itself, rather than allowing ourselves to be hamstrung by the precedent that's been set," she concludes. Mary is abashed and spins around to look at her.

"Wow, you really rocked that!" Mary says. "You're brilliant!" Kate didn't expect to hear that, especially from the stunning Indian goddess.

"Oh, thanks, but yeah, it's all in the books. I'm just a sponge," Kate says, wondering again about her choice of words.

"Amazing work Kate," Lightfoot says, as he turns to look into her big green eyes. "Really, I'm so happy you're here," he gushes.

"It's fun, I love this shit." Kate says, still wrestling with how his smile throws her off the rails. "You know what I mean."

"I know what you mean," Lightfoot confirms. Mary wonders what they mean. She moves on to assuming the role of tour guide.

"Ten more minutes to the Minnesota border, then about an hour from there," Mary calls out from the front, throwing a quick glance to the back. "I hope you're hungry, Kate. Since the quake, my mom's been on a mission to feed the entire tribe."

"You kidding? I'm famished. I only had a cappuccino before my flight and a little bag of something resembling food on the plane," Kate says. She turns to the side window as they pass a large elk, drinking from a natural spring beyond the road. "Oh my gawd! It's a giant deer-like, horse thing!" Kate yells.

"Wapiti," Mary replies, suppressing a laugh while Kate fixates on the alien life form out the window. "Or, 'elk' in English," Mary adds.

"I grew up in Brooklyn," Kate explains. "Biggest animal I've seen is a German Sheppard. Although we did have some rats that are just as big." Kate remains captivated by the 'giant deer-like, horse thing'.

❖　❖　❖

Mary's Bronco rolls into the reservation and stops just short of the three old sisters, who stand in the middle of the road, facing ahead and passing what remains of a soggy cigar. Kate is leaning forward, looking out through the windshield between Mary and Lightfoot when she catches sight of the trio. The Loon sisters glare through the windshield like ghosts from a horror movie.

"Oh, my!" Kate flashes. Mary actually spasms into a belly laugh from Kate's response. Kate likes how her humor can still upstage her own awkwardness.

"Yeah, since I was a kid, I've never seen those three gals separately," Mary says. "My dad calls them 'the flotilla.'"

"Your dad sounds hysterical," Kate exclaims. But Mary is not so sure.

"Yeah, tell me that after you meet him," she says. Lightfoot jumps out and opens the door for Kate, then fetches her wheeled bags from the back as she stands in the road and scans the reservation.

"It smells so good here," Kate says, while taking a deep breath. But Keezheknoi can't pass that one up.

"It's Cuban," Keezheknoi reveals while blowing a billowing cloud of tobacco her way. Lightfoot tries to wheel her stylish bags across the gravel for no more than a foot before ditching that idea and picking them up.

"I got 'em," Harvey Bearheart says, after appearing out of nowhere. He takes Kate's bags and cradles them under each massive arm. Mary motions Kate to her father who stands like a massive woodsy Moses, with his two arms already holding each suitcase like stone tablets.

"Kate Rose, meet Harvey Bearheart, my dad," Mary says with a slightly dubious motion of the hand, as she tightens a bit over what he might say. Kate extends her hand, suddenly realizing he hasn't a free one to shake with.

"Good to meet you," Harvey Bearheart says with a slight nod. "I'll show you to your house, let you get settled." He turns to lead the way. Kate pivots to Mary and Lightfoot and smiles with a shrug.

"Hysterical," Mary says, in a referencing nod to her father.

"Get settled and we'll see you at lunch in about twenty minutes?" Lightfoot says.

"Uh, sure," Kate agrees, turning back and forth from them to her departing bags. With a grin, Kate follows after the large elder, as fast as her city boots will carry her across the lose gravel.

"I like her," Mary admits while they both watch her walk off, taking in the sights along the way.

"She the lawyer?" Keezheknoi inquires.

"She's pretty," Small Duck feels the need to declare. Meoquanee waits to suck a substantial drag before expelling smoke and a question at the same time.

"You paying her?" Meoquanee asks. Mary shakes her head.

"I have to pee," Mary says, in lieu of a reply. "See you in a bit, Billy." She walks off, leaving Lightfoot alone in the road with the trio.

"Morning ladies," he says, as Meoquanee offers a drag of the soggy tobacco. "No, no. That's cool, thanks," he graciously declines.

❖ ❖ ❖

By nightfall, the growing council has finished a feast, and now enjoys tobacco and spirits around another raging fire by the lake. Papa Leo scans the gathering, reflecting on how it took such a disaster to bring everyone together. He considers his grandson and Mary next to him, wondering if anyone other than he knows of their feelings for each other. And then there's Kate, flanking Lightfoot on the left, and clearly interested beyond legal matters. Harvey Bearheart pulls a bottle of Jack away from Small Duck who drinks from it directly.

"Slow down Mindimooyen," Harvey Bearheart asserts, referring to the Chippewa word for old lady. "One spark from that fire and you'll burst into flames," he claims, as he wipes her germs off the rim with his sleeve. Lightfoot keenly examines the dynamics of a people on the verge of hope and on the brink of being plundered for their resources. These are a people who knew the potential of growing filthy rich in a white man's world was as dishonorable as it was impossible. He stops to meet his grandfather's stare, who all the while has been watching him study the group. A giddy squeal pulls Papa Leo's eyes to the side. Lightfoot knew that look. It's something his grandfather did often, practiced from years in the woods, sitting firm and motionless in the deer blind, when only your eyes were allowed to jump across the terrain at the sound of a broken branch or rustle of leaves along a trail. Lightfoot turns to notice Kate, clearly fueled by alcohol, as the source of the contagious squeal. He spies Harvey Bearheart mischievously leaning over when Kate isn't looking and fills her glass, as well as anyone else who isn't watching their drink at the time. Kate pulls the drink up to her lips, puzzled that it still remains full and wondering how she got so shit faced. Mary catches the bewilderment in Kate's eyes, and while feeling little pain herself, looks down to her own *full* glass. She shoots a glare toward her dad.

"It's you!" Mary insists to her father. "Kate, watch out," Mary exclaims. "My 'hysterical' dad is filling everyone's glass when they're not looking."

"Busted!" Kate yells, leaning over Lightfoot to Mary, like a listing mast. "You tell Mister Big-Bear over there, that I'm on to him," Kate says while twisting two pointed fingers from her eyes to his. "I'm done anyway," she slurs as she stares at her glass. "What the hell are we drinking, anyway?" Kate struggles with the coordination needed to place her glass on the edge of the fire pit. "No more, no more for me," she states, as she holds both hands up to the teetering glass, motioning for it to stay put. Mary swings her arm around Kate's shoulders, pointing at her father in an, 'I'm on to you' gesture.

"My dad is NOT hysterical. He's historical," Mary says, proud of her pun. "Get it, like he's old," she says.

"Very clever. Shame on you mister Bear-person," Kate chastises, but the large Bearheart hardly looks bothered and rather seems to enjoy the show. Mary tries to help Kate up and bumps her glass off the hearth and into the fire in a whoosh of flame.

"Watch out, incoming!" Kate blurts through an explosion of laughter. Papa Leo and Lightfoot watch in awe as the two ladies try to prop each other up in an effort to stand and turn in for the night.

"Holy shit, I think we need to call it a night," Mary says, with only slightly better control.

"Fine," Kate slops. "It's a night! You happy?" Mary laughs and nearly falls over backwards.

"It's your fault," Misses Bearheart declares, pulling the bottle from her husband's hand.

"Hey woman?" he protests.

"Don't you woman me Harvey Bearheart. Up, up,

you're done for the night too," she demands with both hands on her hips.

"Somebody's in trouble," Mary chides her dad who hasn't quite mastered his attempt to stand upright either. Misses Bearheart helps him up and walks the grizzly man toward their house.

"Say good night," Misses Bearheart says while dragging him along.

"It was a good night!" Harvey Bearheart exclaims proudly. "Have I told you how glorious you look in the moonlight?" he says, trying to kiss her as she pulls away. Lightfoot looks up to Papa Leo and shrugs, a whadda ya do? They appear to be the only lucid ones in the group. Papa Leo motions with a flick of an eye for his grandson to follow him to the shore. He braces for a stance, placing both hands on his knees to signal his exit. Lightfoot follows him up and toward the water. Mary and Kate remain by the fire, continuing to bang-on about absolutely nothing.

"What's up Granddad?" Lightfoot asks. "How're you feeling?" Papa Leo considers the question carefully.

"Restless," he says. Lightfoot nods in agreement.

"I know. It's too quiet. I'm a bit worried to be honest," Lightfoot admits.

"People like that *Doctor Drummer* guy don't just walk away," he says. Then he motions to the girls at the fire, "Make sure they both find their way inside.

I'm going for a ride," the old man says, turning toward the stable.

"Be careful," Lightfoot says. But Papa Leo pauses and turns back to second his grandson's caution.

"You too, son," Papa Leo says while glancing to the ladies. Whoa, that wasn't subtle at all, Lightfoot thinks as he watches Kate and Mary. He heads to the fire pit, as Papa Leo walks off toward the stable.

"Kate, let me walk you to your room," Mary says, offering her hand to steady Kate to her feet.

"Oh thank you, it gets pretty dark out here," Kate says as she tries to focus beyond three feet. Mary winks at Lightfoot as they pass. He takes a seat by the fire and watches the two ladies weave down the gravel path with Mary slightly leading the way when a cloud of cigar smoke occludes his vision

"It's only you and us again," Keezheknoi observes.

"She's a beautiful girl, Billy," Small Duck interferes.

"Which one?" Meoquanee asks.

"Which one do you think, you old coot," Small Duck replies obviously. Lightfoot doesn't dare ask for clarification, but silently wonders who she meant.

❖   ❖   ❖

Kate's unmistakable laugh approaches the other side of the door leading to her room. First a bump shakes the rough-hewn frame, then another more forceful one manages to suddenly swing the door into the room. Kate catches her foot on the threshold and stumbles headlong into the room. Mary tries to brace Kate's tumble, but winds up crumbling to the ground with her. They don't bother to stand up again, instead they lie in a pile, laughing hysterically. Mary leans back, resting against her elbows. Kate is sloppy, but charming.

"You really are beautiful. No, no really, you are stunning," Kate blathers. Mary is flattered and tries to reciprocate.

"No you are, and so smart too," Mary confesses. "You know, I envy you really, but don't tell Papa Leo I said that," Mary continues. "He'd say envy is.... wait how does he say that? Oh yeah, 'envy fuels the wrong fire'," she says, followed by a puzzled look. "I don't even know what that means," Mary admits. Kate is barely able to look through the narrow slits that her eyelids have swollen into. She tries to be cool and lean back like Mary, but gets too dizzy and ditches the position for a straight-backed plant on the solid floor.

"He's very wise, adorable too. I love him," Kate says before again feeling the need to clarify. "Um, your hysterical dad I mean." Mary smiles.

"I know who you meant," she says kindly. With all inhibitions to the wind, Kate leans forward, deep into Mary's space.

"Okay, there's an elephant in the room. No, I mean, let's... let's discuss it," Kate confides while Mary grins under a puzzled brow.

"Discuss it?" Mary asks, but Kate forges ahead with sloppy confidence.

"The elephant, silly! The one in the room! It's a figure of speech. You know, like there's a giant thing looming in a small place but everyone pretends they don't see it because..." Kate says, thinking hard but not able to come up with a reason. "Because, you know – it's awkward," she discloses. Mary looks around the room for the elephant. Lifting up the sham, she peers under the bed. Kate laughs and slaps at her arm, twice after missing the first time.

"You are so cute. I just love you!" Kate says before gathering herself into what she thinks is sober thought. "Okay, you and..." Kate laughs again. "You call him Billy? Okay, you and Billy. C'mon, you're an item aren't you?" she says, stumbling onto the elephant. Mary tries to play coy but Kate's liquid confidence is running the show right now.

"Oh stop it," Kate says, "I can tell he has a thing for you. Hell, look at you. You're the most beautiful woman I've ever seen. Shit, even I have a thing for you. Wait, I'm sorry, I'm just being nice. I'm not trying to be creepy," Kate says, quickly peddling backward. Mary is charmed though and takes Kate's hand in hers.

"You really are lovely, Kate Rose. I do like you a lot," Mary says. Kate is feeling even more drunk right now, if that were possible. Kate looks at her hand in Mary's, comparing her own ruddy colored skin against Mary's dark complexion. She touches Mary's arm as if examining an exotic creature. The touch turns into a stroke as she moves the back of her hand across Mary's defined biceps. Kate lifts Mary's hand and kisses it. Rather than curb the intrusion into her sacred space, Mary watches in awe. The effects of the alcohol are growing across her body as well, as goose bumps rise against Kate's cool touch. Within moments, they are kissing, cautiously at first and shamefully enjoyable. Kate pauses a beat.

"You know, I've never really done this before. For real!" Kate admits. Without admission one way or the other, Mary leans in and kisses Kate's neck and begins to move a hand along her chest and legs.

"Me either," Mary says. Suddenly Mary stops, and sprouting a devilish grin, says, "I have an idea!"

❖ ❖ ❖

Lightfoot pulls his boots off and flops backwards onto the bed. He lies there alone and aware that while Kate is here, maybe it would be best to keep things quiet between he and Mary. The scent of the bonfire still lingers across the village center, just outside his door. Occasionally a crackling and snap of the embers echo outside in the moist air. But that aside, it's still very, very quiet. A knock at his door startles him a bit, since he had already made peace with sleeping alone tonight. He grins knowingly and rises for the door, confident that when it opens, it'll be... *Nope.* There stands Mary *and* Kate, arm in arm and bracing each other upright. Kate lifts half a bottle of Jack Daniels into the air.

"Can we come in?" Mary asks but enters anyway, pulling Kate in by the arm. Lightfoot pokes his head outside, carefully checking the surroundings before quietly closing the door.

❖   ❖   ❖

Papa Leo sits atop his horse looking across the land below. The eloquence of night has always spoke volumes to his spirit. He considers the many times he was happy up here, and the many more times he wasn't, but he always left the ridge focused and refueled for what the next morning would bring. Tonight though, tension and uneasiness seem to gnaw at him. The uneasiness buzzes around him like an annoying insect that haunts a small room. Except now, there's a direction to the buzzing sound, from just over the ridge. Papa Leo turns an ear toward its source, and furrows his brow. He very gently taps his heels into his mare's side. After all these years, she doesn't need much to know where he wants to go next. They head in the direction of the sound.

Cresting the opposite ridge, Papa Leo's eyes narrow at the nearly impossible sight below. He wonders how such a massive machine could hover so quietly? This was a helicopter, but a nearly silent one. Even the sound of grass rustling from the rotor down wash is louder than the engine or the props cutting through the air. This was a stealth mission under cover of darkness.

The old man dismounts, calming his steed with a gentle pat to her neck, as he slowly moves the horse under cover of some fallen trees, so as not to spook her or expose them to the raid below. Then Papa Leo quietly hikes down into the bowl along the ridge, undetected by the intruders as he has for many years when hunting Wapiti and Woods Bison. Shielded from view, Papa Leo settles into a familiar deer blind, overlooking the valley and the newly formed chasm. Quietly he watches, patiently settling into a tucked-away spot within the foliage for a perfect view of the operation below.

Special Forces Rangers signal to each other in a well-rehearsed mission to recover as much of the floating rocks as possible as they race the clock. They silently hand sacks to each other along a human chain stretching from the crevice, up the hill, and eventually attaching them to a long-line, dropped from the silently hovering chopper.

Papa Leo shows neither surprise nor indignation. He just leans back into the foliage to take in the sight of this covert mission playing out in front of him. He remains frozen, allowing only those dark kinetic eyes to scan the operation below. Even these highly trained rangers, on the lookout through the night vision goggles mounted to their helmets, see no sign of him. One of them pans the valley wall, searching for any heat signature through the trees. Suddenly the ranger freezes and holds up a hand to alert the others, when a buck emerges, followed by his doe and calf. The deer notice the intruders and bound out of the valley as quickly as the little calf can follow. The ranger signals the lack of threat with a flip of a finger to continue on. After a few more bags make their way to form the last bundle, the sentry checks his watch again. Spinning two fingers in the air, he signals the others to wrap it up. The scavengers speed it up and hand the last of the sacks up the chain, and attaching the final bundle to the long-line. One of the rangers rides atop the cargo as the winch pulls them upward toward the chopper.

Papa Leo watches as they climb into the aircraft one by one. The scout is the last to leave the site, expertly continuing to study the terrain around them as the cable pulls him up into the belly of the beast.

Just as quietly, the helicopter rises out of the area with barely an electrical buzz. Branches rustle and pine needles flutter across the ground as the stealth team slowly flies off and over the lake. Without a hint of urgency, Papa Leo leans back into the blind to consider what just happened. It's a long time until morning and for now there's not much anyone can do. Especially considering the state of the tribe right now.

❖ ❖ ❖

Lying on the bed, in a tangle of limbs and few covers, Lightfoot, Mary and Kate are sleeping soundly together. Kate is the first to open her eyes, bewildered for a moment but then beginning to follow a drowsy hunch, she lifts her head to look behind her.

There at the foot of the bed stands Papa Leo, again arms folded and expressionless. Kate turns to nudge the others with a barely audible whisper.

"Hey, guys! Um... hey?" Kate says in a hoarse and spooked voice. Slowly, three pairs of eyes turn in the direction of the statuesque patriarch watching them like a sculpture in the park. The empty bottle of Jack rolls off the bed and across the floor, stopping near Papa Leo's feet.

"When you're ready," he says ordinarily, then turns

and exits the room. Lightfoot can only spasm out a quick chuckle.

"Damn, I wish he'd stop doing that," he says while rising to find his pants. Mary and Kate survey their entwined bodies and with fuzzy embarrassment, silently pull for their clothes and covers. Words are meaningless, possibly even dangerous at this point. Everyone quietly pulls it together, heading out in opposite directions.

❖　❖　❖

Lightfoot meets his grandfather outside by the village road.

"We need to talk," Papa Leo maintains. Lightfoot lets out the breath he's been holding for the last few minutes. He and Papa Leo share a look before both turning to catch sight of Kate and Mary hustling in opposite directions to their own quarters.

"I'm sorry," he says contritely.

"For what?" the old man replies, ready to move on. "We had visitors last night," he says, confirming their worst expectations.

"What do you mean, visitors?" Lightfoot asks. "At the crevice? That means we have pictures of them!"

"Let's hope that matters. Now they have what they wanted all along," Papa Leo says dryly. Lightfoot looks at the ground and nods. He notices his shoes are still untied and kneels to lace his boots.

"Did you see them?" he asks while tying his shoes.

"They were good," Papa Leo says. "Rangers I think, and the helicopter they dropped in from was silent. I didn't know that was possible." Lightfoot stands.

"What did they look like?"

"No uniforms. Everyone was wearing black," his grandfather says. Lightfoot grabs the top of his head with both hands, tormented by the thought of the material in military hands.

"It won't be long before they realize what they have. And determine they need more," Lightfoot says. Papa Leo unties his horse and lifts himself into the saddle.

"You ready to ride up there?" Papa Leo asks.

❖　❖　❖

Both horses are tied at the top of the ridge, grazing on fresh grass while Lightfoot and his grandfather walk the edge of the fissure in the bottom of the valley. Papa Leo stops to grab one of the orange metallic stones left behind from the raid. Lightfoot leans over the edge, noticing the dark crevice is still teeming with floating rocks.

"How much did they get?"

"Five, maybe six sacks full," Papa Leo says. "At least that's what I saw by the time I got here."

"Did they see you?"

"They weren't that good," the old man says with confidence. They watch the massive reserve of rocks continue to bump and float at a common altitude just below the ridge.

"It's time we make a stand, Son," his grandfather declares.

"I agree. But we need an army to stand with us," Lightfoot says. "There's a world of people out there who are being bullied and out-litigated by this government, and they're itching for a poster child." Lightfoot suddenly remembers the cameras and turns toward the tree line. Papa Leo watches him run up the hill and remove them from the base of each tree. Lightfoot returns and hands one of the cameras to his grandfather. "This is our ammunition!" he says. "Luckily I know someone who still develops this stuff." Lightfoot says, while admiring the old technology.

"So, how good is the lawyer lady?" Papa Leo asks.

"She's not a lawyer yet," Lightfoot admits, while noticing Papa Leo cringe just a bit. "She's smart, she has some good ideas and is committed," he says, nodding to himself. "Right now, I believe she's our best shot." But Papa Leo tightly presses his lips together while staring back silently for a dubious moment. He kindly pats his grandson's shoulder and begins walking back up the hill.

EIGHT

"Power Source"

The ten-year-old Chippewa boy peddles his bike purposefully across the village, while a handmade *Shipping Dept.* sign flutters on the basket attached to his handlebars. He waves to construction workers, busily moving ahead on their repairs to damaged structures along the main road.

Arriving in front of the Community Center, the little guy spies Anna Bearheart, wearing overalls and busily painting patched cracks on the walls near the entrance. The young courier peacocks his arrival by masterfully locking his breaks and sliding his back wheel into a power-skid, all for her benefit. He hops off his bike, flips his kickstand, grabs the packages from the basket and quickly prances past the young beauty towards the entrance.

"Hey Anna," he asserts as he passes, with just enough eye contact to see her smile back. He continues inside.

Anna exhales in exasperation of goofy little boys, then continues painting.

❖　❖　❖

The interior of the Community Center now serves as operations headquarters and is sectioned off according to department. Mary directs the enlisted members where to erect folding tables. In the center of the room, the three Loon sisters package and label boxes from a supply of various sized orange rocks, and a stack of leather goods and trinkets. Keezheknoi drops one of the element samples in a traditional trinket bag labeled 'Sacred Stone' and hands it to Small Duck, who inserts the bag and a pair of moccasins into a shipping box. Meoquanee seals the box and adheres a pre-printed shipping label from the Red Rock Chippewa Trading Post.

Across the room, Kate is busy outlining legal strategies at a table in front of a small pup tent with another handmade sign that reads *Legal Department*.

Lightfoot is on the phone and as usual, pacing the room as he speaks. He passes a chain-link lockup area full of scientific and mechanical parts, where Harvey Bearheart is assembling what looks like a large series of plumbing fixtures. Another sign that simply reads *Bear Cage*, designates the lockup area.

"What's it worth to you?" Lightfoot asks of the

caller, while giving Harvey Bearheart the thumbs up on the progress of the contraption. "One hundred-thousand dollars for five grams," Lightfoot replies with conviction. Harvey Bearheart nearly chokes upon hearing the price. "No, we have to do this without exchanging U.S. currency," he insists. "You want fuel and technology, I need equipment for my power station," Lightfoot insists. Mary is also on the phone now and hurries to capture his attention.

"Can you hold one second please?" Mary asks of the person on the other end of the line. She holds her phone to her chest while waiting for Lightfoot to finish.

"Fine, we'll assemble it here," he continues. "You ship what I need from the parts list, and we'll get you material and tech to build your own as well," he says, while noticing Mary pointing to her phone. "Hold on one second," he tells the caller. Both he and Mary cup their hands over their receivers. Mary goes first.

"Steam generator guy again. He says seventy five thousand dollars," Mary explains.

"I got the French lab on the line," Lightfoot says. "I'm trying to get them to trade for the crated parts." He holds up a finger, then returns to the call. "Okay, I'm back, so here's the deal. We both have what the other wants. Think about it and get back to me." He says, before waiting for a reply. "Great, I'll talk to you tonight, thanks," and hangs up. Mary hands him the other line.

"Hey, Professor Lightfoot here. So US dollars only, I hear? I thought we talked about this." He listens impatiently while bobbing his head. "You have it ready to ship, right?" he asks. "Good, then let me get back to you tonight. Yeah you too, bye." Lightfoot hangs up and looks at Mary to suggest, 'what now?' He uses her as a sounding board to think out their predicament. "Doing this without cash is going to be a problem," he reasons, as she follows him down another thought stroll. "So far only the Germans are willing to barter." Mary thinks hard, when an idea sets off a spark in her eye.

"Gold! Everyone likes gold right?" Mary asks. "Can we trade the labs who want the rocks for that instead of dollars and then use the gold to buy things from people who aren't scientists?" The thought clobbers Lightfoot.

"That's it!" he says, grabbing Mary by the shoulders. "That's genius!" he exclaims again.

"Yeah, I thought so," Mary nods assuredly. At her desk, Kate is considering the concept while wagging a finger in the air.

"That might be the ticket we need," Kate says, rising from her post to join the conversation. "You go girl," Kate says, as she slaps Mary's hand in a high five.

"There's nothing in the Indian Commerce Clause that says we can't trade one element for another. We just can't sell minerals or resources internationally yet, without the feds crawling up our ass. At least not until we formally stake our position in court," she notes. "Oh!" Kate exclaims, and hurries back to her landfill of research papers. She fumbles through the messy stack and holds a sheet over her head like a burning torch. "There's something else too!" Kate exclaims. "Even before we prepare a constitutional argument for our rights, it's time we use the photos that you guys got of them stealing the element for an exposé in the media," she claims. "Maybe even start by suing them on totally separate grounds than Tribal Commerce Rights?" Kate says, while grinning mischievously.

"Sue them? How, or for what?" Lightfoot asks.

"Robbery, essentially," Kate says as she hands him the paper. "There's this thing called the *Archaeological Resources Protection Act* passed in nineteen seventy-nine, to protect irreplaceable archaeological resources on federal, public and Indian lands," Kate explains, as Lightfoot and Mary follow along in the report. "It says that 'consent' of the tribes must be received when the artifact is on Indian land, and..." Kate's enthusiasm is certainly contagious, as she flips to a page in the back of the report he's holding. "And check this out," she gleams. "It pertains to skeletal remains, rock paintings, tools, bottles, weapons, pottery and get this... PROJECTILES!" Kate shrugs out a sort of wry expression. "Pretty ironic, huh?" she adds. "And the objects need to be over a hundred years old!" Kate adds, nearly jumping out of her own skin. "I think we got that covered."

"C'mon!" Lightfoot says in total disbelief while tilting his head back past his shoulders.

"Yeah!" Kate exclaims through a hearty laugh. "Whatever they meant by projectile, hell, we'll take it. Like all statutes about Native Lands, the better the legal team, the winner of the definition."

"Kate, you really are good at this!" Mary asserts.

"Oh... thanks," Kate says, pausing with a humble grin before continuing. "So, I'd say with the photos you took, we file a lawsuit now, if only for the publicity." Kate concludes while confirming a plan forward. "We still move ahead with challenging the sovereignty definition, but for now, we make a big splash, by exposing what they did. Fire up the public!"

"But who are we suing?" Lightfoot asks.

"Ahhh, but that's just it," Kate replies while wagging a finger in the air again. "We file it against the Department of Interior, and blast it across the media. We use their own law against them and we use the publicity to prep the narrative for eventually approaching the United Nations. I mean, that's what you want ultimately, right?" Kate looks at the sheet again. "Think about it, we don't even need to win. We need the publicity. Let's make the entire world spend some energy on this. All while they have magic rocks in their hands. Then we just set a price, once everyone agrees on its value and social significance." Kate finishes, holding the papers in front of her in a self-evident manner.

Lightfoot paces, motioning in the air.

"Interesting. Okay, this could be fun!" he says nodding at the potential.

"We still have to avoid U.S. currency," Kate adds.

"Who knows, maybe we could even sell for Canadian dollars, wired directly into banks across the lake if we do need cash." Anyway, I'm digressing. For now we trade for gold, rocks for rocks. In the mean time, I'll prepare a case to challenge the theft."

Kate gawkily fist pumps the air, "Stick it to the man!" she yells, which tickles Mary so much she nearly chokes on her sip of coffee.

"And the Germans will be here soon," Lightfoot realizes. "Ha ha... this could work out after all. They have the gold, and they want more of the one-fifteen element!" he says.

Papa Leo enters the fray and mildly walks up to the team.

"Visitors", he announces monotonously.

"Good visitors or bad visitors?" Lightfoot asks.

"Germans I think," Papa Leo shrugs. "With a big truck, and it's stuck in the mud," the old man mutters without any emphasis. He simply turns to shuffle back outside, as deadpan as he arrived.

"That's Florian," Lightfoot confirms, before rushing outside to meet him. Half the place follows him out the door to greet the arrival. And to see a truck stuck in the mud. Kate and Mary hang behind, as they watch the entire place clean out.

"We don't get many trucks," Mary says with a chuckle. Kate gets up and stretches as she's evidently been at it for a while.

"Oh hell. I don't see many trucks in the mud either. I need a break anyway," Kate says, following everyone out the door while Mary contentedly stays behind.

❖   ❖   ❖

Outside on the village road, Papa Leo watches expressionless as a handful of trendy looking gents surround the rental truck and yelling at the driver in German. The crowd watches as he continues to spin his wheels, digging a deeper ditch. Lightfoot recognizes Florian near the sinking double axle.

"Florian Mayer, you made it!" Lightfoot exclaims.

"Hey Professor, yeah, you mind if we park her here?" Florian chuckles.

Harvey Bearheart arrives with a six-foot plank of wood and motions with a finger across his throat for the guy in the cab to shut it down.

"You're just digging a grave, boy," he calls up to the driver.

"Harvey Bearheart, resident mechanical genius," Lightfoot explains to Florian. "He'll get 'em out. C'mon in," he says, leading Florian to the community center. "You really made good time."

"Yeah well, lucky to be alive," Florian confesses, while motioning over his shoulder towards the driver. "Richter drives faster than our guardian angels can fly." Florian follows the professor towards the makeshift operations center while looking the village over. The space and grandeur of the Great Lakes region is putting a spell on his head. "Wow, this ain't no sausage," Florian exclaims, when suddenly something catches his eye behind him. He turns around to find a goat following him specifically.

"I think she likes you," Lightfoot winks.

"I've always had a thing with the ladies," the German quips. "Except that one doesn't have horns."

"Ah, Kate!" Lightfoot exclaims, pulling her over to meet Florian as she heads to see the daring rescue. "Florian, Kate Rose. Our attorney," he generously claims. Kate will take it this time, reaching out to greet him.

"Pleasure to meet you, Florian," she says, then motioning to the drama surrounding the truck. "I see you found a parking spot."

"No, no, Richter is just drilling for oil," Florian says. Kate laughs and turns to Lightfoot.

"I'll be back in a bit. I have to get a book I left in the room," she says, but really she needs a bit of air.

"Good to meet you Miss Rose," Florian says with a gentlemanly bow as she walks off, but then bites his knuckle without Lightfoot noticing.

Florian, Lightfoot and the goat enter the makeshift operations center.

"Holy shit, Professor. This is crazy, man," he says. Lightfoot walks him directly to the old ladies' shipping table. Currently it's abandoned while the gals observe the rescue mission out front. Across the room, Mary scratches the goat's head as she talks on the phone.

Florian lifts a massive orange rock with both hands, much larger than the one Lightfoot sent him.

"How much of this stuff do you have?" Florian asks, barely able to believe the size of the rock in his hands.

"We're still trying to figure that out. For now, it's a quarry," Lightfoot says. "We think from the Sudbury comet strike that formed the Great Lakes." Lightfoot places both hands on Florian's shoulders, "I have a plan my friend," he says while looking deeply at him. "But I can't do it without you."

"The one who pays the piper calls the tune, Professor." Florian grins devilishly.

Lightfoot notices Mary wrapping up the call. He motions for Florian to follow him to her 'office'. Mary watches them approach and shoos the goat away, but it only circles back with an eye on Florian again.

"Florian Mayer, meet Mary Bearheart," Lightfoot pronounces. Mary extends her hand.

"*Es ist ein Vergnügen, Sie zu treffen Florian,*" she says in perfect German. Florian responds without pause.

"*Nein, nein, es ist mir eine Freude, Frau Bearheart,*" Florian says, clearly charmed.

Lightfoot stares at Mary entirely stupefied.

"You speak German?" he asks, totally astonished.

"Sure," Mary replies in a feasible tone. "I speak German, French, English and Ojibwe, of course." She smiles assuredly. "Oh, and a bit of Swahili," she adds. A dumbfounded haze still blankets Lightfoot's face.

"Why Swahili?" he asks, not sure he wants to hear the answer.

"Amazon sent me the wrong book," she confesses. Florian's eyes dart between them, beginning to catch on to the peppy dynamic between Mary and the Professor.

"God, I love you!" Lightfoot says, surprising himself as well. But as always, Florian never misses an opportunity to offer witty commentary. He simply

141

passes a hand between Mary and Lightfoot's eyes as if to break the trance.

"Breathe Professor," Florian suggests. Mary's barely embarrassed giggle is as adorable as she is. Lightfoot snaps out of it, at least enough to proceed.

"So there's this thing called the Indian Commerce Clause that allows the feds to monitor, and even approve, international transactions with the tribes," he explains. "So to avoid this, we aren't using US dollars."

"Who is, these days?" Florian alleges.

"Then there's that," Lightfoot says. "Now since you want more of the element, and we need equipment from you, let's avoid the money trail and just swap."

"Ah yes, and you need a particle accelerator," Florian says while holding up a finger.

"Doesn't everyone?" Lightfoot replies.

"Exactly," Florian follows. "Just happen to have one in the truck. Well, the parts at least. So yeah, we can trade for that Professor."

"Perfect, that's a great start," Lightfoot says while shaking Florian's hand profusely. "The next thing we need, is a steam generator, say... one hundred megawatts."

"That I don't have access to I'm afraid," Florian says, furrowing a brow in consideration of why he would want such an old-school thing. Harvey Bearheart returns from the rescue mission with Richter and the other Germans in tow. Richter is hardly fashion appropriate for these parts, nor his advanced age for that matter. He's dressed entirely in black, with absurdly tight jeans and severely dyed hair to match.

"Ozzy Osborne over here is wondering where their rooms are," Harvey Bearheart exclaims. Lightfoot pads the sarcasm with an introduction.

"Florian, meet Harvey Bearheart, and this is Florian Mayer, he runs the research lab in Germany," Lightfoot explains.

"Yeah, you're the guys fencing the rocks for us," the big guy says, while wiping the mud from his hands. Lightfoot tries to follow that up.

"Right, something like that," he says, turning to offer Florian another thought.

"So that's the other idea I was going to mention," he says. "What if we could trade some more of the element for, let's say ... another element?" Lightfoot proposes. Florian motions, why not?

"What other kind of element are you thinking of Professor?" But before Lightfoot can respond –

"Gold," Mary exclaims.

"Exactly," Lightfoot seconds the motion, as Florian appears to buy into the logic.

"Ah I get it, but how to get it into the U.S.? That'll take time, maybe through Canada I suppose?" Florian considers.

"You could disguise it as heroin," Bearheart responds. "They seem to have no problem getting that into the country." With that, the big guy heads back to his cage.

"Okay, we won't be doing that," Mary declares. Florian motions to his own head, signaling the formation of an idea brewing deep inside his skull.

"Do you really need the physical gold in your hand? No! Instead we do it like a commodity exchange in the German market," Florian says. "Then I just buy what you need and *donate* it to the tribe? No money exchanged, you just move more of the element our way!" the clever German proposes.

"Like I said, a fence," Harvey Bearheart growls from his cage. Lightfoot turns back from his blank stare toward the Bear cage, and grins at Florian.

"That'll work too," Lightfoot responds.

"How much we talking?" Florian wonders, throwing a number out. "A million, two?" he asks. Lightfoot is ready with the stats.

"I figure a million and a half dollars will buy us all the parts and labor," he says. "That'll get us fifty, maybe eighty megawatts of output. We could fit the generator into a forty-foot cargo container," Lightfoot calculates out loud. "Oh, and we'd need a cooling tower too, so yeah, maybe two million," he says, summing up his list. "And as you can see over there," Lightfoot points to the

Bear Cage. "We're already working on the boiler and condenser."

"I'm shitting my pants right now Professor," Florian declares with a snicker. "So, you're going to use the particle accelerator to..."

"Transmute the one-fifteen to one-sixteen and aim the antimatter result into some hydrogen gas, and POW!" Lightfoot says, finishing his thought. "Shit loads of heat to boil the water, spin the turbine and start pumping megawatts of electricity back into the power grid," Lightfoot discloses.

"For free?" Florian asks.

"Well, at a discount!" Lightfoot replies. "We make the energy companies rich, and we have one of the strongest lobbyists fighting the government on our behalf," the Professor puffs, quite proud of his logic.

Richter, who actually refuses to speak English, has been listening intently. He confers with Florian in his native tongue.

"*Was wollen sie mit all dem?*" Richter asks.

"Richter is wondering what it is that you want to force the U.S. to do?" Florian translates.

"Nothing!" Lightfoot exclaims. "That's the point."

"Yeah right, like that'll happen," Florian replies sardonically.

"Great, I'm glad you agree," Lightfoot says, slapping the funny German on the back. "Let's get started."

❖ ❖ ❖

Nearly a thousand miles away, southwest of the Great Lakes, Doctor Edward Drummond has set up his own mission control, deep within the pines and open sky of the High Desert of New Mexico. This is the Los Alamos National Laboratory, originally founded to design and build atomic bombs as well as housing the Neutron Science Center, which operates one of the most powerful particle accelerators in the world. Today, Doctor Drummond has his bombsights set on a new type of nuclear reaction, using the element one-fifteen that was recently snatched from the Chippewa tribe.

"We know it's stable, until it's not," Doctor Drummond says as he passes a clear plastic bag along the small gallery of briefing participants. "We know when it moves one tick up the chart, it's extremely unstable." Each one examines the strange orange rock then passes it to the next, as the bloated power monger continues.

Turning to the white board, he draws a square and writes the numbers *115* in it. "We think that's the atomic weight of the element you're holding in your hands. Heavy, stable and also emits its own field, a gravity of sorts that when combined in large quantities, the shit actually floats." He taps the dry marker on the number nervously to emphasize his point, peppering the square with black dots. "I want to bombard this thing until it moves up the scale and comes apart. I want to study what this field is when it does. We don't have a ton of it. Not yet anyway. But before we get more, we need to know what radiates from this stuff and the only way we'll know that is to blast it mercilessly," he says, continuing to jab the marker into the square in a compulsive frustration that freaks out everyone in the room. "You're looking at a nuclear fuel that has field properties, the likes of which we've only theorized for the last thirty years." He turns back to the room while unsuccessfully sealing the marker with the wrong side of the cap, and instead painting his fingers black in the process. He tosses the marker to the ground. "Stupid design," he grumbles. The faces across the room reveal a familiar and pained tolerance of his acerbic personality. He holds up a sample of the orange rock for the room. "We pound this fucker until it melts, and then we study the results."

A hand rises from the center of the crowd. Drummond acknowledges the question with an unenthusiastic nod as a small man in his early twenties stands.

"Do we have a hypothesis of what to expect when it does become unstable from the bombardment? What are we looking for?"

"What we don't know or expect to know. Any

other questions?" Drummond says dismissively as if blowing snot on the poor guy. A few hands shoot up. "Nothing? Perfect," Drummond responds, shutting down any further challenges before bulldozing his way to his next point. "Now, we prepare the accelerator for a full-scale proton blitz, with as wide a beam as we can. We prepare to fire immediately," the doctor declares as he closes his briefing book and starts erasing the board. He turns back and looks expectantly across the room. "You're dismissed," he says conclusively.

Drummond turns to strut out of the room, determined always to surpass his pompous entrance with an equally glorious exit. Except today, his foot rolls across the discarded marker and he slips, dropping to the floor like a bag of groceries.

NINE

"Bombardment"

Mary starts the Ford Bronco while watching Lightfoot and Kate approach together, from across the road. Kate wears the same smart city clothes she showed up in, and yet there's something very different about her since she first arrived at Red Rock. There is a new confidence in the way Kate carries herself, more determined and secure in her talents as a strategist and certainly less self-conscious these last few days. Harvey Bearheart arrives with Kate's bags and begins to load them in the back as Lightfoot walks Kate over. Lightfoot feels the changes in her as well. A type of gravity seems to tug at her now, or maybe it's a resignation that propels her - the sort of reluctant acceptance that comes with loving someone and at the same time making peace with all the reasons why they can't love you back. Mary was of course the main reason, and it was Kate's respect of this that made him

149

appreciate Kate that much more. Lightfoot opens the passenger door for her.

"I wish I could go, but I've got to help Florian finish the reactor," Lightfoot says. "Hopefully we can fire it up in the morning."

"I'll call you when I get to D.C.," Kate says, before laying out her plans for the trip. "Itinerary's jam-packed, United Nations science committee then Member Relations. That I'm actually looking forward to. It's the Bureau that's got me concerned the most," she confesses. Lightfoot considers his friend, thinks about the attraction they suppress and all the reasons why the attraction they share will never really merge. He hands her an envelope.

"Take this, our legal *defense-fund*," he explains, nodding for her to take it before she can protest. "You'll be amazing." He gives her a hug as the three Loon sisters shuffle over.

"Next time dress for the occasion," Keezheknoi jabs playfully, even affectionately if that were possible.

"Don't listen to that old crow, we love you just like you are," Small Duck explains, giving her a kiss on the cheek.

"When you come back, I'll take you shopping," Meoquanee promises. Kate isn't sure what the hell that means or how that would work but gives Meoquanee a hug anyway. Papa Leo takes the opportunity to highlight her mission.

"Remember, if you say you're stating the truth, they'll think you're lying. Tell them you can't say for sure and they'll trust you." Kate has come to rely on the old man's wisdom, though half the time she hasn't a clue what he's talking about.

"I'm so going to miss you, Papa Leo. I wish I could take you with me," she says while giving the old fellow a big hug.

"Be careful what you wish for – *Red*," Harvey Bearheart warns, using his nickname for her. "Bags are stowed, you're all set." He gives her his signature hug with one arm, pulling her to his side like a boy's uncle.

"Oh shit," Kate flusters as her eyes begin to water up. "I'm sorry, I'm just tired," she says, and tries to cover with one last hug for Lightfoot. While next to his ear, she whispers, "By the way, what was your grandfather trying to tell me?" Lightfoot places his arms on her shoulders, separating their bodies enough to look deep into her eyes.

"I don't have a clue," he says in an intentionally anti-climactic manner. Kate laughs and hops into the front seat and pulls the door shut. Mary begins to roll as Kate lowers her window.

"See you in a month!" Kate shouts as the Bronco

bounces up the road to the main highway. Papa Leo walks back to Lightfoot, motioning to the front of the community center where Florian and Richter seem to be having a disagreement out front. He offers another of his observations, without taking his eyes off the fracas in the distance.

"Beware of the man who doesn't talk, and the dog that doesn't bark," his grandfather says, his eyes still fixed on Richter. Lightfoot turns to him, hoping for some clarification. But as is often the case, his grandfather's words of wisdom usually end with him walking off into the sunset. Lightfoot looks back at Florian as he throws his hand in a dismissive gesture toward Richter. Florian turns back toward Mission Control, leaving the trendy German to fume silently out front.

❖   ❖   ❖

For Kate, the past three weeks have been a timeless epoch since she first arrived along this long highway. She remembers that day, how she viewed the passing trees, by singling one out in the distance and watching it grow closer until it flashed by her side window. But now, her eyes tend to fix in a single direction, on the vast space between her and the sky, while letting the landscape of nearby trees pass in streaks of color and time with no specific focus on any one thing. Has her way of looking at things changed, she wonders? She certainly turns her head less abruptly now, allowing her eyes to do the work. Did she pick that up from the sage old man? She never thought about these things before. No, she's changed for sure. Why else would she be asking these questions of herself?

"Are you okay?" Mary asks, turning from the highway to check her friend's pensive silence.

"Yeah, better than okay. I'm just thinking, you know – about all that's happened the last couple weeks." She settles into that trance again, but this time with a channel open to Mary. "You know, when I first came here, I thought I was in love." She turns back to Mary. "You know that, don't you?"

"I know," Mary says with a kind rapport.

"Now," Kate continues, "I'm... well, for one thing, I'm convinced that you and he are meant to be together." Mary isn't able to respond. "No really, I'm not trying to be corny, he belongs here, in this world with you. There is a belonging in his eyes now. In Boston, it was just a longing." Kate turns back from her mesmerized state. "You know, I've never had a friend that wasn't a guy before. It's a good feeling," Kate admits. Mary pans back to the road, while shaking her head ever so slightly.

"You blow my mind, Kate Rose!" Mary says, as she turns off the road toward the airport.

❖ ❖ ❖

Mary grabs her luggage from the back of the Bronco as Kate pulls her coat and shoulder bag from the back seat. Kate stops to examine the little airport building, such a funny thing to be called a terminal. Mary comes around with the bags, but instead of heading inside, she sets them down and wraps her arms around Kate.

"Hurry back?" Mary asks.

"I'll be back soon. I promise," Kate says. But Mary isn't so sure. Still, it's best to just go along with the ruse her new friend is selling. Mary breathes deeply and reaches for Kate's bags.

"No, I got 'em," Kate says, but Mary has already lifted them. "No really, let me. Or I'm going to start crying in front of you." Mary gets the point, and hands the bags over. Kate thinks up a bit of logistics to help pull herself together. "Oh, as soon as the power plant experiment is running, we'll start the media blitz. Even get them to travel and do a live interview." Kate expands her chest. "Okay, here we go," then heads for front doors. Mary waits while Kate walks into the terminal, looking back over her shoulder one last time before disappearing around the corner. Mary stands for a moment, thinking about all that's happened over the last couple weeks, before returning to the Bronco.

❖   ❖   ❖

Back at base, Mary enters the retrofit Community Center. Lightfoot notices her from across the room and rushes over.

"All good?" he asks. "She get off okay?"

"Yeah," Mary replies somewhat wistfully. "You know, I'm going to miss her," she says.

"I know, she's a champ," he says. "She'll be back, though." But Mary isn't so sure, still daunted by the hunch that it will be a long time before Kate Rose comes back to Red Rock. Florian scampers into the operations center, roused and ready.

"Ah, there you are Professor. You want to see it?" Lightfoot places his hand around Mary.

"C'mon, it's nearly ready to test," Lightfoot says, pulling her along.

Florian leads Mary and Lightfoot into the woods, toward two large forty-foot shipping containers sitting about where the toppled wind generator used to be. The makeshift steel structures are nestled deep inside the woods, obscuring their view from overhead. Florian approaches the nearest container and swings open the large door open at the end. Mary is astonished at the progress. They step inside to see a long glass tube in the center, running the entire length of the container. At the source of the tube is a large metal sphere and more glass coils. A red danger

155

beacon rotates, casting the interior of the container/ lab with the feeling of a sixties spy movie. The other end of the tube exits the container through a hole, cut into its rear wall. Florian is beyond excited.

"Follow me, you have to see this," Florian says, running out of the container like an excited child. Mary and Lightfoot follow him outside, to where Florian stops at the back of the large metal structure. The long glass tube exits the back of the first container and continues on another few feet before entering a hole into the next steel box. Florian proudly places his hands on his hips and looks to gather Mary's impression. "The dumbest farmer gets the biggest potatoes, eh?" Florian quips. Mary shoots him a puzzled look, having no idea what he's talking about. "Stupid people always win," Florian explains. But Lightfoot cuts through the humility.

"Stupid people didn't make this," he says.

"Okay, let's just say we're too dumb to know what we can't do," Florian replies, while proudly observing the contraption. "She is beautiful!" he says, dazed by the sight of his creation. Not finished with the tour by any means, Florian snaps out of it and motions along the path of the glass tube to the other container, as he continues to narrate the process for Mary's benefit. "So the particles shoot out of the first container, and into the second which houses the reactor, boiler and steam generator." Florian runs to a nearby clearing. Mary is charmed with the odd German's energy as he leads them deeper into the woods. She and Lightfoot follow his eyes to the treetops, where a large water tower has been erected atop the remaining half of the old wind turbine. "The cooling tower," Florian gushes, finalizing the tour. "We re-routed the line from the power grid to the output of the steam generator. Mary is awestruck and shoots Florian a wide grin.

"What was that German saying for, 'I don't believe what I'm seeing'? Mary asks.

"I do believe my pig whistles," Florian blurts with a giggle.

"Yeah, that's it," Mary says. A blast of light pours through the hole in the second container as the vivid glow of a welding torch flickers on and off. The glass tube between the containers lights up the woods with each arc light and bathes the forest haze with an eerie bluish glow. The three of them curiously round the container to the opening at its other end. Inside, Richter braces a large boiler with a log, while Harvey Bearheart finishes an artful bead of weld along the boiler's edge. He pops the torch off and flips his visor when he sees the audience, especially Mary's wide smile.

"I think we're ready for prime time," her dad says with a pained finality that recalls all the back-breaking work up to this point. This container is filled to the extent with the newly installed steam generator and boiler unit. The glass tube narrows to a tuned metal tube that enters the boiler. "Not bad for a bunch of Injuns, 'eh Professor?" Harvey Bearheart says while holding his sore lower back and looking the installation over. Richter on the other hand isn't so chipper.

"*Drei Wochen Florian. Wir drücken unser Glück. Ich schlage vor, dass wir dieses aufwickeln, bevor ihre Regierung diesen Platz in einen anderen Cowboyfilm dreht,*" Richter says, complaining as always in German, yet not aware of Mary's ability to listen in. Lightfoot makes out a few words.

"Something about cowboy movie?" Lightfoot asks. But before Florian can try to dampen his associate's poor taste, Mary translates.

"He says 'he wants to go home before the cowboys kill the Indians '– basically," Mary says with a cringe. A rather embarrassed Florian nods his confirmation of her understanding.

"Mister grumpy pants has been busting my ass in German all day," Harvey Bearheart says.

"*Buck up und beenden handeln wie eine kleine Hündin. Wir sind fast fertig,*" Florian says, scolding his associate, then forcing a smile to the others.

"He called him a little bitch," Mary whispers to Lightfoot.

"Florian said that? Lightfoot asks, surprised to see his little buddy finally reach the limits of his patience. Florian turns and smiles sheepishly at everyone, while Richter skulks out of the container.

"Don't mind the lonely sausage," Florian claims.

❖　❖　❖

"I think we'll be firing up Billy's experiment tomorrow," Harvey Bearheart tells Papa Leo as the two talk privately by the shoreline. They gaze into the sunset while sharing a bag of Fritos. He notices the uneasiness that still haunts the old man. "It feels good to fight back," Harvey Bearheart says encouragingly, while offering him some Fritos.

"This time, it's not a fight, it's a plea. Our hope won't rely on winning against our enemies. It will rely on being heard by our friends - the white tribes who live on reservations called suburbs. And as Billy says, 'all the other nations who have seen loss at the hands of the same conquerors we face'," Papa Leo says, as he tracks an approaching rain cloud across the sky. "We're not alone. That we must remember." He dips his hand into the bag of corn chips while they both continue their gaze out over the lake. "Time for a ride," the old sage nods toward the last few seconds of sunset.

"I'm going to bed," Harvey Bearheart says as he crumples the now empty sack of chips. Instead they stand silent and motionless for the next few moments, as the last sliver of the sun's edge begins to disappear below the lake.

❖   ❖   ❖

Mary and Lightfoot sit together on the small front porch, nuzzled into a crafted birch bark lounge. He moves his hand across the lines of the wide chair as Mary watches him admire the craftsmanship.

"My dad made it when I was Anna's age," she says.

"He's super talented. The Power Plant construction is impeccable," he says. From where they sit, Papa Leo and her father can be seen, still standing at the shoreline and silhouetted against the final seconds of the sun's shift.

"They've been doing that for as long as I can remember, standing out there together, sometimes even in the snow," Mary says, watching as the two men separate and walk off for the night.

"They're good men," he says.

"You're a good man, Billy Lightfoot. You've given up a lot to do this," she says. "That's not easy, I'm sure."

"Maybe. I've always wondered how people work

so hard, making as much money as they can, save it all in a bundle they call a retirement fund, so they can check out of society and live a simple life with nature. By that time, you're too tired to run through the woods. I figure if something means that much, maybe you should go there to live while you can, not go there to die." He glances back at her, she's barely awake.

"I love you," she breathes, settling into his arm.

❖　❖　❖

The next morning came quickly with the anticipation of starting the reactor for the first time. Papa Leo rides into the village, the first to welcome what promises to be a monumental day. He catches sight of Harvey Bearheart near the rim of the woods, already prepping the power station for its awakening. He rides in his direction.

"You're up early, brother," Papa Leo calls out.

"I didn't sleep much," the big guy says. "Had this damn thing on my brain all night." He motions up the road. "Misses B is preparing a meal for the team." Papa Leo looks over the monstrous assembly in the woods and the magnificent cooling tower standing slightly above the canopy of pines. The rusty containers blend into the misty wood below.

"Will it float?" Papa Leo asks.

"I think it just might," Harvey Bearheart replies

while admiring the results of the last three weeks of work.

"T-minus sixty minutes and counting?" Lightfoot calls from down the road. They turn to receive the couple, carrying a basket of food and coffees. Mary hands out breakfast sandwiches to everyone and sets the basket down.

"Couple more in there for the happy German and one for the sad one," Mary says before taking a bite. She looks over her sandwich, catching sight of Lightfoot choking on his coffee. "What?" she says filtered through a laugh. "I was being nice."

"The sad German? It sounds like a George Clooney movie," Lightfoot says.

"We're all set. You nervous?" Bearheart asks him.

"Nope," Lightfoot replies, definitively. "It'll work." Mary reaches for his arm and spins his wrist around, checking the time on his watch.

"Kate should be in Washington by now too," she says, reminding everyone of the forward flank.

❖ ❖ ❖

Kate looks out her taxi window as they pass the Lincoln Memorial while she tracks the road trip on her phone's street map.

"A left at Constitution, it says. Eighteen forty-nine,

C-Street, northwest," she calls out to the front, but the cabbie clearly doesn't need her help.

"Thank you ma'am, been there." Kate rocks her head side to side, mimicking the smug driver.

"Is it usually a busy place, the Indian Affairs Bureau?" she asks, appealing to the cabbie's extensive knowledge of all things Washington.

"That address is the Department of Interior building. Didn't know there were any Indians in there," he grouses, while taking the corner fast enough to slide her across the back seat.

"Whoaaa!" Kate yelps. "Anyway, that's the address so we'll go with it," she says. Thanks for your help by the way."

"No problem lady," the cabbie replies in unenthusiastic monotone. Finally the cab pulls up to the Department of Interior steps and stop just in front of a hotdog trailer, moored out front.

"Here you go," the driver announces, punching the meter. "Forty-eight, fifty." Kate signals her rate shock with a gasp. "Oh my. Okay," she says, as she fumbles for change.

"You have change for a fifty?" she asks innocently.

"You're kidding me right?" the cabbie groans.

"Oh, well if you don't it's okay. Keep the change."

"Oh wow lady," the cabbie snarls. "Maybe you need this more than I do," the driver says and tosses her a dollar fifty, then motions her along. Kate gets out and barely latches the door when the cab lurches away. Kate turns to the front, readies herself and pauses momentarily deciding on which of the five doors to enter. She picks one, and marches inside.

❖   ❖   ❖

An endless lattice work of corridors, form the guts of The Department of Interior building. Each hallway resembles the next, each door an identical copy of its neighbor. Kate rounds a corner, carefully considering the number ranges to exclude yet another corridor from her search. She continues to navigate the maze, until finally in the center of the mausoleum-like structure she finds a single door, labeled U.S. Bureau of Indian Affairs. She thinks of knocking first, but then heads in.

Kate approaches an ancient receptionist at a single desk just beyond the door. The matron's head remains bowed even as Kate approaches her.

"Hi, Excuse me, I'm looking for..." Kate says, stopping briefly to check her notes. "Deputy Director Michael Smith please." The peevish dame manages to look up, examining Kate's business suit first, working her way up to her perky smile. It's clear this granny isn't a fan of perky.

"You have an appointment?" she asks.

"Certainly do, Monday morning, ten AM," Kate grins. My name is Kate Rose?" Kate watches the tired gal conserve all possible energy while she searches the appointment log.

"Have a seat," the receptionist grumbles, making no further attempt to communicate.

"Oh, okay," Kate says. "I guess I'm early it's three minutes 'til," she says, but the matron *harrumphs*, not feeling the humor. Kate wipes the edges of her mouth in a gesture of resignation and finds a seat. No sooner does she settle, when the door opens and a balding fellow in his fifties enters. He nods to the receptionist then looks Kate's way, tossing a creepy peruse of the young Redhead and thinking she's probably the prettiest thing he's seen in these musty yellowed halls all spring.

"Your ten o'clock Mister Smith," the receptionist says, nosing toward Kate. Kate rises and extends her hand to meet his clammy white palm.

"Kate Rose, Sir. I'm here to discuss my client, the Red Rock Chippewa tribe in Minnesota." Pretending to remember, the official wings it, as he's been doing for the last seven years.

"Oh, yes certainly Miss Rose, come on in," he says, while motioning Kate to his office entrance and ignoring the loathing glance of his surfeit receptionist.

The old gal studies Kate's shoes when she passes her desk.

Director Smith's office is an insipid collection of Native American artifacts and badly framed historical images. One would hope these were gifts bestowed upon him by grateful tribal leaders, but chances are that's not the case.

"Have a seat please," he says. Kate makes her way to an appropriately sterile chair facing his desk. "No, no, over here," he smiles while motioning to the couch as he pulls up a facing chair. Kate takes her seat, holding a folder in her lap like a security blanket. "So, how can we help our friends in Minnesota, Miss Rose?" Kate figures there's no better time than now to pull out the guns. She fetches an iPad from her purse, and promptly starts a video of the two Blackhawks overflying the quake-damaged valley. Director Smith takes the tablet and studies the video. "What am I looking at?" Smith asks.

"Sir, you're looking at a reconnaissance mission, conducted by the United States military over sovereign Native American land," she says. Reaching back into her bag, she pulls out a stack of still photos, taken from the game cameras placed in the trees. She hands them over to the deputy director. While still digesting the video which continues to play on the iPad, he tentatively takes the photos, with a pained expression that looks as if he just shit his pants in church. "And these photos show a subsequent operation, let's call it a *raid*, which was conducted a week later, in which commandos took protected artifacts from these lands." Smith flips through the photos, sinking further into his seat with each new image he views. Smith returns his attention to the running video, which Kate still holds for him. "As you know, this violates a number of statutes, including the Archaeological Resources Protections Act, the Indian Commerce Clause as well as the sovereignty of ownership rights relating to resources both natural and 'unnatural'." The director is clearly bothered.

"Where did you get these?" Smith asks.

"We filmed them. As well as motion detection surveillance of the robbery," Kate explains. "I think we can call it that, don't you agree?" she says punctuated by a wide smile. "If you'll remember, there was an earthquake in the Great Lakes region a few weeks back, which created a fissure on Native Land. This slice in the earth, revealed the remnants of a comet impact from prehistoric times. Whatever ejected from that comet, impacted into the center of what is now Native American land." Kate rests her case and switches off the iPad.

"I'm familiar with this now," Smith says in a sickly sounding voice, as he hands the photos back.

"Familiar?   Meaning the comet or the robbery?" Kate asks.

"Familiar as in, this might explain some recent inquiries we've received, into the meaning and limitations of mineral extraction pertaining to "a certain Minnesota tribe, yes," he says, in a clarification of sorts. "How then can I help you?"

"Well, you can start by calling off the dogs, since we've already had a visit from the Army Corps of Engineers, as well as people from your field office, and representatives from the nation's top weapons facilities, under the guise of offering earthquake assistance. We all know what they are after, and when they were denied access to the epicenter, they took it upon themselves to steal it." But Smith falls back on time-tested policy, using the ambiguities of a vague treaty to defend any government intrusion.

"The difficulties we face here, is an often debated interpretation of the meaning of 'sovereignty', 'commerce' and frankly 'rights' of the Indian peoples as it relates to the stewardship by the U.S. Federal government on behalf of Native American tribes," the director says, reciting the babble-politic that has empowered white privilege for years.

"That's it?" Kate asks before launching into a cut-the-crap follow-up. "Director Smith..."

"*Deputy* Director, actually," he interjects. Kate then focuses on the man and not the mission.

"Mike – consider my visit a courtesy call. Before proceeding to the next step in seeking to protect these rights," she reveals.

"Next step?" he queries.

"In light of recent negative publicity concerning the Dakota Access Pipeline injustices as well as oil and water rights abuses by major energy companies across the country, and countless examples of tribal abuse of Native Peoples who were promised protection from this kind of abuse by your very agency, we wanted to allow you the chance to respond, before we publicize these videos across all media outlets. Thought maybe you'd like to get ahead of this now, before all this rolls over your agency in media," Kate discloses in a well rehearsed run that surprises even herself.

"So, you're threatening us?" the deputy director asks.

"Yes," Kate says simply, rather than try to reframe his accusation. "People need to know that this agency is either acting like the protective body it claims to be, or... a front for those who seek to abuse Native land rights." Kate throws shade with the most charming smile. "What can I tell my client about the Bureau's response, Mister *Deputy* Director?" she asks. Smith turns his head like he just heard a silent dog whistle.

"I'll have to take this up with my superiors. In the mean time, can you leave those with me?" he asks while reaching in expectation.

"Sadly, no," she says, returning them to her bag. Kate stands. "I enjoyed our talk," she concludes sarcastically, but actually she did enjoy the meeting, very much.

❖   ❖   ❖

Florian runs from container to container, nervously doing final checks. Richter mumbles his way down the length of glass tubing with a clipboard in hand, checking connections and continuity along the path. For all his bad taste, he's at least passionate about his work.

Harvey Bearheart stands with Papa Leo and Mary, at the observation line, anxiously looking toward the experiment tucked into the woods nearly fifty yards away. Only the cooling tower is visible above the treetops. He fans the cigar smoke from his eyes.

"What if it blows up?" Keezheknoi asks, while dragging a puff.

"That's why we're way back here, stupid," Small Duck retorts.

"I wasn't worried about us, *stupid*," Keezheknoi fires back.

"Shut up, you two," Meoquanee says, jabbing Small Duck in the ribs.

"Thank you!" Harvey Bearheart cries out over his shoulder. Suddenly, a bluish electrical arc bursts from the woods, sending the three ancient ladies to take cover behind the big Bearheart. The glow then settles into a sustained pulsing aurora, illuminating the low hanging fog along the tree line. Mary holds her father's arm tightly. Then the sound of a turbine, winding up and up, until it too finds its mean resonance and begins to hum efficiently likes a jet engine. What feels like a continuum of anticipation is finally broken when Lightfoot and Florian run out of the container, thumbs up and cheering. Even Richter exits with a slight bounce in his gait and high fives Florian.

"Oh my, even the sad German is happy," Mary exclaims. Cheers and applause detonate across the entire viewing gallery as Lightfoot runs over to the gallery and parks in front of Papa Leo. Covered with grease and stained of sweat, Lightfoot looks his grandfather in the eye and extends his hand in a timeless honor all Chippewa warriors have demonstrated to their elders when returning from battle.

"It works, Granddad!" Papa Leo places his palm alongside his grandson's head.

"Of course it does! You made it," he says, proudly vindicated in his confidence that his grandson is the brightest man he's ever known. Mary is beyond ecstatic, joining the applause and stopping briefly when he reaches out to hold Mary's face in hands. He kisses her in front of her father and the entire tribe. The cheering erupts even louder.

"Wait 'til Minnesota Power sees this start flowing their way," Lightfoot beams. "That'll get everyone's attention." Florian and Richter make their way to the viewing theater.

"We're done Professor," Florian says while celebrating with a high five. "It's feeding the grid at thirty now. We're about to open the gates to a full sixty, now that everything seems to be running fine. Then, it's back home for us to do the same," Florian says before turning back to view the glowing woods from a distance. "Hate to leave actually," he says. Florian rotates to Mary. "*Alles hat ein Ende, nur die Wurst hat zwei.*" Mary howls.

"What did he say?" Harvey Bearheart asks.

"He said..." - but she's laughing too hard to finish and tries again. "He said, '*everything has an end, only the sausage has two*'," Mary says nearly crying with laughter. Papa Leo looks confused.

"It's not that funny," the old man says.

"What is it with you and sausages?" Harvey Bearheart asks Florian.

"We're German, we like sausages," he explains.

Mary laughs even heartier as Florian relishes in Mary's ticklish appreciation of German humor. Papa Leo tosses his hands upward.

"I still don't get it," the old man says. Harvey Bearheart shakes his head to second the thought.

❖   ❖   ❖

"Hi Kate, can you hear us?" Lightfoot asks while he positions the phone in range of everyone around the table.

"*Got you loud and clear, Captain,*" Kate replies with cocksure buoyancy.

"We miss you already," Mary calls into the phone.

"Yeah, wish you were here to see the power plant fire up. It's been running all day," Lightfoot says.

"*That's a good thing,*" Kate notes. "*We're going to need a lot of PR now. I spoke to CNN and the local station in Minnesota, they want to send out a video crew.*"

"Okay, I can't take it any longer, how'd it go in D.C.? What did the Bureau say?" Lightfoot asks.

"*Safe to say they're worried about the press. Which is why we need to stay on that,*" Kate states firmly. "*At first they pretended to know nothing about us. I showed him the video of the copters, and he turned white.*"

"Whiter you mean," Harvey Bearheart quips. Mary gives him the eye.

"The BIA is a stooge for powerful people," Papa Leo

interjects. "They were formed to limit our sovereignty, not protect it," Papa Leo laments into the little phone on the desk.

"*You're totally right,*" Kate replies. "*They will do nothing for us. But they can be our foil now, as we expose them in the press for what they really are. We need to pull their teeth by creating bigger allies than they could ever be. And if we back down now, they'll just continue to do what they've done to all three hundred tribes for the last hundred and fifty years. We need to circle their wagons Papa Leo.*"

"You said it sister!" Harvey Bearheart says, as he fist-bumps Papa Leo. Mary and Lightfoot watch the old men in speechless awe, then look at each other as if to ask 'who are these guys?' Lightfoot leans closer to the phone.

"Kate, we're all with you here," Lightfoot confirms. "The power station is blasting enough electricity into the grid to light up a city now. Let's see how long it takes for Minnesota Power to freak out and contact us. They'll think it's an anomaly at first, but with enough energy to light up nine thousand homes, we'll be able to set a competitive price to keep it running, and use the power grid as ammo in the press."

"*Let me know when the media can come out there for a demo and we'll bring the pony show to you. Brush up on your presentation skills Professor William Lightfoot. You're about to go viral.*"

"Go what?" Harvey Bearheart asks, shooting a puzzled look at Papa Leo who simply shrugs if to say 'don't look at me'.

❖ ❖ ❖

The young Minnesota Power Engineer carefully sips hot coffee from his favorite mug. He monitors pulsing node graphics scattered across the electrical grid, displayed on his workstation while tolerating the monotony of the job with his favorite playlist sounding in the background. Another worker, barely pushing thirty years old and wearing the company's blue boiler suit, enters the control station carrying a box of donuts.

"They're still hot," the worker exclaims, calling out the highlight of his day. The box is spotted with oil leaching from inside. The engineer flips out when the Worker sets the dozen donuts on a stack of reports he's working on.

"Dude!" the engineer yells. "You're getting grease everywhere." He grabs the box of donuts and plops the oily mess on a nearby taboret. The worker calmly grabs a glazed jelly donut for himself and dunks it into the engineer's coffee. He squeezes the spongy mess between his teeth. "What the hell is wrong with you?" the engineer barks. "That's my coffee?" He grabs his cup and looks inside. "Yuk! That's disgusting," he yells then leaves his post to wash it out. The worker chuckles, glancing at the online stats when something catches his eye. He turns to alert the engineer but realizing his mouth is too full. In shock, he zeroes into at a certain spot on the screen while working to swallow. Finally he's able to utter a sound.

"Hey man, what's going on at the Red Rock reservation?" he asks. The engineer stomps back to the screen, drying his cup with a utility rag.

"What are you talking about," the engineer asks, still pissed off and half expecting another antic.

"Seriously, you didn't see this?" the worker points to the screen. The engineer focuses on the spot at the end of the lineman's finger.

"That's impossible!" he exclaims while quickly punching up details of Red Rock on the grid. A summary breakdown window pops up, and they both look at each other in pure shock.

"Yeah, that's nearly fifty, hell almost sixty megawatts of input!" the worker exclaims with a mouth full of dough.

"You better get out there. Something's wrong with the sensor on their wind generator," the engineer asserts. "That's going to throw off our switches unless that's fixed."

TEN

"Nation Building"

It's another monotonous morning at Luna Café. The same patrons, wearing the same hats and coats discuss the same frustrations with the same urban lifestyle and the same relationships. Sitting at his usual table, Tyler reads from a proper newspaper, intermixed with the usual mobile alerts all while glancing at a muted TV monitor above the counter. CNN's excessive graphics, tickers and *noisy* images cycle over and over.

A plucky millennial girl with bright orange mittens, places a hand on the back of the chair that Tyler uses for his backpack and notebooks.

"Are you using this?" she asks, feigning politeness, while ready to snatch the chair anyway. Tyler pulls his belongings off the chair without taking his eyes off the paper.

"Knock yourself out, child," he says matter-of-factly. Clearly addicted to the buzz of being offended,

177

the coed pulls the chair in a huff to join a gaggle of girlfriends sitting nearby.

"Oh, my, gawd? That guy is hideous," she says, nearly choking on the word 'hideous'. Tyler grits his teeth, and glances up at the silent monitor. His eyeballs nearly drop from his face, when on the screen he sees his buddy Lightfoot giving an interview with a horde or microphones shoved in his face. The crawl beneath the video reads, "*NATIVE AMERICAN TRIBE DEFENDS ITS SOVEREIGNTY*".

Tyler flies off his chair, squeezing past the gaggle beside him and further prickling the young ladies' over-sensitivity. The girls pull their chairs closer to the center of the expansive ring they've sprawled into.

"Oh, my, gaaaawd, this guy never quits," the mitted coed continues. Tyler reaches over the counter for the remote and increases the volume, well above the precious din. On screen, Lightfoot continues.

"*The rare element is not a natural resource,*" the Professor tells the reporter. "*Rather the result of a comet impact long before living creatures populated the planet. In fact, it's very possible that along with the material we've discovered, the projectile may have brought to this planet, organisms, the building blocks of life itself.*" A reporter retracts the microphone briefly to her lips, inserting another question into the record.

"*Can you tell us why this 'rare element' as you're calling it is causing so much consternation between you and the federal government and exactly what your protest centers around?"* the reporter asks.

"Sure," Lightfoot replies. *"The material is a super heavy, stable element, a sort of nuclear fuel that unlike other radioactive isotopes, plutonium or uranium for instance, this material produces zero waste and nuclear fallout. To say a nuclear power plant produces 'clean energy' is a joke. In any nuclear reaction, only two, maybe three percent of the nuclear material actually reacts. The other ninety-seven percent is released as waste. In the case of an atomic bomb for instance, that waste is released into the atmosphere as radioactive fallout. But this fuel, this produces none of that and can deliver even more controlled heat than messy radioactive material,"* Lightfoot explains plainly.

Tyler is overwhelmed and motionless. Fixated on the screen, he turns to the schoolgirls with a finger to his mouth, motioning for the shrill flock to be quiet – further offending them.

"Oh, my gawd!" they whine again, nearly in unison. He turns the volume up even louder.

"So it's valuable then?" she asks of the professor.

"That's why the government is trying to take it from us. We created a prototype power station on these grounds, and are dumping over sixty megawatts of power back into the grid." Lightfoot replies.

"And why is that important?" she asks

"It's clean – an entirely efficient form of energy. No waste and a thousand times more powerful per pound, than conventional nuclear fuel. Don't take our word for it. Ask Minnesota Power Company. By comparison, a massive nuclear power plant can produce ten times that, but it's dangerous, requires massive waste management," he says, holding up a perfectly milled orange cone, about three inches tall. *"Our system uses a couple ounces of fuel element and operates out of a facility the size of a train car. We mill it into this shape to help utilize its properties,"* Lightfoot concludes. The reporter attempts a witty observation.

"It looks like a little tee pee," she declares. With that, she turns to the camera while Lightfoot steps back, slightly humored by her reflex toward the camera.

Also watching the news in his office is Deputy Director Smith as the reporter summarizes her report for her station headquarters.

"And at the heart of this legal fight, is the definition of Indian sovereignty. Does the United States government, or anyone for that matter have the right to take resources that exist on tribal land? – Wolf," she says in conclusion.

❖ ❖ ❖

Dr. Drummond struts through another bullish pitch to a group of suits in his office. An assistant enters the room, and whispers in his ear.

"Turn it on," he commands. The assistant points the remote to an opposite wall. "Gentlemen, we may have a blip". On a competing news station, another reporter is about to introduce the explosive charge.

"*And we have some video and pictures to put up,*" the next reporter says, introducing the clip. The video of the Blackhawk recon mission fills the screen, as do the surveillance photos, showing the night raid of Army Rangers hauling sacks into the helicopter. "*These images show the recent robbery by government actors, totally avoiding even the most basic protocol outlined in Bureau of Indian Affairs procedures, the body created to protect the rights of indigenous people across the country.*" The screen cuts back to the reporter who mugs an indignant expression for the camera.

Drummond is about to burst a vein in his neck.

"Get the Bureau on the phone," Drummond insists. "No wait!" Drummond says, rethinking his strategy. "Scratch that, get me on the Dash-Nine to D.C."

❖   ❖   ❖

The camera crew grabs B-roll of the tribe, panning to Papa Leo's icy stare into the lens. His face is estranged from any feeling of awe or interest. The shot creeps out the cameraman, clearly feeling the old man's stink-eye insistence to, *point that stupid thing somewhere else.* The operator pulls back from the viewfinder and glances over the camera, hoping to believe his own eyes, but Papa Leo continues to stare deep into his intrusive soul. He quickly pans down the line, finding Harvey Bearheart, then the three Loon sisters, all of whom offer nothing but unresponsive glares into the lens. So much for B-roll. The cameraman swings into a two-shot of Lightfoot and a local news reporter, now ready to begin.

"You're watching Minnesota Network News, my name is Bill Werner," the next reporter begins. "Well, if you haven't heard about the Red Rock Native American Tribe, get ready because it's a story that's soon to become a worldwide phenomenon. I'm here with Professor William Lightfoot on sabbatical from MIT, who has returned to his childhood home to develop an alternative fuel experiment, 'native' only to this small spot of land in the Minnesota border waters region," the reporter says. In the background, the two connected steel shipping containers whine together in choreographed efficiency. "At the heart of this, is a homemade power station, capable of powering nearly nine thousand homes," Bill Werner mentions, before holding the element sample up to the camera. "All this, by using only two grams of a very *unnatural* resource known as element one-fifteen," he declares, completing the intro and now moving his mic quickly to Lightfoot's face. "Professor, tell us a bit about what makes this discovery so special."

❖ ❖ ❖

In the community center, Mary coordinates three more news crews, while holding her phone to her ear in mid conversation. A Chinese team is in the midst of unpacking their equipment while next in line, a Canadian CBC crew is preparing to move outside at a moment's notice for their chance at an interview.

"I'm back Kate. It's as mad as a bucket of frogs over here," she says while flashing an open palm to the Canadian crew, signaling a five-minute warning. "Billy is on his fourth interview of the day and three more are getting ready to go," Mary says.

❖ ❖ ❖

"That's great," Kate replies excitedly as she weaves through the flow of La Guardia airport travelers towards baggage claim. "Publicity is our friend right now." A businessman pulling his bags while checking his phone, barrels into Kate and has the nerve to become indignant. "Excuse me, sorry," Kate says, wondering why she always apologizes for other people's rudeness. She returns to the call. "Sorry Mary. Have you heard from the electric company?"

Mary has stepped out front, noticing the interview in progress is winding down.

"Oh, you bet," Mary says as she returns to the holding area. She cups her hand over the receiver. "You're up!" she tells the Canadians, then back to the phone. "Yeah, they're actually showing up in person tomorrow morning. They don't believe it and want to get a look at the station," Mary says.

Kate has arrived at the baggage claim. She sits on the edge of the carousel for a moment to adjust her shoe.

"I have an introductory meeting with the United Nations Energy people this afternoon," Kate says, as the carousel alarm blasts in her ear. She covers her ear from the noise with her free hand while resting on the belt ridge, totally oblivious to the meaning of the alert. "I'll call you guys after, but the plan is to donate some material and technology to their program, prior to putting them on the spot to support our bid for member status." Kate is knocked sideways when the carousel belt begins moving. She shoots upright, without missing a beat. "We need all the media capital we can get right now. I saw the CNN interview. It was brilliant! Everyone's talking about it," Kate says, craning over the other travelers in order to spot her bags on the belt.

Mary is curiously watching the odd Chinese crew

argue with each other in Mandarin as they prep their gear.

"Yeah, problem is everyone wants to buy the fuel," Mary mentions, while still intrigued with the bickering Asian production crew.

"*Just tell them the United States government is trying to stop you from selling it but make sure you get their names,*" Kate says over the phone. "*We're going to need that kind of leverage when you guys come to New York to address the U.N.*" Mary holds the phone at arm's length to stare at the receiver for a moment in disbelief before returning it to her ear.

"What was that?" Mary asks.

Kate struggles to pull her bag off the belt, as she relishes the opportunity to spring that part of the plan on Mary.

"Oh, didn't I tell you?" Kate asks, knowing full well she hadn't. She begins wheeling her bags out of baggage claim.

Mary walks back out front to find the Canadian interview in full swing while Kate continues.

"*This is bigger than any of us can imagine, and at the center of it will be MIT Professor William Lightfoot a native son of the very tribe the U.S. is trying to rob of their inalienable rights,*" Kate continues in Mary's ear. It's at this moment, that the reality of the situation fully set in for Mary as she continues to listen to Kate, while watching Lightfoot being interviewed across the road. *"You guys are going to be richer than most countries and most importantly, you're about to be the biggest contributor to the World Commission on Sustainable Energy. The meek will inherit the earth, Mary. And right now, the world is fed up with tyranny."*

"Okay," is the only reply Mary can muster.

Kate flags a taxi, while reflecting on her own fearlessness, shaking her skull in astonishment.

"Yeah, this bitch is on fire, baby!" Kate yells into the phone. A couple standing next to her with a small child is appalled. "Anyway, thanks for letting me practice my pitch, Mary," she says as a taxi pulls up. "I'll call you guys when I know more. I gotta go now. Love to everyone there!" Kate hangs up and attempts to heave her bags toward the cab, with no help from the driver. She glares at the guy behind the wheel. "Really?" she says, of the stationary cabbie. Bothered to offer assistance, the driver pulls himself out of his seat and tosses her bags in the trunk. "Thanks," Kate replies with mock gratitude.

Mary takes the time to let everything sink in as she watches her celebrated professor educate another network. A rising treble of unintelligible sounds soon claws for her attention. She rotates toward the high velocity vocals of the Chinese video crew, stepping on each other's voices in a heated squabble.

❖ ❖ ❖

The back-to-back events are beginning to weigh on Lightfoot. He devours the sight and sounds of the odd Chinese news crew, as they hurriedly set up their tripods and lighting. Their cattish demeanor continues while awkwardly stepping over the previous news team, who are trying their best to strike their equipment and get out of the way.

Mary is behind the fracas, motioning with a bottle of water in the air. Lightfoot lights up and reaches over the news team for the bottle.

"Thank you, you're reading my mind!" he says before guzzling the full eight ounces in a single pull. After five interviews so far, and two more in the wings, fatigue is setting in. "Ah, thanks," he says, handing her the empty bottle as an Asian lady pats his forehead with a powdered pad. "I haven't needed that so far," he protests.

"You shiny," she says before scurrying off behind the camera to do the same to her reporter.

"You shiny," Mary says quietly, trying her best not to howl inappropriately. "Kate called," she starts to report. "She said that..." but then Mary bounces backwards as a microphone is shoved between them by the reporter, who's now positioned by the camera.

With one finger, Mary incredulously lowers the tip of the shotgun mic away from her face. "Um, we'll talk about that later," she says with faux calm. "You okay?" she asks. "There's two more after this, you know."

"All good," Lightfoot says while shaking out his arms to get the blood flowing again.

"You're doing great, Billy. It's showing up on all the networks already," she says.

"We weddy naau!" the Chinese reporter exclaims. Mary gets the *hint*, and gives Lightfoot a quick peck on the cheek.

"Don't be shiny," she says before sliding out of the fray. The perturbed makeup lady squeezes back in and powders the spot Mary kissed.

Across the road, the viewing gallery has grown to include the entire tribe. The puffing grannies drag on a fresh cigar, the smoke of which wafts across Harvey Bearheart's nose. He fans the stench away from his face as Mary arrives to find her dad shooting a stink eye at the Loon sisters.

"Yeah, and that stuff on your boots is honey," Keezheknoi says.

"Honey!" Small Duck repeats with a laugh. "Pass that back over here before you make the big man vomit," Small Duck says.

"Okay, quriat preeze!" the Chinese reporter calls out, scolding the audience. Papa Leo raises an eyebrow. He's had enough of the circus and leaves to fetch his horse.

The testy reporter turns back to start the interview and thrusts his mic into Lightfoot's face.

"Okay. Can you state yo name preeze?" he asks.

"Sure, William Lightfoot," he says, leaning back from the intrusive mic. The reporter coaches him to try it again.

"Fuwl name preeze? Plofessa Willum Rightfut!" the reporter corrects.

"Right, Professor William Lightfoot," he repeats while subconsciously enunciating a bit too much.

"Okay plofessa, my qwestin fo euw," the reporter says. "Amarkin govement take yo powaful fewel elment, wifout asking – what will euw do now?"

❖　❖　❖

Doctor Drummond marches through the Department of Interior halls. Casper Elliot tries to keep up, pulled along in the angry doctor's wake. Drummond hurriedly checks the room numbers as he blows past each door, eventually approaching *another* dead end.

"You've worked with these people before and you've never been here?" Drummond bellows. He spins on his heels and barrels back the way he came, leaving Elliot in the dust. He hurries after the doctor.

Moments later the door into the Bureau of Indian Affairs springs open, startling the receptionist.

"Doctor Drummond here to see the head of the agency!" Casper leans around from behind the steaming bully.

"Morning, ma'am - Casper Elliot, Army Corps of Engineers. I'm with him," Elliot says in a tone more befitting the cold call.

"Who exactly are you here to see, if I may ask?" the receptionist *asks*.

"The boss, whoever's in charge – *exactly*," Drummond replies, demanding nothing short of blind compliance.

"Well..." continues the matron. "That would be Director Chambers. He's not in at the moment but our Deputy Director should be in shortly," offering more information to these strangers than she should, before gathering her wits.

"What's his name, again?" Drummond bellows.

"I never mentioned it, but that would be Mr. Smith. Deputy Director Michael Smith. Look it up," she declares, finally starting to pull herself out from under the bully's spell.

"Fine! We'll wait. In the mean time, when do you expect... the top dog, Chambers?"

"Director Chambers won't be in today, but I'm sure

the Deputy Director can help you in his absence," the career employee assures.

"Whatever!" Drummond blows as he takes his seat against the wall and pouts.

❖   ❖   ❖

Deputy Director Smith opens the door to his office, motioning Drummond and Elliot inside. Drummond marches in with such annoyed bluster, that Elliot feels compelled to offer Smith a shamed wince as he follows the doctor in.

"Have a seat gentlemen," Smith says, motioning to the two chairs facing his desk. Apparently only young women get the couch. Smith takes his seat behind the desk. Wasting no more of his precious time, Drummond launches into a pitch, long before anyone has even managed to sit.

"I'll keep this brief," he asserts. "As I understand the law - according to the Indian Commerce Clause, the federal government has the right to regulate the political and economic rights of tribal governments," Drummond posits while seeming to expel so much hot air, he settles into his seat to catch his breath. He leans intrusively forward, placing his forearms on Smith's desk. Smith is hardly fond of the tone, but chooses to let Drummond bully his way into a corner. "Does or does not, the United States have the right to hold Indian land and its resources in trust to do with, as it sees fit?" he asks in a tone more suited for a cross-examination.

Director Smith adjusts in his chair by bracing his elbows on the armrests and swinging his lower torso into the seat. The pained look on his face would have one think it's his bad back acting up again, but really he's buying the time to carefully plan his next answer.

"At the Bureau, we don't see this as a *right*, as you're calling it," Smith says. "But rather a responsibility to protect the values of Native American sovereignty and indigenous rights under the law," he maintains, in perfect harmony with department talking points. "May I ask, is this by any chance related to the Chippewa tribe of Minnesota?" Smith adds.

"Oh, so you're familiar with this after all?" Drummond snorts.

"Mr. Drummond..." Smith starts to reply.

"Doctor Drummond," the pompous ass interjects.

"Of course, Doctor Drummond. It's safe to say at this point, that everyone is familiar with it. Especially as video and images of Army Blackhawks assuming that 'right' as you call it, and removing materials, possibly also covered under Native American Artifacts protections, without any authorization to do so," Smith counters. "And where did that stolen material wind up I wonder?" Smith asks pointedly. Drummond bristles and leans back in his chair in mock outrage.

"Who's side are you on?" Drummond catechizes the mere government official. Smith is hardly intimidated.

"Side?" he questions, in an insulted tinge. Now, up to this point, Casper Elliot had hoped to observe, but seeing this meeting go pear-shaped so quickly, especially with implications of the Corps' raid surfaces, Casper feels compelled to jump in.

"Doctor, if I may?" Elliot asks, turning his focus to the Deputy Director. Drummond crosses his arms like a petulant child.

"Sir, we appreciate your position here. Really do," Elliot says, striking a more conciliatory tone. "The Corps' concern is that the recent quake in the area may have released a highly toxic, extremely radioactive isotope that poses a danger to not only the local Chippewa people, but to the nation as a whole. We simply need access to this material for further study and evaluation," Drummond looks over rather smugly, yet quietly impressed with Elliot's word craft. Except that Smith wastes no time debunking that argument.

"Here's my problem with that," Smith says, while standing to deliver this next bit of rebuke. "First of all, if it was so 'highly toxic and radioactive' as you say, then why were your rangers gathering it up with their bare hands, and hauling it away in canvas sacks?"

he asks, turning to observe no attempt at a response. "Right, I thought so. And second, your assumption of this prerogative you think you have, by marching onto tribal land and just taking what you want, has posed a huge public relations nightmare for us, which makes the Dakota Pipeline debacle look stainless." Casper holds up a finger, about to protest. "Not finished yet," Smith insists. "One last point. If you already have bags of material in your possession, how much more do you need to study these 'adverse effects'?"

"For one thing, there's no proof we were involved in that." Drummond insists.

"You're right," Smith responds. "I'm sure a lot of people have access to stealth Blackhawks!" Smith exclaims. "Stop trying to play me for a fool. I've lost my patience with this entire meeting, especially with you barging into a government office and insisting on anything! Have I made myself clear, *Doctor Doom?*"

"We don't need the insults, thank you," Drummond says, while again feigning the victim role. "So, fine. Let me ask you this," Drummond pivots. "Doesn't the Commerce Clause prohibit tribes from engaging in international trade? We know the Germans, Canadians… who knows who else have been buying up these resources. If I understand correctly that's not only regulated by Congress, it's currently prohibited," Drummond posits, playing his last card.

Smith returns to his seat, begins to scratch something on a memo pad.

"That's just the point. They haven't 'sold' anything." Smith says while continuing to scribble the note. "No money has ever been exchanged. They've only gifted material to research labs, and considerably less material than you... how do we say, have stolen?" Smith asserts, no longer considering politic.

Drummond can't take any more challenge to his alpha status and rises abruptly from his chair. Casper Elliot follows slowly, lifting himself out of the chair with pained effort.

"I can see we're wasting our time with you," the Doctor huffs. "We gave you a chance to save face over this, but you've given us no choice now but to go over your head."

"Save face?" Smith asks, now entirely beyond just annoyed. Smith rips the note from his pad and rises to hand it to Drummond. "This is the contact for the congressional oversight committee in charge of these regulations. Be my guest," he declares. Smith marches to the door and opens it wide. "I have another meeting now gentlemen, thank you for coming," he says, motioning an arm out the door. Doctor Drummond exits quickly, in even more of a huff than when he entered. Casper stops briefly to offer his hand to the Deputy Director.

"Thank you for your time, Director," Elliot says, but Smith just glances at his extended paw and shuts the door on him and returns to his desk to grab the phone.

"Merriam, can we get Senator Finkle's office on the line?" Smith asks. He stretches his jaw, to loosen the muscles, tightened from clenching his teeth the last few minutes. He looks at his watch, noticing it's just only ten in the morning.

❖ ❖ ❖

Kate pays her New York cabbie and turns to freeze in awe at the sight of the United Nations Headquarters. She absorbs the reality of the grand sight, something she'd only seen in pictures before today. The familiar arc of flags representing the member nations catches her eye immediately. Nothing could have prepared her for this feeling, not the force in her gut that fueled her boldness up to this point or even her meetings in Washington. Things were on a grander scale now and it felt very different and hugely intimidating. The thought of all those people who pleaded and fought for their rights at this site weighs heavily on her. So much so, that she begins to question why this struggle would be any different, and worthy of a favorable response?

"Enough of that," she says out loud, reasoning with

her brain to avoid falling back into self doubt. There's no time for those kind of thoughts now. Maybe she's just tired, she wonders. That's it, that's totally understandable she thinks. So, *enough of that* is right. For now it's time to gulp back all those confusing emotions and step brazenly into the next phase of this grand plan. After all, this is her strategy and it merges perfectly with the rare power and keen edge they hold in their hands. Kate expands her chest against the buttons of the smart business suit she picked out for this very occasion, and advances into the main lobby.

The UN-Energy department isn't a large space, merely an office or two at the end of another long hallway. This is a department that relies mostly on donations from private individuals and corporate donors, for the purpose of providing grants and services to nations seeking to adopt sustainable alternatives to burning oil or splitting an atom.

Kate opens the door, peeking tentatively around the corner before entering further.

"Can I help you ma'am?" a kind voice asks, welcoming her in further. Kate gently closes the door behind her and steps up to the receptionist, who this time is standing to greet her warmly. Kate extends her hand, dropping a folder in the process, but it's the receptionist who graciously picks it up and hands it to her.

"Sorry," Kate apologizes again, as the lady rises to hand over the folder. "Oh, thank you! I have an appointment with the Energy Secretary, Doctor Vega?" Kate says, almost forgetting to introduce herself. "Oh, my name is Kate Rose, we spoke a couple days ago. Maybe that was you I spoke with – about donating energy resources to the program?" The receptionist enthusiastically shakes Kate's hand.

"Miss Rose, yes definitely, that was me and actually Doctor Vega is expecting you. Please come this way," the receptionist says, leading her toward another door. Kate looks the humble offices over, still fully dazzled by the hospitality.

❖   ❖   ❖

Kate steps in to find a striking man in his sixties, standing in the center of the room in anticipation of her arrival. Nearly slayed by the juxtaposition of this reception to the one in Washington, she reaches out to shake his hand. Surprisingly, the gentleman greets her by name even prior to an introduction.

"Miss Rose, Doctor Martin Vega, it's a pleasure to meet you," he says charmingly. Kate is stunned. Then again, she is here as a donor so that certainly must have something to do with all this love, she considers.

"My pleasure, thanks for meeting me on short notice!" Kate replies. She considers his simple grey suit, solid color tie and how his frameless glasses seem to disappear over his gaunt, acne-scarred face that bear the signs of his modest childhood.

"Please come in, come in," Doctor Vega says, while gentlemanly holding a chair open for her. He doesn't size her up, nor does he gawk at her chest or legs, instead he keenly focuses into her big green eyes.

"Thank you very much," Kate blushes as she takes her seat. Vega reaches for another chair, ditching the formality of speaking from behind a desk. He takes his seat facing her.

"How can I help you this morning Miss Rose?" he asks.

"Yes so, I'm sure you've heard a lot lately about a certain Native American Tribe in northern Minnesota and a rather remarkable discovery?" Kate says, hoping to avoid rehashing a backstory that by now most people should know.

"I have indeed," he adds. "And if my facts are correct, they've recently proved the potential of a new kind of nuclear fuel, thanks to the work of an MIT professor from that very tribe," Doctor Vega replies.

"Oh my, yes you're up on your news," she says, relieved to hit the ground running.

"That's my job Miss Rose," Doctor Vega says as he leans back in his chair and loosens his jacket button to settle into a longer discussion.

"Please, call me Kate," she offers.

"Kate, certainly," he says.

"Just recently my client, Professor Lightfoot, the man you noted, has brought an experiment online that uses only one gram of this material. The power plant they constructed, although only a proof of concept, is already producing over sixty megawatts of clean, sustainable energy and freely feeding the electricity into the local power grid, all with zero radioactive waste," Kate states.

"How is this possible?" the good doctor wonders aloud. "And how much of this material exists?"

"All of the material *only* exists in a specific geographic area, within the Red Rock reservation land. I guess years ago when the American government relocated the Ojibwe nation, they weren't aware of what lay under the ground."

"Yes, the earthquake, I heard about this," Vega says, nodding while he fidgets in his chair.

"All I can say is it appears to be a massive deposit," Kate mentions without giving up too much, too soon. "This is capable of cleanly powering entire countries." But then Kate catches a crack in Doctor Vega's mood, first with a furrowed brow then glancing downward in a sort of tortured uneasiness. "Is something wrong, Doctor?" Kate asks. He looks up without the slightest attempt to hide the concern from his face.

"And you believe the United States government will just allow this tribe…" Kate can't help but interrupt.

"Independent sovereign nation," she says, before apologizing for the interruption. "Sorry." The doctor nods his head.

"Okay, let's go with the most generous definition of sovereignty for the moment. Do you believe they will allow *any* 'independent sovereign nation' exclusive rights to do what they will with this discovery?" Vega asks, somewhat rhetorically.

"No. Not at all," Kate replies with a sure grin that might even be interpreted as mischievous. "That's where you come in, Sir," she explains. The doctor squints in a puzzled way and offers a curious smile.

"I must say, I'm intrigued, Miss Rose," he admits. "Please continue."

"We believe we have a case, a strong one designed to exploit our rights under the Indian Commerce Clause and define implicitly what sovereignty and resource rights allow in this situation," she says, continuing to take the gentleman down a reasonable path. "But as always, power rules." Kate straightens her back, confident now that she has him sufficiently captivated, she reaches into her bag and pulls out a two-page document, and holds it back against her chest for a moment as she continues. "Now, for the time being, as long as we avoid selling the material and technology, we circumvent existing restrictions imposed from predatory arguments crafted by the U.S. to limit tribal sovereignty." Kate *then* hands over the 'Letter Of Intent' to Doctor Vega. "This is why we are donating three million dollars worth of material and supporting technology to this body, in an effort to call attention to the potential of our case and at the same time, benefit the lives of many others in need."

"What exactly then is your case? If I may ask?" The doctor says, as he leans forward in his chair, highly anticipating the answer.

"Certainly," Kate continues. "We're sitting on tens of billions of dollars worth of energy reserve which can improve the lives of millions, possibly even billions of people on this planet. I don't know about you, but I think that kind of potential just might convince the General Assembly of seriously considering our application for Member Nation Status. Not like that hasn't been tried before, we get that. But in this case, money talks and we need friends outside the U.S. now, more than we do inside," Kate proposes. "And it starts by donating in good faith to prove our worth, in exchange for your friendship and influence with the U.N. Permanent Forum on Indigenous Issues." Doctor Vega appears completely and utterly speechless, when suddenly his stunned expression blossoms into a most anticipatory grin. He lifts from his chair as if offering a standing ovation.

"A magnificent plan miss Rose, albeit dangerously ambitious," he gushes, while wiggling his fingers like a mad scientist. "I love it. We'd be honored to help."

"That's great!" Kate exclaims, nearly throwing her arms around him, before composing herself barely enough to just shake his hand, albeit effusively.

❖   ❖   ❖

Fallen logs and timber have been used to construct a cover over the chasm at what now has become a working quarry. Mary is talking to a sentry at a far end of the fissure. A dozen young Chippewa teens stand guard along the edge of the fissure, in twenty-four hour shifts. Further up into the woods, Lightfoot and Harvey Bearheart overlook the construct, while they watch Mary charm the young Chippewa warriors and hand out water bottles below.

"I had a strange dream last night," Lightfoot says.

"I used to have dreams," Harvey Bearheart says. "When I was young. I would even write them down so I wouldn't forget them."

"And now?" Lightfoot asks.

"I'm lucky I remember to wake up," the big fellow says as he waves to Mary with a firm hand in the air as if he was flagging a taxi. "What happened in your dream?" Harvey Bearheart asks.

"Like I said, it was strange. It was like the beginning of time, when there was only this land and nothing else on earth, except Granddad was there," Lightfoot says.

"Makes sense. He's old enough," Bearheart mutters, while they watch Mary make the rounds below. "Then what happened?"

"It was when the comet struck the Earth. But Granddad just stood there when it hit, as if it was no big deal. It destroyed everything around him, but for some reason he survived the impact and all the land around him started flourishing," Lightfoot says, before turning to look at the big guy. "And then he popped a cap on a Moosehead with his thumb and downed it in one gulp," Lightfoot says. "Then I woke up."

"That's a stupid dream," Harvey Bearheart says plainly. Lightfoot nods in agreement and takes a swig of his water bottle.

"I agree. Felt more like a Pepsi commercial than a dream," Lightfoot says.

"Second shift is all good," Mary calls from halfway up the hill. As she gets closer, her dad reaches down and pulls her onto the outlook ridge. "We'll bring them some food in a couple hours," she says. Together now, the three of them look across the valley as the guards settle into their positions for the night. "They said they'd like to carry guns," Mary reports. Without uttering a word, the three of them consider the futility of any situation that would cause these boys to try and fight back.

"They have a direct dial on their phones to Tribal Police, right?" her dad asks.

"Yes," Mary says. "So far they've only had to worry about our own people showing up after a couple beers and nearly falling in the pit."

"I can't imagine the Corps will make a move now anyway," Lightfoot says. But Harvey Bearheart isn't so sure, worrying they've just managed to poke a sleeping grizzly in the eye.

❖ ❖ ❖

"That's easy, we just need to convince everyone how dangerous this material really is," Doctor Drummond says. Empty coffee cups and half filled water bottles are clear signs that this covert strategy session has been going on for quite a while. Lieutenant "Mac" MacCallion faces the maniacal doctor across the round table. The sun damaged officer motions for Casper Elliot to slide over the blueprint that lies across the table.

"May I?" Mac asks, reaching across the table for a roll of plans. Casper Elliot unfurls the blueprints for the brackish Naval officer and weights the edges down with coffee cups. Mac unfolds a pair of cheap collapsible reading glasses, the kind you'd get in duty free. He leans into its details. "So in other words, we're saving them from themselves," the Lieutenant smirks while studying the layout of the Red Rock reservation.

"Essentially, yes," Drummond replies with the kind of self-assurance devoted to an idea too new to have been vetted properly. Crisis mode fuels this contingency discussion, after returning from D.C. empty handed. "Think about it. Everyone is watching now, wondering how these 'too-good-to-be-true' claims of theirs will stand the test of time. What if, let's say, it wasn't so 'stable' as they keep claiming and it actually reacted in a big way. Hell, we couldn't let them face that fate alone, they'd certainly need expert protection from something that dangerous," Drummond posits with a *wink-wink* benevolence.

"Is it?" Casper Elliot asks, innocently.

"Is it what? Dangerous?" Doctor Drummond replies incredulously. "Of course not, but that's not the point. If the public thinks it is, they'd beg us to intervene. Drummond stands, thinking out loud as his ruse gestates in his large pale skull. "After all, when the world realizes they're sitting on a weapon of mass destruction, a 'nuclear' weapon so unpredictable that it just *blows up* on its own, the public – hell the world will beg us to move in and secure it before it falls into terrorist hands." Drummond circles the room in a trance, while the others squint at the mad doctor. MacCallion signals with a slight but abrupt lift of his hand, to gently wake Doctor Evil from his phantasm.

"And how do you propose we 'prove' this?" Mac asks. Drummond turns back to the room and smiles.

"That's where you come in. We know where it lies. Make it explode," Drummond proposes easily.

"Nuke it?" Casper Elliot asks in utter disbelief. Drummond spins around to glare at the imbecile.

"Do you think I'm nuts?" the doctor blurts, while MacCallion tries to hide the 'YES!' that explodes in his brain. "Just use conventional explosives, a drone strike or something," Drummond says before resuming his seat and leaning across the desk toward the officer. "You spooks do that all the time." MacCallion rises, having reached his limit

"You just get ready to build a case with a bunch of science shit when it's time to explain why it's so volatile," Mac declares.

"So you'll do something then?" Drummond asks excitedly. Elliot on the other hand at least knows better than to expect any spoken confirmation of such a thing.

"I'll say it again," Mac reiterates as if speaking a second language. "When it proves to be unstable, be ready to explain why," Mac repeats, without the *wink and a nod* that Drummond seems to require. The Lieutenant glances at Elliot, who instantly returns a knowing smile, indicating he'd explain it to the petulant doctor later. MacCallion skulks out of the small room without any further eye contact and certainly not another word. But Drummond isn't wired for subtlety. With a wary shrug, he looks to Elliot for some kind of clarification.

"Let's give it some time," Elliot confirms. "I think everyone understands what has to happen."

ELEVEN

"Full Scale Roar"

Bubbles begin rising from below the surface a few hundred yards offshore, just below Papa Leo's favorite lookout spot. First to break the surface is a large black Pelican case. The watertight container bobs silently in the choppy midnight waters of Lake Superior's northwest shore. A couple Great Blue Herons swoop in to check the disturbance, but with no indication of a feeding Walleye or Northern Pike, they continue on toward land. The yellow nylon tether attached to the handle begins tugging from below, pulling half the case under the surface a few times, as an increasing field of rising bubbles surrounds the area.

The Navy Seal diver suddenly emerges and pulls his mask up to his forehead, waiting as a second diver appears moments later. Without uttering a word, the first diver motions with two-fingers towards the top of the cliff, barely visible in the night mist. Wasting no time, they begin to tow the large buoyant case to the shoreline.

Papa Leo crests the valley ridge, overlooking the fortified quarry. From the valley floor below, the sentries tilt up to see the old man's silhouette rise above the ridge line as it has every night since they've started their shifts. Six hours on - six hours off, they stand guard, twenty-four hours a day. One of the sentries, a young Chippewa teenager not more that sixteen years old raises an arm, his palm facing toward the patriarch on the hill. Papa Leo returns the signal, repeating the gesture as the other guards greet him similarly. The fallen debris and timbers in the valley have been repurposed to cover the large trailing split in the earth. Papa Leo considers the futility of mere foot soldiers standing guard against another possible raid. But this was more of a gesture of dignity, to at least meet another incursion with a show of resistance.

Back at the shoreline, both divers expertly secure the mortar tubes at the water's edge and aim them to the peak above. They dial-in their coordinates and confirm the connections before loading the first of two shells laid out before each rocket launcher. The first diver checks his watch and then prepares the open case by the water's edge, standing ready to quickly store the spent hardware before they drag the evidence back into the water. He turns to his partner, approaching close enough to whisper without his voice carrying across the water or up the shear rock.

"On my mark, we both fire simultaneously," the first diver instructs. "Three seconds, then the next pair. We have thirty seconds total to break down and get below the surface," he says, outlining the battle plan and exit strategy. "Got it?" The second diver nods while both turn in unison to man their assault positions.

Papa Leo listens as a Great Horned Owl flares her wings, thumping the air as it flutters onto a branch beside him. He turns back to meet her manic yellow eyes, staring back at him with a look of fixed shock. She closes her eyes briefly, snapping them open again and shifting her massive feathered head side to side.

But Papa Leo notices another thumping in the air, reminiscent of that sound made from pounding a hanging blanket with an oar, to shake the dust from its fibers. Again, two more deep base tones resonate in the trees.

The air above him whistles, quickly growing to a screaming pitch. "Wegodogwen," the old man says as his brow furrows with uneasiness when suddenly the valley floor explodes into a colossal blossom of fire. Papa Leo's senses race to record every microsecond of the blast, when another *one-two* burst of fire and rain complete the destruction. The huge timbers covering the crevice tumble and splinter outward to splash across the valley walls. Time itself appears to stop, reducing his vision to flashes of still images. The montage of snapshots tells a story of innocent faces, frozen in expressions of surprise before terror could even register in their eyes. In a sort of poetic horror, young bodies rip apart like chicken meat pulled from the bone in bursting clouds of crimson.

Papa Leo's mare rears in fright, throwing the old man backwards and to the ground, his head impacting a hard fallen log. He hears his own mind yield to the force, like a coiled spring instantly releasing its tension until all becomes quiet and gentle. He lies there in pastoral bliss as elegant flaming debris slowly falls back to earth around him. Papa Leo fades off to wake instantly in whiteness and with little memory except scattered glimpses and many questions.

Lightfoot jolts out of bed from the sound and force of the blast wave. A bad dream he wonders, then notices Mary also shocks awake. Turning to the open window, they see the orange glow beyond the ridge and leap to their feet. Grabbing just enough clothing to cover their bodies, Lightfoot and Mary run from the small room.

Outside in the village center, Mary and Lightfoot meet Harvey Bearheart and a growing band of tribe members. The bright cloud of debris grows from just over the ridge as the thunder still echoes throughout the foothills and travels across the lake. Small chips of wooden debris and orange rock begin to rain upon the village. "That's the quarry," Mary exclaims. Harvey Bearheart reaches for a young boy standing nearby.

"Tell me if Nimishoomis' horse is in the stable," he asks, as the little fellow runs off.

❖   ❖   ❖

"Tonight NBC has learned of a massive nuclear reaction at the site of that exotic fuel discovery on Native American land in northern Minnesota!" exclaims the matte-finished news anchor. She speaks in tones elevated above the anxiously pounding lead-in music, underscored by a text crawl cycling over and over. *'MYSTERY FUEL ELEMENT SPONTANEOUSLY EXPLODES – SIX NATIVE AMERICANS KILLED, AS NUCLEAR FUEL SITE DETONATES!'*

"We go live to Minnesota where our own Carol Bosworth is waiting for a press conference to begin," the anchor breathlessly announces. *"Carol?"*

The impromptu press conference on the steps of the Federal Building here in central Minnesota appears well planned, as the Bureau of Indian Affairs is remarkably ready with all the 'facts'.

"Thank you, Brooke," Carol says, acknowledging the handoff to the live event. Hank Poysen is about to take his place before the cameras while Doctor Drummond and Casper Elliot wait patiently in the wings for their turn to offer their expert support. The reporter continues.

"Brooke, first to speak I'm told, is Hank Poysen, the local Superintendent of the Bureau of Indian Affairs. For our viewers, we should note that the BIA is a division of the Department of Interior and is designed to protect and facilitate Native American rights and safety for all three hundred and ten tribes in the United States. I'm also told..." Carol stops, noticing Poysen is about to speak to the cameras. "Brooke, let's go to Superintendent Poysen who appears to be addressing the cameras now." Hank settles into position before the news crews.

❖ ❖ ❖

Kate hurries down the hall to her hotel room, while at the same time rummaging through her purse for the room key. She's balancing an armful of books, and holding her cell phone to her ear with the same shoulder currently stressed with a large travel bag.

"Oh, c'mon!" she exclaims. "No, not you, I'm trying to get to a TV," she explains to the person on the other end of the line while unsuccessfully fishing for the room key. "I'm at my room now," she announces, struggling to hold everything together. "Excuse me a second," Kate says before giving up and literally tossing everything in her arms to the floor in front of her. She digs for the key in her purse, while calling into the phone lying somewhere on the pile of debris at her feet. "Found it!" she calls out. "One more second."

Finally the door swings open into the room. Kate drags, kicks and pushes her belongings inside as fast as she can, just far enough to shut the door and run to grab the television remote. Kate stops, remembering her cell phone and runs back to recover it from the heap. With the phone and remote in her hands she runs back into the room and aims the phone at the TV, and holds the remote to her ear.

"I'm back!" she says, just before noticing she's talking into the TV remote and quickly changes hands. "Okay, turning it on now," Kate says while kicking off her heels and scanning the news channels. She stops just as Hank is wrapping up his opening statement.

"*I'd like to turn it over to someone who can speak to the dangers posed by this radioactive element as well as how something like this explosion could have occurred,*" the stooge concludes.

"Oh right!" Kate says, berating the TV screen, "Like we're supposed to believe that?"

"*Doctor Drummond?*" Hank says, motioning him to the podium. Hands shoot into the air from the press corps, amid demands for more information.

215

"Can we expect radioactive fallout from this?"

"Who's to blame for this disaster?"

"What are you doing to protect public safety?"

Hank holds his hands up to the crowd, quickly stepping back to the mic while briefly upstaging the 'good doctor'. Drummond impatiently weathers Hank's inability to exit the spotlight.

"Let me just say that this is early into the investigation," Hank adds. *"We will be informing you all as we learn more. Doctor Drummond?"* Hank says, stepping away again.

Kate tosses her coat on a chair and sits on the edge of the bed, her phone still at her ear. She turns up the volume as Drummond clears his throat.

"My name is Doctor Edward Drummond. I am senior scientist at the Los Alamos Neutron Science Center," he says proudly. *"That's, D-R-U-M-M-O-N-D."*

"For the love of god!" Kate protests. "Get on with it, you pedantic fuck!" Finally Kate thinks better of subjecting the caller to her rants. "Sorry. Thanks for letting me know. I'll call you back after this is over, okay?" she asks, before hanging up. On screen, Drummond continues.

"Let me just start by saying that ever since the discovery of this highly dangerous substance, we've alerted the United States government, urging caution to exercise all federal statutes designed to protect our cherished Native American tribes from the harmful effects of this material. I will also

say that the current climate of unwarranted suspicion aimed at any government or scientific oversight, has hindered our ability to research the dangers posed by this element, due to confused definitions of what tribal sovereignty actually means," Drummond says, waxing politic and expertly controlling the 'narrative', as the media is so fond of calling it these days. Again, panicked hands launch into the air.

"Is that why it's taken so long for the government to properly secure the area?" a reporter yells across the press corps. Casper Elliot leans into Drummond's sacred space, to offer his own explanation.

"For the record, I'd like to add that our national security experts and military personnel must be allowed access to ANY area on our continent, regardless of jurisdiction, that may present a clear and present danger to neighboring human life," Elliot interjects.

Kate is apoplectic, thinking better of throwing the remote at the TV, she lowers the device and instead grabs her phone and dials.

❖ ❖ ❖

Papa Leo lies in a hospital bed, his head heavily bandaged and his arm is in a cast. The heart monitor pings steadily, an encouraging rhythm for those at his bedside. A physician checks his chart and vitals while Mary holds his strong hand with both of hers.

Lightfoot and Harvey Bearheart study the doctor's face, trying to interpret the slightest expression while he examines Papa Leo.

"It's a good thing he's as strong as he is," the doctor says, noting a man nearly a hundred years old. "Most people half his age couldn't have survived that kind of force. We've given him something to sleep for right now. We need him to rest until the swelling in his head recedes," he says. "Also, with all the press reports, we had to consult with the Nuclear Regulatory Commission. Oddly enough there are no signs of radioactive poisoning or even the slighted bit of contamination."

"And there won't be either," Lightfoot strongly asserts. "This was not a radioactive material."

"I'm just going with what's being reported," the doctor points out.

"Which is a fabrication," Lightfoot adds, while leaning to feel the old man's forehead. The doctor doesn't look convinced, choosing rather to go with the media hype.

"I'd like to keep him here for a few days, but I'm hoping he'll be ready to go home by the weekend." The young physician stands quietly for a moment, and smiles reassuringly at the peaceful old man. "Really, I'm stunned he was able to endure such a fall at his age. I'll check back in a couple hours."

"Thank you Doctor," Mary says. Lightfoot slides the back of his hand along his grandfather's cheek. The physician smiles and exits the room.

"I need to get back and meet with the families of the boys," Lightfoot mentions, torn with having to leave his hero right now, but also needing to fill the role of leader in his absence.

"We'll be here with him," Mary assures. "You go, I'll call you if anything changes." He kisses her on the top of her head then starts to leave before stopping half way to look at his grandfather for a while.

"Billy?" Mary's dad calls over, standing and motioning for them to talk outside. Mary stays at Papa Leo's side.

Outside the room, Lightfoot's anger flows a bit freer around the big fellow's normally cynical outlook.

"You know this was an attack. Blatant murder," Lightfoot asserts. "Once again preparing the way for the splendid white man to march in and save us from ourselves."

"I'm not surprised," the big Bearheart says.

"There's no way this was the result of a stable element transmuting on its own," Lightfoot insists. "I'll prove it..." but then Lightfoot stops cold, unable to continue though not limited by anger or sadness. This time, there is something else that triggers his sudden disregard for words of despair or rage.

Harvey Bearheart has seen that look before - that unmistakable sight of a man at the crucial edge. It was at this very moment that Lightfoot became a warrior, and Harvey Bearheart knew it.

❖   ❖   ❖

The young delivery boy helps Lightfoot saddle the palomino at the stable.

"Is it okay to go up there?" the little fellow asks as he expertly cinches the saddle for his champion. Lightfoot isn't much for words right now, instead choosing to communicate with a kind smile and a gentle mussing of the little guy's thick black hair. He mounts the horse and quickly rides off, up the trail to the epicenter. The other tribe members look on quietly, still mourning the loss of life while they continue to prepare for six burial ceremonies.

Further along the shoreline, Lightfoot slows his horse, walking respectfully past family members and volunteers, assembling a line of funeral pyres at the water's edge. The men work silently, delicately constructing the platforms that will hold the bodies of the young boys killed in the attack the night before.

Lightfoot pauses to share a look with the fathers of the fallen boys. Is he the only one struggling with doubts of his own recklessness in standing up to such a powerful aggressor? How could these parents and siblings of these murdered brothers ever consider that giving one's life for riches could ever be honorable? In the end, it's he who bears the responsibility for their deaths and they must know that and resent him because of it. Yet, is it really wealth that they've taken a stand for? No, he realizes, this is bigger than that. This is about dignity, the right of sovereignty. This is but another stand in another battle, against another bully. Maybe even a final battle where the stakes are higher than they have ever been. This time, the Chippewa nation stands at the edge, an aging tribe of decimated clans, finally given the opportunity to right the many years of wrongs. They must see it as he does. But how could they now, and how could he ever expect them to see past this grief, enough to comfort themselves with the idea that their sons died for something greater?

And then, as if hearing his doubt, one of the fathers raises his hand high, holding it there, his palm open toward him, signaling his faith and solidarity. Yes, even at this hideous moment, this father took the time to say that we are all still a clan. Lightfoot knows what that simple signal meant. Soon all the fathers and brothers along the line of pyres, raise their hands high and hold them there toward him, as warriors have done for hundreds of years to signal their solidarity with their elders in the face of an enemy. Lightfoot's spirit lifts with them, and he too raises his hand in return and in honor. Beyond the hysteria, unaffected by the media blitz aimed to whip fear and doubt about their stewardship of the mysterious *Ishkode* element as they call it now, everyone here knows the truth. Just as they have for hundreds of years - and this time, this tribe has had enough.

❖   ❖   ❖

At the epicenter, the young professor forensically filters through the debris, blackened by fire and splintered by explosive force. He looks across the valley at the shards of orange rock, blown across the basin. Most of the timbers have blasted away from the opening of the fissure or have fallen deep inside. He lowers his head and freezes, when near his feet he sees a blood stained sneaker lying at the place one of the young sentries last stood their ground. Lightfoot leans over to gaze into the dark chasm, inspecting the level of floating stones. Oddly enough it appears the explosion just managed to jar more of the element lose. Thousands of orange rocks hover peacefully now, buoyantly forming a thin layer just below the rim of the chasm. Of course, the attack was never intended to destroy the prize. This was merely designed to limit their access to it. Lightfoot notices a shallow crater nearby, possibly a point of impact. *Of course,* he thinks. If this was an attack, then there had to be an origin, a ground zero where an explosive charge would bear some signature of the explosive used. He studies the charred pile of bark and wood near the edge of the crack in the earth, clearly not the result of a reaction from within. It's these telltale scars, the smoking black remains, and the circular gouges in the ground that tell a different story. He picks up a piece of wood and smells it, dabbing a finger in the soot and tasting it with the tip of his tongue. Three other impact points stand out. And then, the drab green shard from a cylinder catches his eye, printed with a bit of stenciled yellow paint, with the lettering, *M83* still visible under the soot.

❖   ❖   ❖

Back atop the valley's ridge, Lightfoot loosens the reins of his horse from the fallen tree and places the charred fragments into the pony's side bag. He swings himself back into the saddle and rides off.

Lightfoot arrives moments later at the power plant, still churning away and pouring massive amounts of electricity into the Minnesota grid. Today is the day he was scheduled to meet with the energy company and discuss plans to move forward, possibly expand in an effort to generate income and leverage in the fight for independence. The palomino continues to walk along the shore, stopping in front of Mission

Control, the makeshift headquarters carved into the Community Center building.

The three Loon sisters carry blankets and white sheets along the shore's edge, no doubt on their way toward the ceremony site.

"Billy," Keezheknoi calls over, leading the other two to meet him, and void of the banter that usually surrounds the trio.

"How's Nimishoomis?" Small Duck asks.

"They're watching him closely," he says. "We'll know more tonight when they wake him up." Lightfoot pulls the charred fragments from the side bag. "I need a favor," he says, handing over the pieces of wood and metal. He scribbles a note in a small pad and hands it to Small Duck. "I need to send this stuff to Tyler Penrose, at MIT. That's the address, phone number's there too. Please mark it urgent, next day," he concludes. "Thank you, ladies," he says.

"It'll be there tomorrow first thing," Keezheknoi assures him, while she examines the burnt debris. "And thank you, Billy," she says, without any of the sarcasm that usually tailgates everything out of her mouth.

"For what?" Lightfoot wonders, startled by her gratefulness.

"For calling us ladies," Keezheknoi explains before turning quickly toward the road to avoid the awkwardness of being out of character for too long. He watches in astonishment as the old birds shuffle off on their mission. As he turns his horse toward the stable, he overhears Meoquanee in the distance.

"We can pick up some smokes while we're out," she suggests.

"Is that all you think about?" Small Duck scolds her red-dressed sister.

"After last night, it reminds me I can still inhale," Meoquanee replies.

❖ ❖ ❖

Six wooden platforms rise nearly ten feet high against the black night sky. The young sentry's bodies lie on top of each structure, wrapped in white linen, illuminated by a single torch planted in the ground at each base. Under these beds of wood and woven bands of birch bark, are dried wood, logs and branches stacked nearly head high as fuel for the fire which will soon be lit to carry the spirits to the heavens within the rising smoke. The moon is merely an arched sliver providing very little ambient light.

Lightfoot stands with Mary and her family by the shore, barely visible in the darkness and lit intermittently by the flickering of the torches. Harvey Bearheart drapes his massive arms across little Anna in front of him, as she leans into her dad and watches first hand, a ceremony she had only read about in school. She tries to comprehend so many deaths at once, lined up along the shore like the slain warriors who fought against the English and French 'traders' long ago. Anna loved the stories Miss Achambo told of their Chippewa ancestors at a time before the immigrants arrived and tried to own the land and sky.

Grieving relatives, immediate to each lost spirit stand near their deceased. Without any apparent cue and as if tuned into some inaudible frequency, each of the fathers removes a torch from the soil and touches it to the dry timbers and twigs under each swathed body. Within seconds all six ceremonial stands grow into bonfires reaching twenty feet into the sky. No one says a word. There are no eulogies, no tears, no scripted send-offs, simply the living standing boldly by as they watch their loved ones ascend from this tortured place to happiness beyond.

Anna's glasses reflect the raging flame, fully occluding her eyes, but appropriately reflecting what must be a metaphor of the feelings that burn in her little spirit. Mary looks on enduringly as anger, rare for her kind demeanor, hardens her normally gentle features. She tightens her grip on Lightfoot's hand while he too braves to hold back emotion, determined never to allow these killers to pull a tear from his eye. Instead he clenches his jaw, tightening features already hardened with insomnia and resolve. His breathing labors to pull into his lungs the scents of smoke and the stench of burning flesh.

❖   ❖   ❖

Kate walks from wall to wall in her hotel room, while dialing Lightfoot's number again. It's morning now and still no word from Red Rock. She sighs completely at the sound of his recorded voice.

"It's Kate again. I'm so worried about you. Please call me... all I know is what I'm watching on the news. We need to talk William." She hangs up, flops on the bed and notices a segment on the muted TV of a sensational female newscaster's silent display of panic. Kate turns up the volume.

"*More now on that massive explosion at the Red Rock reservation, caused by the mysterious element at the heart of a controversy over tribal sovereignty.*" The newswoman says, nearly hyperventilating alongside repetitious video of B-roll and historic stock footage of nuclear disasters worldwide. "*Sources are telling us that the Bureau of Indian Affairs has imposed an evacuation order to clear the area in Northern Minnesota and relocate the affected Chippewa tribe to another nearby reserve.*" The video window next to the announcer switches to a news conference in progress. "*We're just getting word of another briefing in progress. Let's listen in.*"

227

On screen Deputy Director Smith speaks to the press, joined of course by 'experts' Doctor Drummond and Casper Elliot.

"Thank you for your time. My name is Deputy Director Michael Smith with the Bureau of Indian Affairs. I'll read from a statement prepared by members of Congress and in consultation with the Army Corps of Engineers. 'In an effort to ensure public safety both for the Red Rock tribal community and surrounding areas, it has been determined that effective immediately the United States federal government has issued an evacuation order for all peoples of the Red Rock Chippewa tribe. Upon securing the damaged area, the Army Corps of Engineers, together with experts in nuclear containment will evaluate the site for any further actions needed to contain this event and determine the level of radioactive exposure. We encourage the Native American peoples to abide by this order as their safety and that of the affected shoreline area depends on a proper vetting of this event.'"

Kate's phone rings, which she's still holding tightly in her hand. She notices Lightfoot's number on the screen.

"William! Oh, my god I've been so worried. It's all over the news. What the hell happened? Is everyone okay?"

Lightfoot and Mary are huddled around his cell phone.

"Kate it's okay. You're on speakerphone, I have Mary here." Mary leans in to the phone.

"Hi Kate. It's pretty horrible. Six of our kids were killed in the blast. Papa Leo is in the hospital, but he's going to be okay. He was thrown from his horse when the blast went off."

Kate is beside herself, freaking out through the speakerphone.

"*This is horrible, how did it happen, I thought the stuff was safe!*" She exclaims.

"It is safe, Kate," Lightfoot assures, "Someone set off an explosion, this was intentional. I'll let you guess who. This was not a nuclear reaction, that's impossible and by tomorrow morning we'll know for sure when the test results from the explosive residue is complete."

"*They're saying the feds have issued an evacuation order!*" Kate exclaims. Mary and Lightfoot lock eyes, sharing their surprise.

"That's the first we're hearing about that," Lightfoot admits. "We've been at the burial ceremony all night," Lightfoot says, while noticing the sunrise out the window as Kate continues in a panic.

"*The guy I met with at the Bureau was there. And that same Doctor Drummond jackass, and... another Army guy with the Corps! They're saying that the entire place is radioactive,*" Kate says. Lightfoot grits his teeth at the thought of Drummond being at the heart of the media blitz.

"Drummond and that Army Corps guy are the ones who showed up here after the quake. We refused to give them access. Looks like they found another way," he says, as he fits the evil little pieces together.

Back in New York, Kate paces furiously in her hotel room.

"The U.N. Energy Secretary was ready to work on our behalf, but now they're saying they have to wait until an environmental impact study is complete," Kate says, while struggling to click the TV off. "We can't let them get away with this," she declares, feverishly pressing the off button on the remote with no success before tossing the device and walking into the bathroom. She stares into the mirror, trying to train her breathing while Lightfoot tries to console her through the phone.

"*Kate, we won't let them get away with this. Just ask them to wait until tomorrow before they make any decision on this, okay? If what I suspect proves true, this will 'blow up' in their faces' once the world hears what really happened. This was an attack Kate, on our sovereignty. Hell, this was an attack on the truth,*" he says, managing to talk her down, as she concentrates on her breathing in the mirror.

"For god's sake, please be careful," she begs. "These

bastards are capable of anything," Kate says, pausing momentarily to consider Papa Leo. "Please tell your grandfather I'm thinking of him. And Mary?" she asks.

Mary leans into the phone.

"Yes Kate, I'm here hon," she replies, trying to project calm.

"*Mary, we're going to win, you just watch. They're fucking with wrong people!*" Kate assures. Mary glances over while releasing an exhausted but welcome laugh. "You got that right. Good night, Kate, we miss you," Mary concludes.

"Please get some sleep Kate," Lightfoot adds.

"*Good night guys,*" Kate says before clicking off. Lightfoot reaches for Mary and pulls her close. But when in his arms, her strength seems to finally deplete and she crumbles into him.

In the hotel bathroom, Kate remains staring into the mirror. She takes a deep drag of air and heads back into the main room and searches the floor for the discarded remote. Again she flips through the news channels. There's no way she'll be sleeping tonight.

❖ ❖ ❖

Tyler exits the famous George R. Harrison Spectroscopy Lab on the MIT campus and steps into a stiff morning breeze. His nose is buried in the report he's just received - an analysis of the charred remains

Lightfoot sent him. A sudden gust yanks the sheets from his grip.

"Aw, c'mon!" he yelps, pleading with the wind or the papers, or maybe his own inability to hold on. Tyler chases the sheets across the quad, as they seem to dodge every swing of his arm. Of course, another flurry tosses the report in an opposite direction. "Stop it!" he cries out, trying again to reason with nature.

A young coed reaches for the report as it blows across her path, grabbing it quickly as he approaches while hunched over, his hand raking across the ground after the sheets.

"Here you go," she says, offering Tyler the report. He tilts up from her feet.

"Wow," he exclaims, more mesmerized by her than the rescue. The young lady smiles and walks off, leaving him holding the sheets and admiring her gait. "Man!" Tyler says, before eventually snapping out of it and continuing to read the report. But when he flips to the second page and lays eyes on the final result of the analysis, he's clobbered by what leaps off the page. "Sweet Bobby Jesus!" he blurts, while digging through his pockets. His freezing fingers grapple to dial the mobile phone.

❖   ❖   ❖

Mary is seeing Lightfoot out the door, on his

way back to the hospital when his phone rings. As is customary, he has no idea what pocket it's in, and while he pats himself down, she reaches in and pulls it out for him.

"Oh, thanks," he says timidly while noticing the call from Tyler. "Hey Tyler, I'm on the edge of my seat over here. I assume you got the package?" he says.

Tyler holds his oversized phone to his skull while reading the report and continuing to walk across the quad.

"Hey Lightbulb! Man, what the hell is going on over there? Everyone here is talking about you!" He looks back at the report, "Yeah, got it here. Just like you thought man, the residue is definitely military grade C4 explosive," he says. He holds the report in the air, shaking it as if Lightfoot could see the emphasis. "And you're right man, the report confirms the metal casing was from a mortar round."

Lightfoot has the phone on speaker mode so Mary can hear.

"That's great news," Lightfoot says while shooting a thumbs up to Mary. Tyler panics on the other end.

"*Great news?*" Tyler exclaims. "*Someone dropped a bomb on your ass, dude. This isn't good.*"

"No I know, I mean it's great news we can prove it," Lightfoot says, wagging his head. "I didn't have any doubt, but I need the data to support it. How soon can you email the report to me?"

Tyler looks at his watch.

"I'll do it now, no problem, man," Tyler says. "The copy center opens in about ten minutes, so you should get it right away." Tyler starts marching across the quad, "William, seriously you're picking one bat shit crazy fight here," Tyler announces, while quickly rubbernecking as another female passes. Tyler recovers, focusing back on the call. "Anyway, sure, I'll come out there. You know me. I'm always up for a chance to poke the man in the eye. You say when and I'll be there," Tyler pledges.

Still standing in the doorway, Lightfoot checks Mary while inviting Tyler to the reservation.

"How 'bout now?" Lightfoot suggests. Mary shrugs, why not?

"Uh yeah, how's the weekend looking?" Tyler asks.

"Perfect! I'll send you the travel info. Mary and I will pick you up at the airport," he says before realizing he hadn't exactly filled him in on everything.

"Mary?" Tyler asks. *"Okay, I gotta get out there now,"* Tyler declares. Mary grins as Lightfoot takes it off speaker mode.

"Yeah, we've got a lot to catch up on," he admits, tenderly moving a strand of hair from over her eye while he talks privately now. But Mary is well aware he's dodging the possibility of an inappropriate comment flowing from Tyler's unregulated thought stream. "In the mean time, send the report. And Tyler? Thanks again, really this is an enormous help. Bye." Lightfoot hangs up. "I was right. It was the Army that blew up the site. And we have confirmation of a shell fragment."

"So now what?" Mary asks.

"Now, we set up a press conference," he says, quickly running a checklist through his head. "We have to let Kate know so she can set it on her end."

"I'll let her know," Mary says. "You get going. When will you be ready for the press?"

"I'm ready now, as soon as Tyler sends the report." He leans in and kisses her. "Right now, I better get to the hospital. You can bet Granddad will start terrorizing the staff as soon as he wakes up and finds out where he is." He heads out the door, calling back over his shoulder. "I'll call you when I get there."

❖   ❖   ❖

Papa Leo hasn't just woken up, he's wearing the floppy hat over his bandaged head and trying to put his pants on while surrounded by protesting nurses.

"Sir please, you've had a serious fall, you need to rest!" the head nurse implores, while another tries to stop him from pulling the tubes from his own arm.

"I already have a healer. She's a hundred and three years old," he argues.

"Sir, we appreciate Traditional Indian Medicine, we really do, and even adopt much of it here, but you need to lay low right now and let us monitor this. You took a strong blow to the head," the Nurse continues.

"At least it was my head," he says. He lifts his extensively plastered limb to illustrate the absurdity. "And what's this concrete on my arm? I just need a splint," the grumpy old man protests. Papa Leo freezes with his arm in the air when he notices Lightfoot enter the room.

"Granddad, what are you doing?" Lightfoot says from the doorway. The head nurse shrugs while the young RN pulls her hands back and into the air after he bats her away.

"Boy, tell them I'm okay!" he insists, fully expecting his grandson to share his incredulousness.

"You are okay," Lightfoot concedes. "But maybe just one more day. You have fluid on the brain right now, and need to stay still." Instead, Papa Leo finishes putting his pants on, then holds out his tube-tethered arm to the nurse.

"You going to take this out, or am I?" he insists, rather than asking. The nurse looks to his grandson for help, but Lightfoot is resigned and finally just nods. Against her best judgment, the head nurse removes the tube. Papa Leo watches the needle come out of his arm.

"That's probably where all the fluid in my skull is coming from," the feisty old fart postulates. The nurse ekes out a condescending smile, rather than argue with him any further.

❖ ❖ ❖

A large orderly rolls Papa Leo in a wheelchair to the curb, followed by the nurse. The old man doesn't look too pleased with the ironsides, while he taps on its flimsy construction. Lightfoot runs outside through the main lobby doors with the discharge papers in hand and catches up with the prison break in progress.

"I'll go bring the car around. And don't move!" he orders his grandfather, in a last attempt to show some kind of resistance for the old man's good. And of course, no sooner does he run into the parking lot, does Papa Leo start to pull himself out of the wheelchair.

"Sir, please stay seated," the nurse insists in the most authoritative voice she can squeak out.

"I'm fine," Papa Leo insists, but this time, the very large orderly, also Native American, places a firm hand on the old man's shoulder in a somewhat kindly *don't mess with me* gesture.

"Sir, this has nothing to do with how you feel. It's all about lawyers, and you know how stupid they are. Just sit there, until you get into the car and then you're on your own," the clever brother says, offering the cranky elder a platform instead of a pass. Papa Leo nods, grateful that at least this boy respects his justified incertitude with stupid procedure. He releases his grip, allowing Papa Leo to plop himself back into the chair on his own accord. The orderly gently places his large mitt on Papa Leo's shoulder from behind and gives the nurse a nod of victory.

"Lawyers!" Papa Leo says, in a tone synonymous with idiots.

"You got that right, Ogimaa," the massive orderly says, patting his shoulder warmly.

❖   ❖   ❖

"How many boys?" Papa Leo asks while fixated on the long highway ahead.

"All six," Lightfoot says. Papa Leo gazes forward. Quite a distance passes before the next words are spoken. Lightfoot glances over, watching his grandfather examine the cast on his arm, then feeling the bandages on his head. "How you feeling?" Lightfoot asks.

"Inside, or out?" Papa Leo replies.

"Both," Lightfoot replies quickly. Papa Leo thinks a bit before answering.

"My body is fine for an old man. I'll feel even better when I see the healer and get some real medicine," he insists. "Inside?" Papa Leo considers, but then doesn't continue except to shrug out a 'whatever'.

"It was military explosive," Lightfoot notes plainly. Papa Leo wags his head in disgust. "They also issued an evacuation order, so they can protect us from the 'dangerous' and 'explosive' material on our land," Lightfoot adds. Papa Leo isn't surprised, but again sees no reason to speak further. "They want to make it look like it blew up on it's own," Lightfoot says, inflecting the absurdity of the idea. Lightfoot looks over again to find his grandfather seeming to fade off. The old man's head begins to sink a bit, mesmerized by the moving lines in the road.

"Do you remember anything from that night?" he asks his grandfather, trying to keep him alert. Papa Leo perks up again, struggling to visualize that night, prior to the explosion. He strains, tightening his eyes and gazing into his hands.

"The last thing I remember was waving to Jimmy and Noodin, and Ogichidaa's boy," Papa Leo says, then suddenly turning to his grandson with pleading eyes. "Ogichidaa's son? Jimmy and Noodin?" he says, showing a level of emotion Lightfoot has never seen in him. Lightfoot meets his grandfather's tired and horrified eyes with a sadness of his own, crushed at the sight of his hero's sudden realization. Lightfoot can only shake his head.

"I'm sorry, Granddad," he says. Papa Leo slowly turns to stare out the side window and not speaking another word for the rest of the day and into the night.

TWELVE

"Vengeance"

Doctor Vega opens his door, not at all surprised to see Kate return so quickly after the latest news.

"Doctor Vega, I wanted to follow up in person," Kate says.

"Certainly Miss Rose, come in," Vega replies, while motioning for her to have a seat. But Kate declines, choosing rather to project urgency and stay for only a moment.

"Thank you, but I have to catch a flight. I just wanted to assure you of two things," Kate says earnestly. "First, we'll be providing you with an analysis from the world's five top nuclear research labs, confirming the 'unprecedented stability' of the fuel material. Second, please check the news in about..." Kate notices the clock on his wall, "...two hours, for an even more *explosive* charge, regarding the so-called 'nuclear event' at Red Rock."

"Can you give me a preview, Miss Rose?" Vega asks.

"Sure," Kate says. "Simply put, military assets were used to conduct a covert strike on the reservation in order to make you, and everyone else think that the fuel element is unstable. All designed to evict the tribe and take control of their resources." In a move designed for dramatic effect, Kate checks her watch then heads for the exit while glancing back to add another point. "Oh, our offer of support still stands, Doctor," she says over her shoulder, before stopping briefly in the doorway. "And, if I may ask, maybe you could inform your colleagues at the U.N. to tune in? It should be on all the networks."

"Okay, yes certainly," Vega says, fully engulfed in her wake turbulence.

"Thank you, Doctor Vega," Kate concludes and with that she quickly leaves. Moved by her haste, Vega heads to his desk and grabs the phone.

❖   ❖   ❖

Kate smiles confidently as she exits the U.N. building. She dials her phone while descending the stairs toward First Avenue and misses a step, nearly breaking her ankle in the process. She continues to limp to the curb, while flagging an approaching taxi.

"Mary, we're set up at the U.N.," Kate shouts into her phone over the sounds of rush hour. "Looks like we'll have an eager audience for tonight's press conference." The cabbie pulls to the curb. "I've got about two more hours to get the word out. Good luck tonight hon, call me when you get this message. Bye bye." Kate hobbles to the cab and flops into the back seat. "New York Times building please, before five if you can," she says while rolling her window down and settling into her seat. She breathes the cool air off the Hudson flowing through her window while the noise and grandeur of Manhattan fills her senses. "God I love this place," she says, her body tilting side to side as the driver slaloms through traffic.

❖   ❖   ❖

Two Tribal Police vehicles block the Red Rock Reservation entrance from the main highway, holding at bay a dozen news media vehicles, lined up at the barricade. Reporters wait anxiously under extended microwave antennas, while submitting live reports in anticipation of what is promised to be an 'explosive' revelation. Production and technical staff busy themselves, checking and double-checking their equipment while waiting for the gates to open. Various camera crews line up along the shoulder, focused on an opposing line of reporters.

"We've been assured there is no radioactive activity in the area, where we're gathering for the interview," a stylish reporter claims while holding in his hand a yellow Geiger counter. "As you can see here, we're seeing absolutely no sign of radiation, but are prepared to turn back as soon as this needle begins to move."

Also returning to the scene is the reporter from the Minnesota affiliate, who interviewed Professor Lightfoot previously.

"As we've announced earlier today, the United States government has issued an evacuation order, which went into effect this morning and gives the Red Rock Chippewa tribe one week to fully abandon the area," the affiliate reporter says, as a growing rant of protestors begin to drown him out. "So far, we've seen no sign of this happening. Tonight, we're expecting a statement from tribal elders, including the now famous Professor William Lightfoot who you'll remember left his position at MIT to support his tribe, in this moment of opportunity, and now it appears - crisis."

Across the street, Minnesota State Troopers are blocking two bands of opposing protestors from rushing the reservation entrance, as well as each other. One group chants furiously while the other group calmly motions with large graphic signs.

"*In with experts, out with squatters. In with experts, out with squatters,*" the opposition shouts angrily at anyone who'll listen. The more supportive group, clearly sympathetic to the plight of yet another

Native American tribe being tread upon, hold signs that read - *Native land, take a stand!* But perhaps the most popular statement among the opposition is a professionally designed sign of bold black letters on a yellow background that simply reads... *BULLSHIT!*

❖ ❖ ❖

At the reservation village, Mary is setting up a table near the first of two containers, which hold the buzzing particle accelerator and electrical generator. Lightfoot arranges scientific equipment in just the right position for maximum impact for the cameras. Even the field worker from Minnesota Power helps him move equipment into view, having also set up some metering devices nearby, ready to corroborate any claims made to the press. The power worker proudly wears his company colors, with the Minnesota Power logo emblazoned on his chest.

Harvey Bearheart hangs from the rungs of a ladder, about fifteen feet up the cooling tower. He's adhering a logo to the tower surface that reads *THE REPUBLIC OF TRIBAL PEOPLE*, featuring a magnificent modern graphic of a golden eagle.

Misses Bearheart lays out refreshments on a stand near the media bullpen, a small area separated by a roped barrier delineating the camera limits. Harvey Bearheart calls down to his wife.

"Why are we feeding them?" he asks.

"Because reporters are people too, and if you want them to say good things about you, I suppose feeding them might help," she says, as she studies the placesetting with both hands clasped together in approval. Up top, Harvey Bearheart grimaces with a 'good point' gesture by pursing his lips and bobbing his head from side to side.

Two Tribal Police Deputies, actually a teenage boy and girl, wear oversized police shirts and not quite filling the extra cloth originally designed to accommodate a middle-aged belly. Together they set up cue ropes to direct the reporters from the road to the media bullpen. At the other end of the bullpen, the Loon sisters meticulously stuff small clear plastic bags with a tiny piece of the orange *Ishkode* rock, no bigger than a grain of rice. Meoquanee adheres a sticker to the bags, displaying the new Republic's logo.

Mary moves from station to station, expertly coordinating the media event while Lightfoot practices his *moment of truth* delivery.

❖ ❖ ❖

At the valley epicenter, older tribe members are positioned with rifles, high along the ridge line. These marksmen are capable of splitting a sapling from a hundred yards with a single shot. The fissure below has been cleared of debris and covered with new timbers.

❖ ❖ ❖

Papa Leo sits comfortably in an overstuffed chair on the porch of the community center. He has a blanket across his legs and a Winchester over-and-under rests across his lap, 'just in case'. His old broad rimmed hat still covers most of his bandaged head and the cast on his arm has been traded in for an expertly crafted splint. Even the hospital staff has been swapped out for a 'more capable' medicine woman who sits nearby. She's a sinewy looking old gal with enough muscle to force the patriarch into compliance for his own good. From Papa Leo's vantage point, he can view the entire event in the village center. His mare eats hay from a nearby trough, just off the porch, again - 'just in case'.

❖ ❖ ❖

The crowds and media at the main entrance have grown in number and impatience. Every time one of the tribal policemen answers his mobile phone, the reporters brace, should the order be given to open the gates. Producers study the body language of the gatekeeper on the phone in a growing sense that this call might just be the one. After all, it's merely a minute or two past the designated start time and the sun has already started to drop below the ridge. Sure enough, the officer hangs up and nods to his partner who then proceeds to the gate's lock. Fussy producers launch into action, hurrying their crews to pack up. The news teams fold themselves into crowded vehicles and slam their doors in a rhythmic ensemble that sounds like a circus drum roll.

The two officers remove the pad locks and pull both swing-arms to the side as news vans roar to a cacophony, but still blocked by the tribal police vehicles in the road. The Officers jump into their Broncos and begin to slowly escort the media convoy down the narrow road to the reservation center.

❖   ❖   ❖

With the media bullpen full and the light from the setting sun perfect, the press event is finally ready to begin. Cameras are ready and trained on the table in front of the homemade power station. Lightfoot steps into the shot behind the table, which now is covered with various pieces of 'evidence'.

"Thank you for your time tonight," Lightfoot begins, soberly focusing down the barrels of lenses. "Many of you were here a few weeks ago, when you covered the discovery of the fuel element as well as the subsequent robbery. Since that time, we've learned a lot and aim to share it with you now. I'll start with a statement, and then will take your questions," he says while motioning with a report in his hand. "You've heard a lot about an explosion at our quarry, the area exposed by the recent quake. This was not a 'nuclear' explosion nor was it the result of some dangerous material, as many in the government would like you to believe. The material we refer to, element one-fifteen on our Periodic Table of Elements, is a stable one. It does not react unless it is bombarded with protons in a controlled environment and even then it totally converts to energy, in proportion to the acceleration applied," he explains. "How do I know this? I teach particle and theoretical physics at the Massachusetts Institute of Technology. The very field of study that in part, determines how radioactive elements behave. He holds a Geiger counter up to a large sample of the element, indicating that the needle doesn't move. "Again, this is a 'stable' element. It is not radioactive, and it does not just explode on its own"

Mary watches near the media gallery with her father and other members of the tribe.

"I am also born here of the Red Rock band of the Chippewa tribe. This is where I grew up. This is my home".

Papa Leo watches from the small TV that the medicine woman set up for him on the porch. He follows along, anticipating his grandson's plan to first make a bombing run of allegations, then wade through the blast wave of questions in its wake. Papa Leo watches Lightfoot on screen, holding up the report he received from Tyler.

"This is a report, an analysis from MIT's Spectroscopy Laboratory on the debris, specifically the residue from the explosive material used to blow up our quarry," Lightfoot affirms, while Papa Leo nods.

Back in the media pen, producers and reporters are anxiously taking notes, texting and motioning to their associates to get a copy of the report.

"We will make this report available to you all. In it, you'll see that the explosion was caused by a military grade C4 explosive. NOT, a nuclear reaction. NOT, a spontaneous event. This was an attack by rogue elements in the U.S. government to make you all believe that our mining operation poses some sort of threat to our well being. When was the last time you saw the American government show such benevolence and urgency for our welfare?"

❖   ❖   ❖

"Fuck yeah!" Tyler yells, raising a fist in the air and startling the other staff members who watch from the faculty lounge. Tyler lowers his arm, settling into a demeanor more appropriate for a professor. The staff and faculty slowly turn back to the press conference playing on the large monitor.

"*You've seen the surveillance video and images of Army Blackhawk helicopters raiding and stealing our property. Violating a number of tribal related laws as well as invasion of property. You've seen the evacuation order, seeking to remove us from this land, so they could move in and 'evaluate the danger' as they claim"*. Lightfoot looks into the lens. "*Why are they doing this? Why would they want to remove this nation from its rightful place? Simple. They know what we are sitting on. They know the power of this fuel source, a clean, powerful, non-radioactive source, and enough to power many countries on this planet in a sustainable way.*"

❖   ❖   ❖

Doctor Vega watches from the United Nations, with a dozen other U.N. officials as Lightfoot continues.

"*The Bureau of Indian affairs was built to protect the rights of indigenous tribes. Yet over the years, they've demonstrated a rich history of allowing their mission to be driven by large oil, gas and water companies to buy up tribal land on the cheap, and turn it for huge profits. And now, they are simply acting as stooges for a small sector of the military machine.*"

❖   ❖   ❖

Doctor Drummond is about to burst every vein in his neck, while watching the news report on TV from his office in New Mexico.

"Exactly, who's doing this?" Lightfoot asks, before following up with the answer. *"The Army Corps of Engineers, in collusion with Doctor Edward Drummond from the Los Alamos Neutron Science Center, a leading weapons facility serving the U.S. Military, aided and abetted by officials from the Bureau of Indian Affairs. That's who. The very people you've seen on TV, claiming the need to protect us from ourselves. You've heard the denials of the raid on this land, even in the face of photographic evidence showing rangers in Army Blackhawks stealing this element with their bare hands,"* Lightfoot says to the camera, knowing full well Drummond is watching on the other end. Drummond fumes.

❖   ❖   ❖

Lightfoot notices the reporters nod, scribble and talk excitedly among themselves. Glancing briefly at Mary, he lifts an item from the table toward the camera.

"And this is a shell fragment from the explosive device used to attack our reserve," he says, moving on to lift a stack of reports. "These are reports from the leading nuclear research labs in the world, concluding the element in question is in fact stable, and an extremely valuable source of clean, waste-free sustainable energy. All of these reports, sources and contact information will be provided to you after this conference." Lightfoot turns to the Minnesota Power worker, who stands near the particle accelerator. "Remember our proof-of-concept power station, the one you see behind me?" Lightfoot asks. "It's still running, since the day you first reported on it. Simply by using a standard particle acceleration process, to change the element just enough to generate a total conversion of matter to energy. The heat is used to boil water, which produces pure steam, and in turn spins a turbine generator, producing electricity. Since this experimental station was brought online, our tribe has been sending our friends at Minnesota Power, a continuous stream of electricity, capable of powering nearly ten thousand homes and businesses for half the price of other methods," Lightfoot says while tossing the harmless element into the air and catching it to punctuate his point. "And it all starts with less than one gram of metal, capable of lasting for thirty years." Lightfoot grabs some sample bags of the 'token' element the Loon sisters have prepared for the guests. He steps in front of the table and walks to the media bullpen and hands out a few bags of rock, before returning to his spot in front of the camera. "You will all be given a sample of this material as well, to have analyzed for yourself. Compared to other available power sources, not as efficient or clean, a small amount of this material is valued at one hundred thousand dollars a gram," he announces to the rumble of reporters. "A lot of money, I get that. Yet substantially less than any other source of comparable output, including oil, coal, solar, wind or even radioactive isotopes," he notes, while lifting yet another document to camera. "Also, we are currently donating hundreds of millions of dollars worth of this fuel source to responsible nations, and scientific industry partners to develop large scale power fixtures to remove their dependence on fossil fuels. And this work is already underway in many parts of the world."

❖   ❖   ❖

In her hotel room, Kate is dancing like a fool around the bed and throwing sucker punches into an invisible opponent.

"Yes, yes, yes, yes!" She rounds the bed toward the TV, and clobbers her shins on the bed frame. She hops back to the TV. "Ow, ow, ow!"

❖   ❖   ❖

Lightfoot pauses for effect and scans the line of media. Lightfoot knows the time has come to face the camera again, for that final declaration. A promise to his grandfather and the members of his tribe that stand so proudly in the wings, as well as all the brave warriors before him. "Effective immediately, the Red Rock Chippewa Nation declares its refusal to comply with any evacuation order imposed by this or any other *foreign* government. We decry the crimes committed against humanity both current and in the past. Tribal sovereignty, though vaguely defined, has been debated for years."

❖   ❖   ❖

Doctor Vega grins widely, as do many of the other U.N. members he gathered and prepared for this announcement tonight.

"*Native American nations were constitutionally granted equal protection by the federal government to that of member states. Except that these tribal lands are claimed to be held in trust by the federal government, to be run sovereignly by the tribes themselves. This TREATY has been broken. Tonight, our nation - the newly declared REPUBLIC OF TRIBAL PEOPLE, officially informs the United States federal government that we are seceding from this union and are applying for full member status with the United Nations.*" Vega turns to watch the room explode with shock and disbelief.

❖   ❖   ❖

Lightfoot watches as the news crews come unglued, as producers pull back to call their stations and camera crews check their media and connections to confirm these explosive claims were actually recorded safely. Lightfoot ends his statement as simply as he started.

"Thank you," he says humbly, stepping toward the media line and presenting himself for their questions. Hands shoot upward into the air from the media bullpen, in a rush of cheers and questions.

"Professor Lightfoot, how do you plan to defend your sovereignty from those who will certainly seek to use force?"

"Mr. Lightfoot, Professor –do you plan to file murder charges?"

"How much of this stuff do you have, Professor?"

❖   ❖   ❖

It's after hours at the Interior Department in Washington. Deputy Director Smith slumps in his office chair while on the phone and scanning various media reports on his computer.

"I'll let you know when we hear something, but right now nothing changes," Smith assures yet another concerned official. He tries his best to juggle the calls pouring down on him like an over-stacked closet. As soon as he hangs up, the receptionist rings through the intercom again.

"Mr. Smith, I have the Director on the line?" she says, her weariness evident through the speakerphone.

"Put it through," Smith acknowledges, with a glance across the desk to Hank Poysen, who waits nervously and dreading this very moment. As the phone begins to ring, Smith drags his palm across his face, squeezing his flesh into doughy shapes before sucking in enough air to plunge into the deep end. He lifts the receiver with a wince. "Mike! Good evening," he says, hoping to set a tone that he knows full well will never stick. "Actually I have no way of knowing if the stuff is dangerous or not. That's what the Corps and those guys from Los Alamos claim." Hank sinks further in his chair, folding his hands and swallowing so many times he's depleting saliva faster than his cheeks can create it. "He's here with me now," Smith replies. Hank glances up from under his brow without lifting his head. "Sure, I'll put it on speakerphone," Smith says while motioning for Hank to join in. "This is BIA Director, Mike Chambers, he'd like to..." but Chambers explodes with rage through the speakerphone, cutting the introduction short.

"*I'd like to understand what the fuck is going on?*" Chambers screams. Smith offers a thin smile, and motions to Hank, as if to say, 'you're up'.

"Uh sir, this is Hank Po..." but the Director slashes through the niceties.

"I know who the hell you are! You're the idiot that took it upon yourself to chaperon those bastards into Red Rock. I want to know why you thought it was a good idea to bullshit this tribe into thinking that these guys had any interest in 'offering earthquake assistance'," Chambers bellows. *"Don't you see what this looks like? The tribe says go away, the next thing we know Blackhawks raid the place and take rocks in their bare hands that they now say will destroy mankind."* Hank attempts to explain further.

"Yes sir. Uh..." but Hank can't get past a few vowels before the speaker slices through the crap.

"Yes sir, bullshit!! You know who these people are! When was the last time you saw the Army Corps of Engineers, much less government scientists give a shit if Indians are suffering? Explosion my ass! What's going to explode is our reputation, and you're at the heart of it, Mister! I want a full report by morning. Screw that, you have one hour to give me all the names and backgrounds of the moles you took out there, the tribal leaders involved and how this MIT Professor fits into all this!" Hank is too afraid to speak and simply nods yes. *"Are you there, HANK?"*

"Yes... yes sir. I'll have that for you right away," Hank follows.

"FUCK!" the Director blares through the phone. *"And Smith, what's this crap about evacuation? Pick up the fucking phone!"* Smith grabs the receiver, while making a writing gesture for Hank to get on it then sweeps

his fingers across his desk, motioning Hank out of the room.

"I'm here Mike," Smith says in his best sounding attempt of like-mindedness he can rally. But the rage keeps on coming so strongly, he can't even hold the phone to his ear.

❖ ❖ ❖

"Slam dunk, bitches! Take that!" Kate screams at the screen while rubbing her bruised shins, when suddenly her cell phone rings. "Whoa!" she says when noticing the caller ID. "Hello? - Yes, Doctor Vega! I trust you've seen the news?"

In Vega's office, he motions to the surrounding members that he has her on the phone.

"Oh yes, we've seen it. You're right Miss Rose, pretty explosive stuff. And I have to say, your Professor Lightfoot makes a stunning case." One of the other UN secretaries points to the floor, nodding his head enthusiastically. "So much so, many of my colleagues here would like to invite the professor, and you of course, to meet here and discuss how we might move forward. Would that be something we could arrange in the near future?"

Kate walks to the window with a view of the U.N. headquarters.

"Yes, I think the professor would appreciate that

opportunity very much," Kate says. "I'll check with him and get back to you immediately, Sir."

"We look forward to that Miss Rose. This could prove to be an historic event," Vega states passionately. *"Please offer our congratulations to Professor Lightfoot on a brilliant presentation and compelling event. Bye for now."*

Kate hangs up and continues staring at the U.N. building in the distance to gather her thoughts. She dials the phone.

❖　❖　❖

Doctor Vega hangs up, silently waiting for the others in the room to voice their thoughts. But the demeanor across the gathering is hardly a consensus. This is a complex bunch of diplomats, their expressions ranging from enthusiasm to dour indifference, as well as shear bewilderment.

"This could prove to be the catalyst for the kind of human rights movement we've been imagining for sixty years," says an older dignitary as he holds his elbow with one palm while the other hand fiddles with his white goatee.

"Dream on," another less hopeful diplomat exclaims. "There's no way the *host nation* will allow them to split," he predicts. "They did nothing today but paint a target on themselves."

"I hope you're wrong," Vega states.

"Hope all you want," the cynical diplomat expounds. "Nothing good will come of this, but the destruction of another indigenous group," he says definitively. But Vega isn't so sure this time. "Seriously, Vega. What makes you so sure they have even the slightest chance?" a younger attendee asks.

"Money, power, and a mountain of press, my friend." Vega replies. "Show me any occupied nation that can match that."

"They need powerful friends to pull this off," declares a portly German Ambassador. "The U.S. will certainly package this as a security threat and clobber them if they go this alone."

"Well, I suppose that's where you come in Mister Braun," Doctor Vega suggests pointedly.

"I still don't see this ending well, Vega," the first dour diplomat insists. "I get that you like them, but I'd advise you to be very careful here."

"Careful of what?" Vega asks.

"Of whom, my friend? Of whom?" the diplomat replies. Instead of buying into the doubt, Doctor Vega smiles boldly and with such confidence that it would appear nearly sinister if one didn't know him to be such a gentleman.

JON D. ANTHONY

THIRTEEN

"The Republic"

Over the next two years, the small Red Rock Chippewa tribe became one of the richest and most powerful 'occupied' nations in the world. Of course, the United States still refused to let an apparently insignificant speck of land along its northern border split off, but in light of the press and international attention, they had to practically assume a hands-off policy. Red Rock refused to acknowledge the treaty and now had the financial resources to milk this détente for over twenty-four months with no end in sight. At risk of blow back from military intervention, the United States was stuck in a mess of their own making. For now, the newly formed 'Republic' seems to enjoy all the prerogatives of sovereign statehood, including the right to negotiate, (or not) with an openly hostile southern neighbor.

Mary's idea of selling their unnatural resource to other nations of the world in exchange for gold proved to be the lynch pin for the new Republic's accumulation of wealth. A transaction for the orange fuel element usually takes the form *of receiving the buyer's gold bullion or commodity, into the tribe's German bank accounts. At which point a shipment is delivered directly to the purchaser via Republic aircraft, one of two Airbus jets, obtained as a trade with the French. As the mining operation went into full-scale production, it revealed a much greater deposit than originally thought.*

❖　❖　❖

This morning, Papa Leo rides his horse up the well-traveled slope to his spot overlooking the reservation. Another set of approaching hooves claps the soil behind him.

"Good morning Son," Papa Leo says without turning, and focusing across the lake as he has every morning since Lightfoot joined him in this ritual. Lightfoot's horse steps into Papa Leo's peripheral.

"Morning, Granddad," he says, without needing any further words. They silently share the view, turning their gaze to the waking village below. Predictably, the dogs run free to terrorize the roosters and chase shorebirds feeding in the breakwater while the crows play above the treetops. Now though, the old Community Center has transformed into a large and brilliantly designed log structure, modern in scope but still true to the culture of what it means to be Chippewa. Further up the shore, the little experimental power plant has given way to a much larger operation, ten times the size and artfully tucked within the timbers. Four high-tech cooling towers, textured with rough lumber and each emblazoned with the eagle crest of the new Republic rise above the tree line.

Within the village center, and in keeping with the architectural theme, a magnificent school serving all grades from pre-school to high and stands in tribute to the priorities of the new Republic. This is Lightfoot's vision, of a free school, steeped in the study of math, the sciences and certainly the tribal art and history the indigenous students from across the continent deserve.

A pack of children and teens laugh and bicker in the distance, on their way to the school. They arrive from the outskirts of the reservation through nature paths, carved just for them through the woods to connect the school to their living areas further up the shore. This is a proud and unpretentious utopia, designed by these people in honor of a new generation. A community in balance, where technology serves nature, and people learn to think before speaking. A dream world where a child's self worth is advanced and measured by the boldness of their questions, not the brashness of their statements. An Erewhon whereas Papa Leo continues to note, people never stop wondering if the sun could reason as consciously as the grey meat in their skulls.

But for all this, they are still not totally free. They

merely live, separated by a demilitarized zone known as a 'hands-off-policy' practiced for the time being by a federal government and only because of the enormous embarrassment from a couple years earlier. This was a policy formed by public opinion, fueled by a continued position in the news cycle and always challenged by a federal hope that with enough time, the world might cease to care and look the other way when the eagle's wings are clipped.

The sound of flight turns their head upward to see the arriving bird. Lightfoot smiles at the sight of the fearless eagle graphic of the Republic, painted across the entire underbelly of the large aircraft from wing tip to wing tip. They watch together, the morning return from another *Ishkode* shipment delivered somewhere in the world. The jet circles and lines up on final approach to the new two mile runway just beyond a line of cleared timbers.

"We should hear today," Lightfoot notes while his eyes drop to his interlocked hands, a pensive gesture he adopted recently, of palms turned upward like an open book. Papa Leo silently pulls his reins to the side, turning his mare toward the ridgeline. After a moment's glance across the reservation, a final reflection of how far they've come these last two trips around the sun, Lightfoot turns and follows him up the hill.

❖   ❖   ❖

The now famous quarry at the base of the valley has transformed over the last few months as well. A fortress of timber and stone fully surround the fissure. An elegant forest green aluminum roof stretches from one end of the structure to the other, blending thoughtfully with the surrounding vegetation. Along the walls of the valley, artfully terraced ridges support a new growth of pine and poplar trees, in a demure and obliging approach to land management. Even now, at the height of their power, wealthier than the Federal Reserve – there exists a simple, respectful sense of one's place in nature.

Papa Leo is the first to arrive over the ridgeline. He dismounts, a bit slower than he did months ago and ties off his horse. Papa Leo walks with much effort to rest on a favorite fallen log. He smiles, as his grandson's shadow casts across the ground in front him. Papa Leo loves these times alone with his grandson. His stories and proverbs often recur these days, while his normally sharp wit and instinctive insight can give way at times to repetition or sudden reflection. Lightfoot sits down next to him and joins his gaze into the valley below.

"Today, if they make a point to tell you that they aren't lying, then you know they are" Papa Leo warns as he has a few times before.

"And if they say they're lying?" Lightfoot asks attentively.

"Believe them," Papa Leo says, turning to him with a snicker. Lightfoot scoops a handful of small pebbles from the soil and organizes them in his hand as he speaks. "What's bothering you, Son," his grandfather asks.

"We've got twelve out of fifteen votes in the Security Council on our request of membership. Usually enough to pass, but five of those fifteen have veto power. And the U.S. continues to vote against us."

"The other four?" Papa Leo asks.

"China, France Russia, England...all in," Lightfoot says as he lines four pebbles across his palm to represent each of the supporting nations. Our application can't go to the General Assembly for a vote until it gets out of the Security Council and for that they need all five." Papa Leo searches his memory for something relevant, maybe a lesson from struggles past. He strains to listen to the voices of his elders and wise men before him, who faced similar obstruction from these powerful white 'immigrants' who now rule the land. But these days the voices of those times feel like faint whispers. He holds out his hand, motioning for Lightfoot to dump the pebbles into his. Lightfoot watches his grandfather slowly move the four little stones along his leathery palm. Since Papa Leo's fall, Lightfoot has watched his hero disappear at times into small things, mesmerized by the growth rings of a tree stump or lost while following the lines in his own hand. The light colored stones glisten a bit more against the old man's dark sun-soaked palm.

"Remember the story of the two opposing warriors?" Papa Leo asks, still moving the four stones across his palm, replacing one with the other and back again. "Both were the strongest of their opposing tribes. Both were chosen to be the best, each strong enough to take the life of the other. They were equal in might. They were equal in mind. They had the same weapons," he says, considering the zero sum of the match.

"So who won, Granddad?" Lightfoot asks. Papa Leo smiles at the four stones.

"The one that chose not to fight," the wise old fellow says, looking up now in a moment of keen lucidity. "A negative vote in any 'security council' would naturally come from the *insecure* member," Papa Leo states. "But what makes them feel insecure?" he asks his grandson. Lightfoot thinks, about this.

"Empty greed maybe?" his grandson replies. Papa Leo considers the idea, but he was hoping for another answer.

"What don't they have, that to others do?" the old

man asks rhetorically as he picks a small orange stone from the ground, possibly debris still littered along the ridge from the explosion. He places the stone in his hand, next to the white ones. Lightfoot's face lights up with the realization Papa Leo intended. The wise elder continues his thought. "You bought the loyalty of the other four nations, maybe now it's time to buy their loyalty as well," Papa Leo says. "All we've done is succeed in keeping them out, by shaming them to the world. And, that's had its place, surely. Look what we've accomplished," Papa Leo explains, motioning to their surroundings. "But now, we hold the cards. Now it's time for a gesture," his grandfather suggests.

"A piece offering," Lightfoot realizes.

"Yes," the old man says pointedly. "Yes, they know they can't touch us or steal our wealth while everyone is looking. All they can do is block our path because they have nothing to loose, and nothing to gain if they don't." Lightfoot jumps up and places both hands on each side of the lovely old man's face and kisses him on the forehead.

"You are the smartest man I have ever met," he declares excitedly. "I have to make a call."

"You go ahead, son," Papa Leo says. "I'm going to sit here a while." Lightfoot places a hand on his grandfather's shoulder, then turns to hurry toward his horse. Papa Leo watches him climb into the saddle and ride off and over the ridge toward the village. The old man lifts his eyes across the valley and raises a hand to the *elderly* sentries armed and ready along the rim of the crater. They return the gesture, greeting their *Nimishomis,* as the old man once again allows his mind to wander off toward the sun over the ridge.

❖   ❖   ❖

Lightfoot gallops into the grounds of the Red Rock School and ties his pony off at a hitching post, labeled *Professor Lightfoot.* Amidst the urgency, he still takes the time to calm the palomino and check her supply of water and hay in the covered 'executive parking lot'. He then hurries inside.

While walking through the rustic wood lined halls of the school, Professor Lightfoot is stopped and greeted by faculty and students alike. He smiles as he passes a flock of teenage girls who nearly melt into a puddle of gush when they see him. Eventually stopping at a rough-hewn wooden door labeled *FACULTY LOUNGE,* he places his palm on the hand reader, artfully mounted in the center of a crosscut log. The digital lock disengages and he enters.

❖   ❖   ❖

A young Chippewa boy works the cappuccino

machine and greets the professor, handing over a freshly brewed coffee in a mug labeled *CHIEF DUDE*.

"Nice one, Amik," he says, while examining the custom mug.

"My dad sent it for me to give you," Amik says. Lightfoot takes a sip.

"You ready for math finals?" he asks the young student.

"I'm gonna slay it brother," the student exclaims. Lightfoot enters the faculty lounge where Tyler sits, reading a paper, scanning his phone between sips of coffee and glancing to the muted news broadcast over the bar. Lightfoot arrives at the table and pulls up a chair.

"Yo, Pro!" Tyler says, raising a fist, which Lightfoot follows with a bump. Tyler blows it up with a flourish of fingers and a verbal 'whoosh'. "Did you see the news? Congress says we pose a threat to global security." Tyler chuckles, hardly fazed he takes another sip of his coffee before moving on to more pressing topics. "Hey I got to tell you man, these kids are killing it," Tyler notes. "My Boston students didn't care this much and subsequently, neither did I."

"I'm glad you're here," Lightfoot says, motioning to Amik at the counter. "They are too."

"Dude, this means something. I'm energized man," Tyler admits.

"I had a thought, well... my grandfather had a thought, I'm just running with it," Lightfoot says, leaning forward into Tyler's space. "Check this out. So, our bid for member status is held up getting to the General Assembly for a vote, right?" Lightfoot summarizes.

"Yeah," Tyler says, holding up his phone. "It's all over the news today about the Americans vetoing it in the Security Council again," he says, showing him the story on the browser.

"Oh, that happened already?" Lightfoot asks, surprised to hear the news so soon.

"Sorry, I thought you knew," Tyler says. "Story just broke twenty minutes ago. I figured that's what you were talking about."

"No, but whatever – that's the point though," he says. "What if we do talk to them? Forget the whole *you're dead to us* thing, and actually buy their vote?" Lightfoot proposes. Tyler isn't so sure about that idea.

"Uh, but isn't that why the feds have stayed out of your pants so far? And, don't you think that's what they want you to do?" Tyler reasons. "All this didn't come because you played nice, not that they deserved it, after all that shit they pulled."

"Yeah, that was then, and sure it worked, but now... they're butt hurt. The whole country, hell the whole world saw what they did and sure, we won. But now, we hold the cards to maybe force the Security Council vote," Lightfoot continues. "Hell, they don't even need to vote *yes*, they just need to abstain, and not veto."

"How do you 'force' that then?" Tyler asks, still not convinced of Lightfoot's reasoning.

"Think about it," Lightfoot says excitedly. "We continue ignoring the Bureau of Indian Affairs just like before. Except now we go directly to the State Department. Since they're the ones responsible for 'foreign' policy. The Bureau was formed to avoid that very constitutional assumption, since allowing the tribes to talk to the Secretary of State implies their true sovereignty," Lightfoot affirms while rising to pace the floor around Tyler's chair. Tyler's shit eating grin betrays his understanding now.

"Dude, can I have sex with your brain right now? That's fucking intense!" Tyler blurts out, but stops quickly for a second thought. "But wait, why would they allow that? Especially now?" he asks. Lightfoot then holds up the small orange rock he got from Papa Leo's palm and takes Tyler's hand, opens it and places the pebble in the center. Lightfoot then continues to pace the floor around him.

"We have something they want," Lightfoot claims. "Something we've so far, refused to give them. And you can be sure like every other country we've been trading with, that they want it bad enough now to open a dialogue in any venue, so they can get their hands on it, up and up."

"What if someone says you bought their votes?" Tyler asks with caution.

"We don't 'buy a vote', we 'negotiate for abstinence'," he replies. "Then they have deniability. It's perfect!" Lightfoot says, continuing to circle Tyler's chair.

"And just by entering into a negotiation with the Secretary of State..." Lightfoot says, before motioning for Tyler to finish the thought...

"That establishes the sovereignty precedent you need, to negotiate a solution like any other sovereign state," Tyler summarizes and *realizes* at the same time. Lightfoot takes a huge swig from his 'Chief Dude' mug as he circles the table, deep in thought.

"Can you stop orbiting, I'm getting vertigo," Tyler requests.

"Sorry," Lightfoot says. "We're going to need a detailed legal strategy for all this."

"Speaking of which, you heard Kate passed the bar now? Even got an offer to be a partner at some big law firm in Manhattan," Tyler notes.

"Yeah, she's done well," Lightfoot says, before taking another sip. He glances at Tyler over the rim of the cup. "So, how you two doing?" Lightfoot meddles. But Tyler seems wobbly, finding it hard to offer a definitive reply.

"You know, I mean sure I'm nuts about her, but her life is in New York and mine is here now," Tyler says. "I think she's still crazy for you, man!" he says. Lightfoot thinks through another sip, hiding behind his mug, while Tyler continues. "I mean it's always 'Mary and Billy, Mary and Billy. I know she truly respects what you have with Mary, but... you know man."

"I know," Lightfoot admits, mulling through his friend's words. Tyler looks at his watch.

"Shit man, class starts in five minutes. I gotta go." Tyler grabs his coat and stuffs his computer into the backpack. "Math finals today! I'll catch you later.

"Good luck," Lightfoot says, while settling back into his seat and washing down his thoughts with the last sip of coffee. He checks his pockets for his mobile phone and dials a number.

❖   ❖   ❖

Kate fits well into the Manhattan scene. Smartly dressed in a wool overcoat and boots, she walks across forty-seventh street, her head high and eyes focused on the sunburst reflections across a thousand squares of glass panes. Her phone rings and she answers it without taking her eyes off the view or looking at the caller ID.

"Hello?" Kate says, before stopping in the middle of the street in shock. "Oh my god! Billy Lightfoot, I was just thinking about you. How weird. How are you? How's Mary, how's Papa Leo?" she asks, peppering him endlessly with questions. "Okay sorry that's a lot of questions at one time." Concentrating fully on the call, Kate barely avoids being hit in the middle of the intersection. She hurries across the street, finally sliding up to a cornerstone as she listens to his voice over the wire.

"*All good here, Papa Leo's still riding, I'm sure he'll outlive all of us,*" Lightfoot says. "*Mary says hi as well.*" Kate wiggles her head and twists her brows, wondering what motivated this call after so many months. "*So Kate, how 'bout you come by for the weekend. It would be great to see you.*"

"It would be great to see you too - and Mary!" Kate replies, still leaning against the cornerstone for scale and a bit of structure. "So this weekend, huh?" she considers, her eyes now focusing street level on the traffic and congestion. My how perspective can change in an instant. "Hell, why not?" Kate says. "I'll check into flights today," she agrees.

Amik slides up to Lightfoot's table and refills his mug before heading off to class. Lightfoot muffles the mobile phone against his chest. "Good luck today," he says encouragingly. Amik heads back to the counter as Lightfoot continues.

"No, let us pick you up at Teterboro, Atlantic

terminal. We'll have our plane bring you here," Lightfoot says. "Let's say Friday night, around six?"

Kate shakes the thought of such a thing from her skull and laughs.

"Whoa. Look at you, mister fancy?" Kate hollers. Punchy from the sound of his voice on the other end of the line, Kate still wonders, *why now?* "Is there anything I need to be prepared for?" she asks. Kate waits through a longer than normal pause on the other end and even covers her other ear in case she may have missed something under the noise of morning rush hour.

"*We're going to make a move, to try and sway the Security Council,*" Lightfoot says over the line as a pained suspicion begins to carve itself into her face. "*I think we need your legal mind Kate. And can pay your firm, whatever you want,*" he says, crushing her soul in the process. And there it is, she thinks. But quickly she tries to comfort herself with the possibility that maybe he just needs some kind of plausible deniability, a clever way of seeing her again, she wonders. In either case, nothing will be answered over the phone, and her curiosity to know for sure, exceeds her spiraling emotions right now.

"Friday at six, Teterboro it is. I'll be there William," she says, reverting back to his formal name.

Lightfoot looks around the room, noticing all

that has changed and while listening to her voice, considering everything that hasn't.

"You won't recognize the place, Kate. Just warning you. But we're trying real hard to, you know... keep it real. I really look forward to seeing you Kate," he says, also beginning to question his own motives for calling her.

Kate steps away from the cornerstone, inserting herself into the flow of foot traffic again. She chooses an awkward silence instead of a quick reply, a legal tactic she's learned in order to force the other party to keep talking. Lightfoot continues to reveal his hand - or his heart in this case.

"I don't know what I'm trying to say. Much of what we have now is because of you," he confesses over the phone, clearly he's searching for his words while fighting with appropriateness. Kate continues to listen, silently. *"Maybe we can work together again. Start a law firm for indigenous rights - I don't know. Hell, it'll just be good to see you again. I feel bad it's been this long."*

"See you Friday, Billy," she concludes, unable to wrestle anything effusive from her lips, except to return to the more affectionate form of his name.

"Bye Kate," Lightfoot says. *"See you soon."*

"Bye, bye," Kate says, then hangs up and pauses a beat at the curb. Kate purses her lips in consideration of yet another resurgence of doubt, then quickly gathers herself and continues upstream of foot traffic.

Lightfoot stows his phone without thinking again into which pocket it lands and heads out of the lounge, confused and wondering what just happened.

FOURTEEN

"Oninan"

(To assemble things in order)

Kate opens her eyes, having dozed off during the night flight. She lifts the shade to look out over the wing of the private jet and leans into the glass, her lids fluttering to focus into nothing but darkness below. She can feel the descent in her gut and knows they must be close. Kate tries not to snicker as she examines the cabin, decorated in a clumsy attempt at appearing woodsy and one with nature. After all, this is a forty-five million dollar plane and decorating it in wood and tapestries just felt like over compensation for the guilt of being so filthy rich.

Kate closes her eyes, thinking of that morning this all began in Café Luna. And then there were all those battles in Washington, the trips to the United Nations and the image of Lightfoot charming the world with his brilliant grin and exotic story.

"Stop!" she says out loud, hearing the sound of her

voice echo in the empty cabin. She checks herself, no room for fantasy she insists, life has moved on. The plane banks to the left sharply, causing the water bottle to topple and roll off the tray. She catches it on the way down at about the same time a young Chippewa flight attendant reaches from behind to catch the bottle as well. How long has she been there? Kate wonders. Long enough to hear her blurt a command to an empty plane?

"Prepare for landing," the pilot announces over the intercom, when from under her seat Kate feels the bumping of landing gear dropping into the wind.

❖   ❖   ❖

Papa Leo squints into the darkness, catching sight of the red and green position lights just before the bright landing lights fire up.

"She made good time," Lightfoot notes in a plain timber to mask his anticipation. Papa Leo knows better, sliding his wary eyes to the side to study his grandson's hidden enthusiasm.

❖   ❖   ❖

The Airbus jet taxis to a stop in front of Papa Leo and Lightfoot and within minutes, Kate dances down the flight-stairs, craning her head from side to side in disbelief. Strategically, she runs first to Papa Leo and wraps him in a huge hug, which seemed to her the perfect order, a proper segue to condone a deep embrace of Lightfoot thereafter.

"Papa Leo!" Kate exclaims, then extending her arms to take a good look at him. "You look so..."

"Not dead?" Papa Leo quips, before pulling her to his side in a *papa* type of hug.

"Great to see you Kate," Lightfoot says genuinely.

"A runway? A jet? Holy shit!" Kate exclaims. She gives Lightfoot a hug and instantly she feels a heavier weight to his soul. Missing is that bold and cynical spirit, normally running in contrast to the bondage of an oppressive government. Maybe she's reading too much into it, she wonders as she considers his sleepless eyes. The pilot walks Kate's luggage over. She turns back to the massive jet, clearly overwhelmed by the sight, prompting Lightfoot to justify the extravagance.

"The only way we can fulfill the orders without incurring blockades through U.S. territory," Lightfoot rationalizes, embarrassed by the display of wealth. But Papa Leo moves everyone along, grabbing her luggage as a golf cart pulls up, driven by a younger, chipper version of Lightfoot – the same boy who made deliveries on his bike when they were based in the retrofit Community Center.

"No way," Kate screams at the sight of her little legal assistant, now a stunning teenager in only two years. "Look at you!" she yells, as she musses his hair, something he doesn't appear too fond of any longer. "Sorry," she says.

"It's okay, Miss Kate," he says while rearranging his hair. "Hop in, I'll take you to your apartment," he says, still feathering his locks. Papa Leo wedges her bags onto the storage rack and climbs into the front seat. Kate hops excitedly in the back, and extends her hand to the old man's shoulder.

"How are you feeling?" she asks.

"Normal," Papa Leo state plainly as he places his large hand warmly over hers while continuing to look forward. Lightfoot jumps in beside her as the youngster steps on the gas, nearly burning rubber on the ramp. He turns to catch Papa Leo's stare.

"I disconnected the governor," the little driver admits.

"So you're a powerful lawyer now," Lightfoot says, trying to focus life's changes back her way.

"I don't know about powerful," Kate says modestly. "But yeah, a real lawyer. Go figure." She feels her silent stare into his eyes lasting a bit too long. This was not supposed to be this hard. Can the sensibility of just a close friendship really feel the same way it did the first day she laid eyes on him in that stupid café?

"I can't wait to see Mary," Kate blurts awkwardly. "How is she?" Inert and aimed forward, Papa Leo mystically reads every inflection coming from the back seat.

"She's happy and fearless as always, practically runs the school now," Lightfoot says proudly, and still evidently very much in love with Mary. Kate reaches back to stop her wind-blown red hair from bullwhipping Lightfoot in the face. But he too is struggling, not sure with what though – either with ghosts of feelings past or with the guilt of only picking up the phone when he needs something of her. Or is it when he finds enough of an excuse to connect with her again, for no reason except to see her?

❖   ❖   ❖

When the golf cart pulls into the village center, it isn't the magnificence of the rustic wealth, the glorious school facility or even the sense of peaceful power that strikes Kate. No, what arrests her attention is Mary, standing before her in the center of the road, glowing in advanced pregnancy! Harvey Bearheart is nearby as are the three Loon sisters, now puffing on their own individual E-cigarettes. The golf cart power-slides to a crunchy stop in the newly layered gravel. Papa Leo stares at the boy's break pedal then up to his sheepish grin. As Mary waddles to greet them, Kate's eyes begin welling up. She jumps from her seat and extends her arms in disbelief, quickly repackaging her confused and uncontrollable tears into those of joy at the sight of Mary's belly.

"Momma!" Kate shouts, throwing her arms open wildly, then taming her embrace to something more suited to Mary's state. Mary had wondered how Kate would feel, and now faced with buckets of emotion, wonders even further.

"We missed you, Kate," Mary says, sincerely excited to see her. "You look amazing!"

"Me?" Kate says, still wiping away tears. "You look stunning!" Kate spins around to find Lightfoot. "You guys, this is amazing!" she says in a lathered expression of confusion, aimed at his eyes only. Was he that aware of her struggle, that he though she might not show up if he mentioned this over the phone? Or was he really that clueless to have left out that bit of information? Kate turns back to Mary. "Do you know... like, a boy or a girl?"

"I can only guess at this point, but two weeks to go and, surprise!" Mary exclaims while patting her tummy in anticipation and fatigue. Of course she wouldn't know, Kate thinks. This is a different culture after all, she reminds herself. What's the rush to paint the room pink or worry about the registry at Giggle? "Let's get you settled," Mary says, motioning toward the reconstructed village.

Kate gulps back all her questions and confusion

for now, acting upon her best, *how to be gracious* angels. She takes Mary by the arm and together they follow Harvey Bearheart, who's already moving toward the new lodge with her bags. Papa Leo and Lightfoot share an uncomfortably blank look.

❖   ❖   ❖

Senators and their assistants filter in to find their seats along the semi circle of the Senate Hearing Chamber. Deputy Director Smith anxiously sits at a testimony table in the center of the room, facing the Special Committee. Joining him, Casper Elliot fidgets with a lukewarm glass of water while rehashing talking points in his head. Next to him, Doctor Drummond puckers in disgust at the ongoing bureaucracy, while separated from the other two by his legal advisors. Drummond leans back in his chair, impatiently watching the committee prepare to bring the proceedings to order.

At the center of the platform, the Chairman of the Committee pulls his fingers through his thinning dyed hair while reviewing his notes. As his engraved nameplate states, this is Mister Hollis, Senator from Illinois and Chairman of the Senate Committee on Indian Affairs. He removes his reading glasses and focuses his attention toward the testimony table.

"Good afternoon, I call this meeting to order,"

287

the Chairman Hollis begins. "Today we will be considering a resolution as twenty-nine, eighty-four. This resolution as stated, 'supports efforts to stop the theft, illegal possession or sale, transfer, and export of tribal cultural items and resources of Indians, in the United States and Internationally'," he says, pausing to refer to his notes. "This resolution is drafted by Senators Campbell of New Mexico and Ligget of Texas." He nods to the five 'gentlemen' (sic) facing him. "Thank you for being here today," he continues, while adjusting his mic for maximum effectiveness. "Let me start by saying I find your position, as expert witnesses of this honorably-titled resolution to be – ironic and frankly, out of character." He stops a moment to consider the smug silence of the men facing him. Drummond even dares to project a bored disregard for the process. "Right," the Chairman says resignedly. "After an opening statement, I'll yield to my colleagues to begin questioning," he says, while motioning to the committee members flanking him. "First off, it is not lost on this committee that you three have been at the center of a rather embarrassing and disturbing set of circumstances, regarding the Red Rock, Chippewa nation. We've all seen the video of plain-wrapped government personnel and hardware, 'invading' the sovereignty of one of the very Native American tribes that this resolution is supposedly designed to protect.

288

Over the last twenty-two months, the allegations brought against each of you, of theft and even manslaughter is disturbing to say the least," Chairman Hollis maintains, as one of the legal advisors next to Drummond lean into his mic.

"Unfounded allegations Mister Chairman, and we can prove these are merely tactics designed by lawyers representing the tribe, to try and stall..." But Chairman Hollis holds up his hand, as if to stop an oncoming car.

"I don't recall asking your opinion at this time" the Chairman interrupts. "Mister...?"

"Wayne Alexander, counsel to Doctor Drummond, Mister Chairman."

"I see," the Chairman says dismissively, while donning his glasses to check his notes again. "And why does staff council for the Los Alamos National Laboratory feel the need to represent Doctor Drummond?" Alexander leans in but before he can respond, the Chairman waves him off, "Forget it, that was rhetorical," Chairman Hollis says as he sniffs the bad air in disgust. Hollis turns to a colleague while leaning back to yield. "Senator Campbell, would you like to start?"

"Thank you, Mister Chairman," the senator from New Mexico says, flipping on his mic halfway through the gratuities. "For nearly two years, a rare fuel element, a *natural resource* protected by a number of federal statutes, has been sold on the black market by the Red Rock, Ojibwe Tribe, totally without authorization, regardless of prohibitions cited by the Natural Resources Committee, the Indian Commerce Clause as well as the Archaeological Resources Protections Act of nineteen, seventy-nine," the senator puts forth. "This is no insignificant act, Mister Chairman," he says, while he filters through a stack of reports. He produces a heavily highlighted briefing and begins reading from it. "According to recent discovery, over nine-hundred million dollars – close to one billion dollars, has been sold to foreign governments, all while excluding the Bureau of Indian Affairs from monitoring and regulating such sales."

From further across the arc of senators, a kindly man in his mid fifties quickly inserts.

"Do you blame them?" he says. "Mister Chairman if I may please respond to that initial statement?"

"The chair recognizes Senator Finkle from Minnesota," Chairman Hollis announces.

"Thank you Mister Chairman," the Minnesota senator says. "First off, there is nothing 'natural' about this resource. We're talking about something that never originated on this planet, but rather the result of a meteor impact, many years ago and only on this sovereign nation's land. Secondly, the BIA forfeited their 'sacred duties' as they seem to imply, when they colluded to invade sovereign territory and then covertly blew it up to fool the public. An attack that killed six Chippewa children. They then lied to the American people about it being dangerous, all so they could evict the tribe and take it for themselves.

Drummond's lawyers nearly climb over each other to interject.

"Again, Senator, none of those allegations have ever been proven," Alexander claims.

"Save it for the courts, Counselor. You'll have your opportunity to deny the obvious then," Chairman Hollis says. "In the mean time, shut up!" Chairman Hollis insists before yielding back to the senator from Minnesota, with a nod to continue.

"Now, my question for *Deputy Director Smith* of the BIA is, who authorized you to work in concert with these players, to conduct the intervention designed to evict the Red Rock Tribe from their land?" Senator Finkle continues. Deputy Director Smith leans into the microphone.

"Sir, our department was informed by the Army Corps of Engineers, and scientific experts that the area posed a clear and present danger to the Ojibwe tribe as well as surrounding U.S. land," Smith says.

"So you're saying, then..." as Finkle follows along. "That you were 'misled' by the gentlemen at the table sitting next to you?" Smith takes a deep breath, and blows it all out before answering.

"Yes, that is correct," he snitches. The attorney for Drummond dives into the fray anyway.

"Sorry Mr. Chairman, I cannot stand by and quietly watch this farce," Alexander insists. This line of questioning implies that the Red Rock Tribe actually has the right to any protections by the federal government, or even my client for that matter. By their own admission, the elders of Red Rock have refused to abide by the federal authority, and even waived any protections by the court when they stated that they have no desire to be part of the United States any longer." But Senator Finkle can't pass this up.

"And I'll say it again. "Do you blame them?" Senator Finkle asks, then turns to address the senators from New Mexico and Texas who authored the bill. "Quit pretending this is a resolution to protect us all from 'theft' when you are the thieves these people need protection from! History has shown we've done plenty to destroy tribal rights with such self-serving 'resolutions' as this. It's time this rape of Native American land and resources comes to an end. We stole their way of life, forced them onto the least desirable land we could carve out, and now that you've discovered that land might have value, Interior wants it back." Finkle fumes, nearly screaming into his microphone. "I find it ironic that finally, a Native American tribe has acquired enough financial resources to fight back with the very law we used to decimate them with." Finkle flips his mic off and flops harshly back into his chair. Casper Elliot with the Army Corps leans to add his voice, when Senator Finkle keys his mic and jumps back in before he has a chance to speak.

"Mister Chairman, I propose an independent investigation, into the allegations of collusion, corruption and... *murder* perpetrated by the so called gentlemen sitting before us. This is appalling and this resolution should be rejected." With that, Senator Finkle rises and exits the chamber.

❖ ❖ ❖

The tradition of gathering around a rustic fire near the shore hasn't changed in over a hundred years and nor should it, especially now. With their backs to the grandeur of the wealthy Chippewa village, Mary, Lightfoot and Papa Leo gaze over the fire to the lake, onto a scene untouched by human hands. This is a time for reflection, when nothing matters but the natural world before them. It's more than chance that their backs are turned to the infrastructure of the village. This was tradition, even during humble times.

"Professor!" a panting voice shouts out from behind

them. The call repeats, growing in volume and urgency. "Professor!" Amik, the young math student stops between the fire and the water's edge, out of breath and holding a laptop in the air. "Professor?" Amik exclaims while flipping his laptop open. "You have to see this." He hits the play button while presenting the screen to the group. On screen, a C-SPAN video replays the congressional hearing while Amik narrates. "I've been scanning news about the Indian Affairs Bureau, and this came up from today". He maximizes the video to fill the screen.

On the screen, Senator Finkle is winding up his rebuke, flaming the advisory panel of Drummond, the Bureau and Corps.

"I find it ironic that finally, a Native American tribe has acquired enough financial resources to fight back using the very law we used to decimate them with." Finkle flips his mic off and flops harshly back into his chair.

Amik pauses the video as an approaching grind of footsteps in the gravel road signal the arrival of Kate and Tyler to the fire pit.

"Ah, perfect! Kate, check this out," Lightfoot says, motioning for her to join them at the council meeting. Amik hands Lightfoot the laptop who then resumes the video.

On screen, Elliot leans into his mic, just as Senator Finkle cuts him off.

"Mister Chairman, I propose an independent investigation, into the allegations of collusion, corruption and... murder perpetrated by the so called gentlemen sitting before us against the Red Rock tribe. This is appalling and this resolution should be rejected."

"Whoa, when is this from?" Kate asks.

"Two hours ago," Amik remarks. Tyler realizes Kate has never met his star student.

"Oh, this is Amik, our top math major," Tyler effuses. "Nailed the finals today!"

"I did?" Amik asks, apparently not yet receiving a graded report.

"Oh, that's right," Tyler says. "You'll find out tomorrow officially, but yeah dude. Ninety-eight percent," Tyler adds, while fist pounding the young student.

"That's a great name, Amik," Kate says. "I wish I had a cool name like that."

"Thanks. It means beaver," Amik declares proudly. Tyler suppresses a belly laugh, knowing this is just too easy to comment on. He covers by returning to the more pressing topic at hand.

"So, what resolution are they talking about?" Tyler asks Lightfoot, but it's the young student who assumes the explanation.

"These guys, the scientist from New Mexico - Drummond and the Indian Affairs guys are testifying about a bill to stop the 'looting' of natural resources by foreign governments of the *Ishkode* fuel," Amik explains. "They're citing archeological acts, or something."

"Looting? But they did the looting!" Kate declares through clenched teeth. "There's no end to these pricks.

"They think by pretending to 'protect' Indian resources, they can sneak a resolution in, allowing them to shut Red Rock down," Lightfoot says, glancing over to Papa Leo.

"Man they picked the wrong tribe to screw with," Tyler says, feeding off the drama. Papa Leo twists his head, his eyes suddenly becoming distant and disconnected from the group. He rises to stoke the fire with a stick, apparently becoming lost in his own memories again.

"Kate, let's think this out," Lightfoot proposes, while closing the computer and handing it back to Amik, a gentle gesture signaling the conclusion of the young man's presence at the council.

"Great work," Lightfoot says. "This is exactly the kind of research we need. Thank you, Amik."

"No problem Chief Dude. I have to get back," the student claims, fully sensitive to their need for privacy. He spins to run off but stops mid turn. "Professor?" Amik asks. Lightfoot turns to him and nods.

"I'm Sioux, but the battle Red Rock Chippewa is

fighting makes me more proud than you will ever know," Amik says. "I watched my dad lose his hope, and my grandfather before him. I'm proud to know you, Sir," Amik says, then motioning to Papa Leo. "All of you." Amik turns and runs off. Lightfoot watches his grandfather look up from stoking the fire. Lightfoot notices Papa Leo suddenly becoming alert again, as he tracks the young Sioux boy toward the dorm where Amik meets up with a Chippewa girl and a Western Cree boy. Even through his roughcast eyes, an epiphany can be seen striking to the old man's core. Lightfoot studies the old man's interest in Amik, wondering what exactly his grandfather is feeling at that moment? But just as quickly, Papa Leo's eyes turn back toward the fire to daze into the flicker, secluded again in his thoughts.

"So how's this sound?" Kate says cautiously, fully aware of her position as an outsider at this council. "So far, you've tried this case in the media. And it's worked to the extent that they've been hands off to avoid further embarrassing headlines here, and negative reaction from their allies. So far, the tack to reject their authority has worked as well. But what if now, you acknowledge them - *by going after them?* Sue them on a scale larger than any legal actions we took in the beginning when we challenged the statutes. This time, name the Bureau, the Feds, the Army. Hell, sue the President if we have to. If they want to insist that you're still a part of the U.S. then call their bluff and use your rights as a 'member' of their club, to sue the shit out of them – now that you have the resources to do so."

"Sue them for what?" Harvey Bearheart asks, overhearing the conversation as he arrives at the gathering.

"Murder, robbery and violations of treaty," Kate states in certitude. "Make it so difficult for them to acknowledge you have any legal recourse, that they agree to cut you loose to avoid the pain inflicted by your prerogative to sue them!" she asserts. Papa Leo glances from the fire pit, anticipating his grandson's response.

"I don't know about that," Lightfoot says. "I'm with you on trying to acknowledge them," he says, preparing to redirect. "But I was thinking more along the lines of a peace offering. They want access to the fuel, so we give it to them, IF they agree to abstain from the Security Council vote," he proposes.

Mary is also concerned with Papa Leo's apparent retreat from the group. He continues to stoke the fire, mesmerized by the flicker. Is he lost again, she wonders? Or is he keenly aware of every spoken word and instead feigning a preoccupation for some reason? Then she notices that signature gesture, those keen eyes, darting side-to-side with his head pointed in a different direction.

"Money is all they understand anyway," Lightfoot says, continuing to press his 'olive branch' strategy. Mary watches as Papa Leo appears to struggle with his grandson's reasoning at the moment. No, of course he's listening Mary realizes, when a knowing smile breaks across her face.

"My point exactly," Kate says. "Except we take their money, not give them more of it. Hit them where it hurts, until it forces their hand," she concludes. Papa Leo stops poking the fire and gently *snaps* his stoking branch in two. The crisp sound abruptly grabs everyone's attention. They all turn at the same time to watch as Papa Leo inserts both pieces of the stick into the coals, leaving them there to burn side by side.

"We do both," Papa Leo says quietly to the silenced group, like an orchestra yielding to the solo of an oboe. "At the same time," he adds. The group watches the two prongs burn equally in the same fire. With that, the patriarch simply brushes the soot from his hands. "I'm going for a ride," he says. Then Papa Leo simply walks off. Everyone around the fire stares in astonishment as the nearly century old sage walks away and down the road.

"Okay, that man just totally freaked me out right

now," Kate says as she watches him slowly make his way to the stable.

"An olive branch and a club," Lightfoot realizes aloud. "We give them a choice."

❖ ❖ ❖

It's another sunrise atop the overlook. Lightfoot and Papa Leo sit in their saddles, seeing together across the lake below, through eyes that span three generations. They face into a substantial wind, rising swiftly from below the shear cliff. The cold air pushes streaks of indifferent tears along the sides of Papa Leo's face and into he ears.

"Last night, when Amik spoke of the hope he feels," Lightfoot says, setting up a question. "I was watching you. There was something on your mind when he said that." Papa Leo briefly turns from his gaze across the water to smile at his grandson, then returns to stare toward the sunrise.

"He reminded me of a friend, a long time ago," Papa Leo recalls. "A Sioux medicine man – Black Elk from South Dakota." He pauses to reflect again, tightening his eyes as he digs deeper into his memories. "He was the keeper of the Sacred Pipe of his people. He told me of a dream, a vision of himself, standing on the central mountain of the world. In his dream, he was seeing in a sacred manner, the shapes of all things, in the spirit, and the shape of all things as they must live together like one being. He saw the sacred hoop of his people was one of many hoops that made one circle as wide as daylight and starlight combined. In the center grew a mighty flowering tree to shelter all the children of one mother and one father." He turns to face his grandson. "And then he realized, that anywhere is the center of the world."

"Okay," Lightfoot says, hoping for a bit more clarity. "And Amik, a Sioux boy in Chippewa land, living with Cree and other tribes," Lightfoot wonders. "Those are the many hoops?" he asks.

"It made me see," Papa Leo continues. "With eyes as sharp as my youth, that we are not doing all this for Red Rock alone. We are here to hold the sacred pipe, for all Original Men to pass among themselves. This is not just about our independence. We need to think much bigger, just as you mentioned before. But not only by forming a common bond of resistance with the rest of the world who are oppressed by these people. Instead, we join in a circle with all the tribes. It is our destiny to *represent*, and not only resist." Lightfoot looks into his own hands, opening and closing them as if seeing the mechanics of his grasp for the first time.

"I wondered the same, in a different way," Lightfoot says. "And worried that if we do *convince* the government of our right to live independently, out from under their thumb, that it will only create a larger problem for them. Because then, there will exist a precedent, for all the tribal lands held in 'trust' by the feds, to be returned. That will frighten them into rejecting our case for real independence, as it might start a chain reaction they aren't willing to bear."

"The time will come my son," Papa Leo states as sure as the sun. "After they step aside – that they return to us with this problem. And ask us to soothe the other tribes." Papa Leo zeroes in on his grandson's eyes, "We need to be prepared for that."

"How do we prepare for that?" Lightfoot asks.

"We add an 'S' to our name," the old sage replies. "The Republic of Tribal People, should be 'Tribal Peoples'. All of them." His grandfather says. Papa Leo looks up as he tracks a V-formation of Canadian Geese across the sky. "We're nothing special. We only bear the Sacred Pipe," he says, as he watches the gaggle disappear across the water.   Suddenly, the old man snaps out of the dream. A pragmatism glows in his eyes now, more suited to a battle commander. "But not yet! Let the State Department as they call themselves...let them come to us and ask for our help with the other tribes.   By then, we will have diplomats, and we will be allies with the government."

"So we continue as planned, with an eye on a

different prize than we admit to now. Got it!" Lightfoot nods in confirmation.

"And Kate?" Papa Leo asks.

"Well, we let her start the proceedings," Lightfoot outlines. "She has a law firm in Washington ready to take us on. Ready to inflict some pain. So we move ahead, and she drops the cases when they drop their claim over us."

"That's not what I meant," Papa Leo says. "She doesn't impress me as one who can let go of a bone once it's in her teeth," he adds, before trotting off, leaving him to ponder the meaning of Kate's ambitions.

"He did it again," Lightfoot says aloud. Was he implying she couldn't drop a legal case once she started or, could he really see the personal struggle between them? As he watches the old man walk his pony down the hill, he settles for not asking further.

❖　❖　❖

Director Mike Chambers, head of the BIA calmly sips a coffee at a small table outside Greenberry's Café near the Department of Interior building in Washington. It's a mean solar afternoon, a rare time of day, at a rare time of year when the sun's rays flow directly down East Street, unobstructed by buildings. With all he's been through lately, he savors the rare moment of tranquility. That's until his phone rings and he notices the caller on screen.

"Oh, for heaven's sake," he cries out, while placing his ear buds in. "Can't I get a fucking break without..." He answers the phone. "Hello, suicide crisis center."

From across the street, passersby watch as Mike repeatedly and frantically pumps his angry fists in the air like a crazy person, silently raging to the voices in his head. He grabs his phone and launches up from the table when his headphone cord wipes the table clean of his coffee and plate. He rushes off down the street, while his cup and a half eaten muffin, roll in a puddle of Columbian blend on the sidewalk. Mike continues to power walk across East Street, chanting to himself.

"SHIT, SHIT, SHIT, SHIT..." he says, like a mantra timed to each footfall. Turning down Nineteenth, the blurting ceases when the Department of Interior Building comes into view. Braking to a standstill at the sight of reporters surrounding the entrance, Mike begins pacing in a tight circle on the sidewalk as concerned pedestrians consider the nut. "FUCK, FUCK, FUCK!"

Again, Mike stops cold, his eyes bulging out of his red flared face. He breathes not once, but over and over, replacing the rhythm of his blurts with deep rushes of cool air, until he achieves a moderate decorum. With one last breath, which he holds in his lungs before diving off the board into the media waters, Mike continues on towards the main entrance. When the reporters catch sight of the director heading their way, they turn like a flock of seagulls descending on a single French fry.

"Director Chambers, do you have any comment about the class action suit against the BIA?"

"Director, now that the Red Rock tribe possesses unlimited financial resources, do you plan to go to court over this?"

"Mike! Mike, how do you respond to the murder charges levied against your department and the United States Army Corps of Engineers?" But as a man fighting his conscience, Mike weaves through the fray, while flailing his phone and ear buds over his head as if holding them above water. Slowly approaching the main entrance, it's the last question that actually slows him to a pensive crawl.

"Director Chambers, do you expect to lose your job over this?" Thinking better of engaging, Mike then presses harder, accelerating through the swarm and exploding into the building.

FIFTEEN

"Miigaadiwin"

(A battle or war)

"Professor Lightfoot and Leo Lightfoot, I'd like to introduce you to the Deputy Secretary of State, Miss Baumgardener," the cultured aide says while motioning reverently. Papa Leo feels out of sorts in his business suit and tie. He removes his broad floppy hat, to shake the diplomat's hand. Baumgardener turns to the younger and more approachable Professor Lightfoot.

"Please call me William," Lightfoot says, while offering his hand. The State official's warm glow exceeds the stuffy perimeter of status that surrounds her position.

"Of course William, and please, call me Carolyn. Let's have a seat," the diplomat says, while motioning to a low couch and table area in the center of her office. "As I'm sure you're aware, we have to consider this an *unofficial* meeting. As you know the Bureau of Indian

Affairs was established to perform the diplomatic role with Native American nations."

"In all respect, we can no longer recognize the BIA's authority, frankly that's where our problem starts. Already bad treaties have been broken, not to mention the elephant in the room right now," Lightfoot notes.

"The elephant?" Baumgardener asks.

"We're suing them for murder, robbery and collusion," Papa Leo explains. The Deputy Secretary nods her head, obviously aware.

"Yes, then there's that – the elephant." She turns back to Lightfoot who takes the cue to continue.

"The idea that native tribes have an inherent right to govern themselves is at the foundation of our constitutional status, we all get that. Regardless of the fact that unless Congress limits a specific right, it is assumed the tribal nation possesses that right - that doesn't always work in practice, since any argument on behalf of tribal sovereignty has failed in the face of unequal power."

"And that's where you come in, I take it? The official asks. "If there's another elephant in the room, it would be the enormous wealth the Red Rock tribe has acquired?" Miss Baumgardener says. Papa Leo perks up, continuing to insert short bursts of 'grumpy cop' observations.

"Wealth we intend to use to defend our rights in

court," Papa Leo motions further. "Nowhere does Congress say they have the right to a meteor that strikes our land. We therefore 'assume' to possess it."

"Exactly" Lightfoot rounds, more encouraged with the lucidity his grandfather possesses right now, than the grumpiness of his delivery. "My Grandfather speaks the truth and states the basis of our case against the U.S. Government. However, we also would like to extend a proposal, one we believe is best delivered through your office, since our lawyers have told us it would be inappropriate to communicate with the entity we are currently suing in court."

"Of course," The Deputy Secretary smiles admiringly. She glances over briefly to an aide who stands nearby, recording the conversation in a notebook. The trusted aid raises a brow and smiles, clearly implying that these guys know their shit. The aide returns to his notebook.

"You have my attention gentlemen," the Deputy Secretary affirms. Lightfoot adjusts in his chair, leaning forward with his elbows on his knees as he focuses into her eyes.

"As you know, we've donated three million dollars of fuel and resources to the United Nations Energy Commission to support their efforts across the world. We've exchanged fuel resources across the world for other precious metals, and never have taken a dollar of

U.S. currency. But today we'd like to make a proposal, and open our arms to offer the United States up to one hundred million dollars in fuel resources and supporting technology, in exchange for a gesture from the U.S. State Department," Lightfoot respectfully proposes.

"A gesture?" she asks, again humored at where this is going. "Let me guess. You want the U.S. to vote in the Security Council to allow your bid for U.N. recognition to proceed to the main body?"

"No, ma'am," Lightfoot confirms. "We just need the U.S. to *abstain* from voting. Why make it any more difficult than it has to be? We're not here to rub their noses in this," he says. Baumgardener laughs heartily, sincerely captivated by their approach. She thinks it though for a moment while Lightfoot and Papa Leo look on silently.

"And what about the ongoing litigation," she asks.

"We'd be forced drop that as well," Papa Leo states solidly. We'd have no jurisdiction in the courts as citizens once we are truly an independent nation." Again, Lightfoot studies his grandfather's bang-on focus and sharpness.

"You understand..." she continues. "By doing so, you're asking the United States government to fully cut you loose from this union. You are asking approval for secession. There's no precedent that's ever happened, or even possible," Baumgardener says. Ah, but Lightfoot motions toward his next point.

"Article one, section eight of the Constitution implies that 'Indian' tribes are separate from the federal or state governments, and that they are 'only' as sovereign as another state," Lightfoot notes. "Whatever degree of sovereignty a tribe has, it's at least on par with any member state. That being said, if a state can 'hypothetically' secede from the Union, then why can't a tribe? We believe we have that right, and the resources to defend that right in the courts."

"Except gentlemen, may I say that the odds of any state successfully seceding from the U.S., is near zero," the diplomat argues. "There aren't many options. You either withdraw by force, or you amend the Constitution, or you wait until the collapse of the federal government." Papa Leo holds an open palm between them.

"Or, we simply ask nicely," the old man suggests.

"We think we have the upper hand here," Lightfoot follows. "They get access to a much needed resource which up to this point has been blocked by the embarrassing news around the world of their efforts to take it by force," he posits. "They avoid another media nightmare over criminal allegations as well as a financially exhaustive battle in the Ninth Circuit court, the Court of Appeals, and eventually the Supreme

Court. Not to mention, we've already filed charges with The International Criminal Court."

"And avoiding further international backlash over the United Nations' Declaration on the Rights of Indigenous Peoples, which the U.S. shamefully voted against," Papa Leo says, before adding one last point. "And by the way, the nations that *have* voted for it – are our customers," the old man concludes. Lightfoot swallows a bit of shock, tempered again by the encouraging sign of Papa Leo's sharpness today.

"For the U.S. to allow United Nation recognition, it would essentially imply absolute independence of a land-locked nation within another nation,"

"Except our land borders Canada, we aren't land locked," Lightfoot notes, further stirring his perfect-storm of logic.

"Right," she acknowledges. "You've thought of everything, haven't you?" The diplomat leans back in her chair, considering the deal before her. "And all litigation goes away if the United States simply abstains to vote in the Security Council and allows your application to proceed to the General Assembly?" Baumgardener asks. "Again with no guarantee that the General Assembly would even vote in your favor?" she adds. Lightfoot simply nods. She smiles, betraying a bit of 'unofficial' admiration. "Some might assume this to be, blackmail. You're aware of that?"

"Yes, but we think the hundred million dollar gesture might, how do I say...temper that assumption?" Lightfoot ads. Baumgardener stands, followed by Lightfoot and Papa Leo. She offers her hand.

"Well, you seem to have thought this out," the Deputy Secretary respectfully concludes. "Gentlemen, I will take your 'proposal' in advisement and you can be assured I will pass this on." She pauses to scan her brain for any further disclaimers. "Unofficially of course," she reaffirms.

"Of course," Lightfoot says charmingly.

❖   ❖   ❖

You can always tell a tourist in D.C. They're usually the ones looking everywhere but the sidewalk ahead of them. Papa Leo is no exception, as he strolls with his grandson down Seventh Street at dinner hour. Having never set foot out of Minnesota, he studies the strange dissonance of lighting, window advertising and traffic. This is a town dripping in wealth and bloated with power, yet there is nothing impressive or redeeming about these surroundings for Papa Leo. He watches the odd 'civilization' animate around him like electrical bonfires lit up to warm the masses from the chilling reality of their routines.

"Up here, just past that corner," Lightfoot says while navigating to his mobile map. "Food is supposed to be great." He looks up from his phone to watch his grandfather stare at the suited oddities that pass by.

❖   ❖   ❖

A trendy young maître d cheerfully greets the out of town guests, clearly evidenced by Papa Leo's tattered broad-rimmed hat and trail worn boots.

"Welcome to Blacksalt Fish Market, Gentlemen," the maître d says. "Do you have a reservation this evening?"

"I've had a reservation for ninety-five years," the crusty elder replies. Of course the moonlighting *president-in-training*, takes the old man literally.

"Excuse me?" he asks.

"William Lightfoot for two at seven-thirty," Lightfoot says, while the maître d examines his log.

"Yes, exactly Sirs, we have you right here," the host says with faux dignity. "Let me check your table, I'll be right back." Lightfoot leans to his grandfather.

"You couldn't pass that up, could you?"

"This is a 'fish market'?" Papa Leo asks as he looks around and catches sight of the patrons staring back at him. His wolf-lined hooded jacket over his suit and leather boots speak volumes to the other diners, who quickly return their gaze to their plate once the old man's piercing eyes match their stare.

"Statistics say, one out of ten people in here are lawyers," Lightfoot notes.

"Is that why it smells like fish," Papa Leo quickly replies.

"Wow, you're on tonight," Lightfoot claims. "Also I have to say, you really nailed it in there today!"

"You think I'm not listening?" his grandfather declares as the maître d returns.

"This way please," the host says. They follow him through the gauntlet of gawking diners as the young host motions to their table.

"May I take your jacket, Sir," he asks while presumptively extending his hand to the old man's collar.

"No," Papa Leo replies.

"Oh, okay then. No problem," the maître d says before pulling out a chair out for the senior gentleman. Lightfoot looks on affectionately as his grandfather shoots a puzzled look to the boy with the chair in his hand.

"Are you going to sit there?" Papa Leo asks.

"No Sir. This is your chair," the maître d says while flashing a shit-eating grin. Papa Leo takes his own chair.

"Thank you, son," Papa Leo says, then seats himself, wolf-lined jacket and all. With both men seated, the rattled host hands them two large leather-bound menus. The host pauses for a moment with the wine list, looking back and forth between the two men before finally handing it to Lightfoot.

"Your server will be with you shortly. Can I get you anything in the mean time?" Lightfoot steps in to assure the nervous fellow.

"No thank you, we're great for now," Lightfoot says graciously.

"Okay perfect." The maître d says as he high-tails it back to his post.

"You think they have moose?" Papa Leo asks, while examining the leather menu cover.

"Granddad?" Lightfoot questions. He nods to the wolf-lined coat. "Don't you want to take your jacket off?"

"And let people see me in this stupid suit?" Papa Leo says.

"Maybe just the hat then?" Lightfoot grins. "You're attracting a crowd." Papa Leo looks around to notice a dozen or so people stare while speaking sideways to each other. Begrudgingly, the old man removes the soiled, floppy leather hat and hangs it from the breadsticks in the center of the table. Lightfoot gives up and returns to his menu, when a couple of gawkers tentatively approach the table.

"Excuse me, sorry to interrupt," a young lady in a

business suit announces. The guys look up to consider the thirty-something couple.

"I couldn't help but stare," she states rather awkwardly. "But you're the Indian Professor right? Professor Lightfoot? I saw you on TV." Papa Leo turns his look from the couple to his grandson, eagerly anticipating the response.

"Um, yes I am. And you are...?"

"Oh, nobody really," she says, suddenly realizing the sound of that. "I mean, not nobody, I just work here in D.C. in a law firm." She motions to the bearded hipster next to her, "This is my friend Calvin, he's a lobbyist," she mentions before thrusting her hand abruptly at Lightfoot. "My name is Kelly. Kelly Lindquist. It's a real pleasure to meet you." Lightfoot still has no idea where this is going, but as always plays the gentleman.

"Good to meet you Kelly, and... Calvin?"

"Calvin Collins, yes," he confirms, extending a limp wrist in his version of a handshake.

"I just wanted to say how impressed I am," Kelly says, while motioning to her sheepish escort. "We both are." Papa Leo puts his hat back on his head. "I mean, seeing you stand up like that to oppression, is like, so inspirational. What the government has done to your people over the years, the land grabbing, the genocide, it's just not right," the young counselor asserts.

"Yes, genocide is a bad thing," Lightfoot replies, just

barely managing to keep it light. Papa Leo tracks the conversation, panning his eyes rapidly from side to side. He notices the hipster appears to be working up a statement.

"If there is anyway we can help with, please let us know," Calvin says, while whipping out a business card. Not quite sure who to hand it to, he offers the card to Papa Leo. "Seriously, no lie. If there is anything we can do to help your cause, please let us know." Papa Leo takes the card, studies both sides then shoots a puzzled look to his grandson who smiles absolutely. A waiter arrives at the table.

"I can come back?" the server suggests.

"No, no," the young lady replies. "We were just leaving," she says. As they turn to leave, the hipster flips a pointed finger to Papa Leo in a weird attempt at coolness.

"Love the hat, man. It's awesome!" he exclaims with a creepy smile. Papa Leo holds the card in his hand, frozen in bewilderment as he watches them return to join their friends at a nearby table. Stupefied and still holding the card in the air, he looks back to check his grandson.

"Gentlemen, have you had a chance to review the menu?" the waiter inquires.

"Haven't got that far yet," Lightfoot says. "But maybe we could get a couple beers first."

"We have quite an assortment," the server cautions.

"Well, we're in D.C. so make it two Sam Adams," Lightfoot proposes, but his drollery doesn't resonate with the server.

"Of course," the server replies with a tight-lipped smile.   He flutters off to the bar.   Realizing he's still holding the card, Papa Leo hands it over to his grandson. Lightfoot examines it.

"Seriously, no lie," Lightfoot says.

❖   ❖   ❖

Three beers each have passed, when the impatient server returns. Papa Leo's cheeks are rosy, his hat floppier, his wit a bit more cutting. He looks up at the server and squints.

"So, no moose on the menu?" Lightfoot jolts mid-swig, choking back a soggy laugh. He hands his menu over and finally orders.

"I think we're ready, I'll have the John Dory," he says, as his grandfather decides to sing.

"Hang down your head John Dory, hand down you head and cry..."

"Granddad, we better order," Lightfoot says, with a pained grin.

"Fine," the old man says. "Moose!"

"He'll have the Salmon," Lightfoot covers.   He

motions affectionately for his hero to take it down a notch.

"Another beer?" the server asks as he taps the order on his iPad. Papa Leo glances at the menu one last time before handing it over.

"Sure, two Mooseheads," the old man declares, while laughing at his own joke. The server forces a smile and rushes off.

"Granddad, it's good to see you having a good time," Lightfoot says while lifting his glass to him.

"I'm with my favorite grandson, of course I'm having a good time," Papa Leo says.

"I'm your only grandson."

"I remember your naming ceremony, your mom was so proud." But Papa Leo stops at the thought of his daughter. It isn't long before his eyes well up, pulling shades of tears over the merriment that just moments ago felt so freeing.

"Granddad, I know. I'm sorry". But the old man sits, looking straight ahead, neither turning away or bowing his head, he just looks forward through moist eyes fighting through his emotions and the last three pints of brew.

"She was a beautiful spirit," Papa Leo says calmly. He looks around the room again, at all the lights and the signs of modern civilization so apparently out of balance. He considers his fleeting years and all those departed spirits that passed so quickly, leaving him behind. But when he turns back to see his grandson, his face begins to glow again. Lightfoot's emotions are getting the best of him as well. Neither of them can blame the feelings they share together on a couple beers. Lightfoot knows at this instant, while looking into his grandfather's conflicted eyes, that this will be one of those memories you hear people talk about years later – that kind of defining flashback of the happiest and most meaningful time in one's life. The waiter returns with two more beers.

"Your orders will be ready shortly, gentlemen," says the server. He again rushes off to juggle a few more plates. Papa Leo lifts the glass for a closer look. Lost in the color of the liquid, the mirrored gold reflecting the lights of the room. Thinking deeply, so deeply that Lightfoot wonders if his grandfather is fading again into one of those dream states he's frequented since he smacked his head months ago.

"You remember John Lame Deer? Sioux Lakota," his Papa Leo asks.

"No, not really," Lightfoot replies.

"Yeah, might be before your time," Papa Leo considers. "He used to say that, before the white brothers arrived to make us civilized men, we didn't have any kind of prison. Because of this, we had no delinquents. Without a prison, there can be no delinquents. We had no locks, no keys and therefore, there were no thieves among us. When someone was so poor that he couldn't afford a horse, a tent, or even a blanket, he would simply receive it – as a gift. We were too uncivilized to give any importance to civilized property. We didn't know any kind of money, so the value of a human being wasn't determined by his wealth. We had no laws written down, no lawyers, no politicians, so we weren't able to cheat and swindle each other," Papa Leo says, then pauses to take a sip of his beer. "We were really in bad shape before the white men arrived. I don't know how we were able to manage these fundamental things that they tell us are so necessary for a civilized society," he states. Lightfoot has so much admiration in his eyes, considering how he's cherishing this rare moment with Papa Leo.

"He sounded like a wise man," Lightfoot says.

"There were a lot of wise men at one time," he says. His name really wasn't John. It was *Gikinoo'amaagewinini* Lame Deer. But they gave him the name John for some reason."

"That means *teacher man*," Lightfoot notes.

"Ah, so you haven't lost your Ojibwe tongue." Finally the server arrives with their food order. Lightfoot catches the waiter's eye as he sets the plates down.

"Miigwech," Lightfoot tells the server.

"That means, Thank you!" the old man proudly declares to the server.

❖ ❖ ❖

Kate and Tyler are eating breakfast together in the Red Rock Café when Amik arrives to refill their coffee. Kate is on the phone as she mimes a 'thank you' to Amik. Tyler reads from his paper, half listening as Kate dresses down the listener on the other end of the line.

"Let me put it to you this way," Kate says. "You are on the wrong side of history here, not to mention the wrong side of the law. Do you know the United Nations' definition of genocide? It's a crime against humanity. Identified as an activity against a national, ethnic, racial or religious group with includes at least, killing members of the group, causing serious bodily or mental harm to members of the group, or inflicting on the group conditions of life calculated to bring about its physical destruction," Kate posits as Amik's eyes widen in astonishment. "Furthermore, and unfortunately for you, your client has managed to fulfill every one of those activities against the Red Rock tribe. Have I made myself clear?"

"Ouch!" Amik whispers before returning to the counter. Kate wraps it up.

"Good, you do that. Also, you can let your client

know that there will be no settlement. This is going to trial!" Kate catches Tyler gawking at her in awe. "Enjoy your day," she finishes, and hangs up. Amik applauds and cheers from the counter, as Tyler joins in. Kate takes a bow, then a huge swig of coffee. She catches Tyler googly-eyeing her.

"What?" she asks.

"I am so in love with you," Tyler says completely without inhibition. His statement is so outrageous and matter-of-fact that it gives her (and him), the opening for a comfortable dismissal.

"Oh stop it," she responds, contorting her eyebrows in absurdity. Tyler notices Kate glance over his shoulder to the front door behind him. He turns to see Mary enter and waddle over to the table.

"Can I join you guys?" Mary asks. No sooner does Mary approach the table, does Tyler bolt from his seat and pull a chair up for her.

"Of course Mamma," he replies, while presenting the chair. "How are you feeling?"

"Like a frog," she admits while leaning over to give Kate a hug. "Good morning Counselor," Mary says. Kate snorts at the title. "This all happened so quickly, so why now does it feel like an eternity?" Mary wonders out loud, having never before experienced the wild ride of emotions that accompany the hormonal rush. Now, everything feels... well, just *feels*," and that in itself is enough to shake her world. "We were supposed to be married first, that's how it usually works. Last thing I want to do is have a ceremony looking like this."

"You look beautiful!" Tyler exclaims. "Besides, it's a new world. Marriage is a sheet of paper you can fill out later." Mary places her palm over Kate's hand.

"Speaking of ceremonies, we have a tradition, called a 'Naming Ceremony' when the medicine man, in our case it's a medicine woman..."

"Thus my point – progressiveness," Tyler injects before motioning to excuse himself for interrupting. Mary nods certainly, then continues.

"When a child is born, the father and mother ask the healer to seek a name for the child. She goes off and fasts, meditates and the spirits give the name in a dream," she says of the tradition. "I know it sounds corny. But we thought it would be nice to honor my dad, and Papa Leo's tradition. Anyway, in the ceremony the parents ask four men and four women to be sponsors for the child, who vow to support and guide the child in life." Mary says, looking tentatively at the two of them, noticing they are just starting to catch on. "We were wondering if you Kate and you too Tyler, if you would be sponsors to our child?" Tyler of course explodes with excitement and appreciation.

"Are you kidding, I'm honored. I'd love to, although I have no idea how to guide myself through life but yeah, I'd be glad to learn, thanks!" he effuses. Mary looks to Kate who responds just a beat slower.

"Of course," Kate confirms soberly. "I'd be thrilled – and honored as well." Somehow, Kate manages to accept without Mary seeing into her tortured soul.

"That's great, thank you, both of you. This really means a lot!" Mary claims. Suddenly moving her hand to her side, Mary's brow ripples with slight concern. She quickly pats her stomach and side.

"Are you okay?" Kate jumps. Tyler stands, motions for Amik.

"Is it time, are you having the baby? Holy shit!" Tyler panics. Amik grabs for the phone, just as Mary breaks into laughter at the anxiety that surrounds her. She struggles with her girth as she pulls her cell phone from her pocket.

"It was my phone. I left it on vibrate," she explains, while noticing the screen. "Oh, it's Billy!" Mary exclaims. Tyler motions for Amik, to stand down, who's already holding the phone in one hand with his other ready to dial. Tyler and Kate start breathing again.

"Billy, how's it going there?" Mary asks while Kate and Tyler listen patiently for a sign.

"I'm with them now, I'll put it on speakerphone," Mary says, then sets the phone in the middle of the table.

"Hi guys. It seemed to go well with the State Department last night," Lightfoot says over the speaker. *"They appear to get it, even seemed impressed with the argument, and proposal. Should hear something soon."* Lightfoot reports. *"How's it going there?"*

"Hey man, Mary's phone just started vibrating in her pocket and we all freaked out, thought the baby was coming. How you doing?" Tyler starts.

"Hi," Kate says, leaning over the table. "Just got off the phone with the Interior Department lawyers. They're not happy, which is good I suppose."

Lightfoot and his grandfather listen from the hotel room. Papa Leo is looking a bit after-effected from the drinks the night before. He's wearing a courtesy bathrobe over jeans and boots and still dons the floppy hat. They listen to Kate continue her report over the speaker.

"They want to settle out of court, but I told them no way – that this case is going all the way. We need them to think that we don't want money and that we only want justice." Papa Leo rubs his throbbing head. *"So, tell us? We can't wait to hear how they responded at the State Department!"* Kate says.

At the café, Mary, Kate and Tyler continue to huddle over the phone as Lightfoot follows with the update.

"They could have seen it as blackmail. But when our

request was backed with both a gift as well as the offer to stand down, it seemed to catch them off guard," Lightfoot maintains. *"We let them know that all they have to do is abstain in the Security Council, and all the lawsuits go away."* Mary notices that Kate doesn't appear too eager to avoid 'winning'.

"I get that," Kate says. "But I'm even more convinced now that we can win this case," she insists, checking Tyler who most certainly will motion his approval for almost anything she proposes.

In the hotel room, Papa Leo sits up and tosses one of those cautious eyebrows in the air as he listens to her zeal to 'win' the case. Kate continues over the phone.

"Even if we don't care about the money, it sends a strong signal," Kate says as Papa Leo shoots a concerned eye to his grandson. *"It might be we'll have to take it to judgment before they give in,"* she says hopefully. But Papa Leo rotates his head like a wolf hearing a distant intruder. Lightfoot wonders silently, then shares the old man's concern with a wince.

At the table, Mary also studies Kate's newly lawyered confidence as she continues to state *her case.*

"Just don't rule out winning in court first," Kate adds, gently debating her point. "I really believe the world is ready for a hero, someone who possesses the resources to finally bite back in a big way," she says, wrapping up her closing argument. Kate, Mary and Tyler wait around the table for what feels like an eternity before Lightfoot responds.

"*Sounds great!*" he says, much too simply, if not noncommittal. "*We'll be back home in a few hours. Hey Mary?*" Lightfoot asks. Mary retrieves the phone and disengages the speaker.

"Hey hon. I'm off speaker so you can talk freely about Tyler now," she says, but Kate isn't fooled. Tyler is clueless of course to any complications, and laughs at Mary's humor.

Back in the hotel room, Papa Leo is examining the contents of the mini bar as the conversation wraps up. He flips a tube of Pringles around, comparing it to a lovemaking kit in another tube, as Lightfoot continues offline to Mary.

"I'm worried that by hoping to get a deal before going to trial, it's going to be a blow to her as a lawyer," Lightfoot says. "Now that she has something to prove. Lawyer's are wired to win, even if it means settling out of court." Papa Leo glances away from the packaged items to share a look with his grandson.

But Mary smiles at Kate while responding to Lightfoot's concern on the other end of the line.

"Yeah I know, she's amazing isn't she. Really glad she's on our side," Mary says keenly, perfectly selling it to Kate who now blushes appropriately. "I love you too Billy, see you soon." Mary hangs up as Kate gathers her battle plans into a neat pile. Tyler jumps to assist when he notices Mary begin to lift herself out of the chair.

"No, no, thank you," Mary insists. She looks at Kate warmly. "I have to check in on some of the parents of the boys who died. I was hoping I could introduce them to you guys."

Back at the hotel, Lightfoot looks over to find Papa Leo lifting a couple geometrically perfect Pringles chip from the can, comparing the identical chips to each other.

"Well. What do you think?" Lightfoot asks as his grandfather chomps down on one of the chips. Papa Leo's eyes seem to indicate that they're not all that bad. He tries another chip before answering with a full mouth.

"It's pretty clear she sounds more like a dog with a bone, than one running with the pack," he says while blowing a few crumbs out in the process.

SIXTEEN

"Okaadakik"

(The Treaty Kettle)

Mary sits on the porch with the parents of two brothers killed in the attack. Kate and Tyler are nearby, silently watching as the grieving mother remembers her two boys. She's a small but strong woman with a long black mane of hair, tied in a loose ponytail, which she nervously braids as she speaks.

"Jimmy and Noodin are so proud, I know they are happy where they are now," she tells Mary. "They watch over us, and..." reaching over to touch Mary's hand, "they love our Professor Billy." Her husband places his hand over hers, nodding in agreement. "I know they died so that we would live to be free," the woman says. Mary gently kisses her forehead, looking deeply into her eyes before motioning to Kate and Tyler.

"Our brother and sister, Tyler and Kate are helping to tell the boys' story. To hold those responsible for their crimes," Mary explains, while knowing exactly

how the mother will respond. But the woman bears
no bitterness, no anxiety for revenge or longing for
closure. Her closure came the hour her beautiful boys'
spirit left to the happy place together.

"We don't seek revenge in our boys' name, we all
just want to be left alone to live our own lives, by
our own dreams. Peace and dignity cannot live with
revenge," she states. Her husband clenches her hand
a bit tighter, struggling to feel the same by the look in
his eyes. Kate tries to reconcile such a position against
her desire to strike back.

❖　❖　❖

Mary and Kate walk together toward the next
home while Tyler lags behind on the phone.

"I couldn't be so forgiving," Kate confesses. "I
mean, don't get me wrong, it's truly honorable, but
these criminals are taking advantage of their honor
and passivity, just as they have for years. Sometimes
bad people need to pay for their crimes," Kate insists.
Instead, Mary just smiles, pointing to an old man who
opens his door to greet them.

"Ogichidaa, good morning my brother!" Mary calls
out from the walkway. Kate considers the mountain
of a man, standing nearly seven feet tall with hands as
wide as most men's head. Mary leans over to Kate.

"Ogichidaa means warrior," Mary explains. "His

son, Nibaa Little Bear was standing closest to the explosion when it hit. There wasn't enough of him to recover for the service. You would think his father would be furious," Mary explains, all the while setting Kate's heart up for an awakening. Tyler finishes his call, stows his phone and catches up as Mary introduces both of them to the big fellow.

"Kate, Tyler, meet Ogichidaa Little Bear. His son was taken in the attack," Mary explains. "Our friends are helping with our bid for independence," Mary explains to the father. Kate reaches out with her hand.

"Mister Little Bear, I'm so sorry, Sir. We are working hard to get justice for your boy," Kate says sincerely. But like the mother of the other two boys, Ogichidaa sees these events through different lenses, focused far beyond retribution.

"His murderers have already been judged," Ogichidaa declares. "My son's spirit has left them behind to suffer in their own prison, when they could have known him and learned from his kindness. They've lost bitterly." But Kate needs to know for herself.

"Don't you want these people, the monsters that did this horrible thing, punished for their crimes?" Kate asks.

"Punished?" the father questions. "Punished by who?"

"Well, by the courts, they broke the law," Kate exclaims.

"White man's laws are already broken. And they certainly can't bring Nibaa back, so what good are these laws?" Kate can barely move. She stands stupefied and breathing heavily. Mary gives the enormous man a bear hug. He looks down at her belly. "I would be honored to sponsor your child at the ceremony, little Bearheart. If you'll have me?" Ogichidaa offers kindly, possibly even needing a connection to a new life. Mary is so touched, she takes the man's massive paw in hers and kisses the back of it.

"We would be so happy for that. You would be a very wise guide, Ogichidaa." Tyler leans into Kate and whispers.

"Man, I'm having a tough time holding it together right now," he says, while gently shaking the awe from his ears. He glances at Kate, who can only stand by silently, her arms hanging at her side. Yet in all this, a cloud of restlessness still gnaws at her. Even when faced with such unimaginable insight and forgiveness, Kate still fights with a desperate need to win – at something.

❖　❖　❖

Senator Finkle arrives at the local Minnesota Power station, nearest the Red Rock reservation. The engineer hands Senator Finkle a white safety helmet, which he places awkwardly over his greying nap of thick curly hair.

"How do I look?" he asks a female aide that follows him around the power station.

"Absurd," she admits. Finkle knocks on the top of the hat with his knuckles.

"They should make kippahs out of this stuff," the senator suggests.

"What's a kippah," the engineer asks innocently. Having gone off script enough, Finkle dodges to refocus on the purpose of the trip.

"So, let's see what our Red Rock folks are up to," Finkle says. "Can you show me how much electricity they are actually generating?"

"Certainly," the engineer says. "Take a look over here." He walks the delegation to a workstation which displays nodes and connections across the entire Northern Minnesota area. Finkle's hard hat tumbles off his head when he leans in but he manages to catch it just in time. "See, right there," says the young engineer. "That's the input from Red Rock, nearly two thousand megawatts."

"So, how much is that worth?" Finkle asks, not knowing a megawatt from a lightbulb.

"That's enough electricity to power over three hundred thousand homes. Just from their four generators," the engineer replies, appearing just as shocked as the senator is at the moment.

"Holy shit!" Senator Finkle bellows.

"Yeah, exactly," the engineer agrees. "And that's from only four grams of their fuel element. Which I'm told will last twenty, maybe thirty years!" Finkle opens his mouth to speak, but finds himself entirely mute. "And they're giving it to us for half the cost of any other facility on the grid," the engineer adds. Finkle pulls up a chair and flops into it with such force it rolls backwards a couple feet while dragging his shaky legs along the floor.

"And you've been there?" Finkle asks.

"Jeremy has, it's his account," the engineer notes, nodding to Jeremy, the worker who appeared with Lightfoot on camera nearly two years ago. Finkle stares at the flow statistics, which continue counting upwards at an accelerated rate.

"I need to meet them," Senator Finkle says. "Can you take me there?"

❖   ❖   ❖

Flying quickly over thick cumulous cloud tops that extend off to meet the horizon, the Red Rock Airbus begins to settle lower into the clouds. Soon, only the dark eagle graphic that covers the wingspan is visible, as the surrounding white fuselage begins to blend into the clouds creating an optical illusion of a giant eagle in the air. That was Papa Leo's idea.

The woodsy interior of the plane and the hand woven rugs that line the aisles, as well as the bright earthen colors and pictographs along the walls were also added upon his insistence in a way to thumb his nose at the extravagance. As it turns out, this was a bold statement from a satirical old man, and not the weak attempt at over-compensation that Kate attributed to Lightfoot. Papa Leo watches his grandson, soundly sleeping and dressed as a farm hand, apparently unaffected by the immense wealth that surrounds him. And if there were any doubt of that, the baby goat the flight attendant chases down the aisle certainly reinforces the idea.

"Prepare for landing," the pilot calls over the intercom. Lightfoot opens his eyes, bewildered and disoriented, still not used to waking up in a private jet. He lifts his shade, and squints into the blinding light before pulling it back down again. He looks up to notice his grandfather sitting straight-backed, boots flat on the ground and his hands folded in his lap. The goat bleats from the back of the plane as the flight attendant moves him into his cage.

"What's up with the goat?" Lightfoot asks, knowing full well it has something to do with his grandfather.

"Therapy pet!" the old man replies, motioning to

the flight attendant. Lightfoot lifts his shoulders with
a *why not?* and closes his eyes again. Papa Leo looks
out the window, watching the green forest appear as
the plane descends through the clouds.

"It's still hard to believe, isn't it? Lightfoot considers
aloud with his eyes still closed.

"Only when the last tree has died and the last river
has been poisoned and the last fish has been caught,
will we realize we cannot eat money," Papa Leo utters
in typical proverbial fashion.

❖ ❖ ❖

Mary bumps around the kitchen, preparing a meal
when Lightfoot enters. He drops his bag on the floor
and moves quickly to embrace her before she can
even remove the spoon from the pot. He kisses her
playfully, then places his hands on her tummy and
lowers his head to speak to the little person inside.

"I missed you both," he whispers to her stomach.

"You hungry?" Mary asks, while holding the
wooden spoon away to avoid dripping it on his head.

"Yeah, Granddad and I didn't really eat anything
since last night. Well, he did raid the mini bar of all
the chips and granola bars.

"That's all?" she laughs.

"I sort of got him drunk at dinner, yeah I think
that's all he was up to today," Lightfoot admits. "How

are you feeling?" he asks quickly, before she can scold him for getting his grandfather shit-faced.

"Good, seven more days," she says. "Oh, and Ogichidaa Little Bear, Tyler and Kate will be sponsors at the naming ceremony."

"Kate offered?" he asks before quickly realizing the unfortunate sound of surprise in his response.

"I asked her," Mary says, returning her spoon to the soup. "You're worried about her aren't you?" she asks while stirring the pot. Lightfoot pulls up a stool and rests his elbows on the counter to hold his weary head in his hands.

"I don't know if worried is the right word. I *am* concerned that she needs to win. I get that. She's a lawyer now and we're using her to just soften them up, so that we have something to bargain with. I'm thinking maybe we're not being fair to her." Mary covers the pot and leans over the counter, as best she can, touching her nose to his.

"She's never let go, you know that don't you?" she says kindly. He nods, knowing she's right.

"Yeah, another reason why I'm feeling guilty, like I'm using her loyalty. There's nothing in it for her. She needs something of her own. If they do take our offer, we call her off. I don't know, I feel like I made a mess of things." Mary leans in and kisses his eyes, which he closes just prior.

"And you?" she asks.

"Me? Me what?" Lightfoot asks, hoping she isn't asking what he thinks she is.

"She's a good woman, Billy. I know you still care for her and yeah, I know not like you care for me. But I just want you to know I get it," Mary says with the confidence and maturity of an ancient soul. "You need to go to her, talk it out, or it will eat you both alive. And I love you too much to see you struggle with it." Lightfoot rattles his head from side to side in total awe. He settles his eyes on her smile and scans every inch of her face.

"I love you Mary Bearheart. Will you marry me?"

"You asked me that already," she giggles.

"I know, I just want to hear you say yes, twice." Suddenly Mary remembers something.

"Oh!" she jolts, as does he when she scurries around the island to the small table by the phone. "I almost forgot!" she says, grabbing a note from the table. "Remember that senator that went off on the Bureau and the evil Doctor Drummond at the senate hearing? Senator Finkle?"

"Yeah, sure – love him," Lightfoot says, straightening upright with curiosity.

"He wants to come by tomorrow, see the Power Plant, and talk to you. With the Minnesota Power guys too!" Mary hands him the note. "I told him you'd let him know tonight when you got back from D.C." she says.

"He knows I was in D.C.?"

"Yeah, is that okay?" Mary says, cringing a bit.

"That's perfect! Just ups our credibility and if he's such a fan, we might be able to get him to apply some pressure from his end," Lightfoot says while looking at the note. "This is great!"

"Give him a call," she says handing him the phone. "I'll finish dinner."

❖   ❖   ❖

Kate and Tyler walk along the shoreline together. Tyler holds his empty beer bottle to his lips, trying to blow a tune in the neck.

"There was this guy at MIT that could play *Seek and Destroy* from Metallica on a beer bottle," Tyler mentions, while trying to squeak out even a single note. "It was better than the original."

"The MIT students were the craziest people I ever met," Kate says.

"Students?" Tyler spouts. "It was Doctor Kerns, head of the Math Department. The students were the normal ones."

"You're incriminating yourself, Professor," Kate blathers from the single beer and lack of sleep. She watches Tyler continue to try and form a note, while laughing at his miserable attempt. "Give it up," she says, before suddenly stumbling over a piece of driftwood, "Ahaahaah!" Tyler drops the bottle and rescues her inches from the ground. He lifts her back up to her feet. "I'm cool, I'm cool," she says, trying to convince herself more than him.

"You know, you really were awesome on the phone with those feds," Tyler says. "No seriously, if it wasn't for you, none of this would be possible." He watches as his words have the opposite effect than he had hoped. She swigs the last of her beer in an attempt to cover. "I'm sorry Kate. I meant that as a good thing." He turns his head sideways to look up at her hanging head. "Kate, look at me." She looks at him for certain, truly for the first time since she's known Tyler. Without any warning, she leans in and delivers in one kiss all the passion she's reserved for every perfect man she fantasized about since she was twelve. Tyler is happy to reciprocate as both fall to their knees in the sand, ripping at each other like wild ducks.

From the line of trees near the power station, the three Loon sisters stand in a row, silently watching the action at the shoreline. They each puff from their E-cigs and watch stoically as Kate and Tyler sink lower into the sand, entwined in a mass of arms and legs.

❖   ❖   ❖

"It's pretty simple really," Lightfoot admits to the awestruck and still confounded Senator. Finkle follows along as Lightfoot gives a tour of the power plant and motions through the process of generating electricity. "The protons travel down this path, to strike the fuel element in a reaction chamber inside that boiler over there," he explains while walking down the length of the particle accelerator tube. Finkle begins to realize the significance of how such a simple design can rival that of a larger nuclear or hydro station. "When the reaction chamber heats up, it radiates heat from a heating element sphere inside the water tank. That's what boils the water and the steam turns the turbine which produces electricity. Really, it's not unlike a nuclear power plant, except in this case we use a very small amount of electricity to elevate a very small amount of the raw element to produce a *massive* amount of heat.

"Except this clean?" Finkle considers "This has no radioactive waste?"

"Exactly," Lightfoot confirms. Finkle mulls over the sight of the huge Harvey Bearheart, rough hewn and standing firmly at the end of the line in his white lab coat and work boots. There isn't a modicum of pretention or extravagance amid the immense wealth of these people, Finkle thinks. Harvey Bearheart nods upward towards the senator as they arrive at the generator.

"We watched what you said at the hearing. Thank you," Harvey Bearheart says, while extending his enormous hand. The senator tilts upward to shake the human sequoia's hand, like a child meeting the Hulk at Comicon.

"You're welcome," Finkle replies. "So, how's the weather up there?" the senator quips with a goofy charm, causing the burly guy to crow at the little fellow's humor.

"Harvey Bearheart is our chief mechanical engineer and master chef," Lightfoot mentions. Finkle quickly shifts to the foremost concern among them.

"Regarding your proposal to the U.N.," the senator says, noticing the start in Lightfoot's eye. "Yeah, I know, word travels fast," Finkle says. "Look, we all know that our state, any state, has no jurisdiction over tribal matters. That's for the feds. I get all that. But as the Senator of this state, I should be asking you to consider our proud support for you remaining a part of Minnesota," Finkle says, while raising his left palm into the air. "Now on one hand, I shouldn't want Red Cliff to break away as it were, and leave this state because you're an example of the kind of change this country needs to champion," Finkle explains before raising the other hand. "On the other hand, and off the record, I want you to know that whatever happens with your desire for international recognition, I will do everything I can to help. Either as an ally and neighbor to your great nation, or as your senator," Finkle says.

"Can I ask you a question?" Harvey Bearheart says.

"Certainly," the senator replies.

"What do you think is the best for us, assuming some day our children may not have someone as honorable as you representing the state?" Harvey Bearheart asks with a question that seems to answer itself. Finkle's face twists a bit.

"Wow. I guess if you could manage to get the U.S. to allow your plea to move to the General Assembly, then go for it," Finkle says. "But even if it did get that far, I'm just not convinced the GA will vote your way." But Lightfoot hopes the United States government feels the same way, and therefore agrees to let their application go before all the member nations.

"That's a chance I'm willing to take," Lightfoot says.

❖   ❖   ❖

Over the next few weeks, all the forces came to bear on the U.S., in a blurring montage of publicity, legal moves, international pressure and olive branches, all designed to release the Red Rock Chippewa tribe from their bindings to the federal government. Ultimately the State Department agreed to step aside from their Security Council veto, allowing the recommendation of statehood to proceed to the General Assembly for a vote of all one hundred and ninety-three nations, many of which were benefactors of the new *Ishkode* fuel source. And it certainly isn't lost on the other nations of the world that the price they pay now, is sure to be less than if the United States controlled access to the fuel source.

❖   ❖   ❖

Miss Achambo's class of students ranges from eight to twelve years old, all under one roof in the same modest classroom. This is probably the only institution at Red Rock, still unchanged by the influx of riches. As far as she was concerned, this simple method of learning has worked to create some of the most thoughtful and intuitive minds so far, including their cherished Professor Billy, so why change now? Today, she gives one of her highly animated lessons on government and commerce. By the sight of the little minds leaning forward in their chairs, she's successfully working the room with arresting skill. Watching her pace from one wall to the other while emphasizing simple learning, it becomes clear how her influence shaped Lightfoot's teaching style.

"Can you imagine what it would be like visiting the earth from another planet, never having seen the place before?" Miss Achambo asks the class. "If you showed up a few million years ago, you'd see giant bird-like beasts called dinosaurs running all over the place and little monkey-like creatures trying to avoid being eaten or stepped on," Miss Achambo says, to the laughter in the room. "Or, maybe you came to earth millions of years later, when all those huge beasts died off, and their bodies turned to thick black liquid oil to be captured underground," Miss Achambo says, spinning around with her arms stretched outward to the class, a dramatic gesture she used often to impart her contagious enthusiasm. "It might even impress you how much these little monkey people could do simply by lighting the dead dinosaur oil on fire. It wasn't long before the little monkey people made cars that burned the oil, electrical generators that burned the oil, planes and jets that burned oil, plastics made of oil. A whole world, powered and propelled by dead dinosaur goo!" she says, pausing momentarily for effect and to catch the eyes of the little learners. "Well, I think you'd be amazed! I think these space travelers would be even more shocked to see how hard the little monkey people fought to control the dead dinosaur juice. Soon, they invented another explosive substance called gunpowder that could be used to throw pieces of metal at each other so some of the little monkey people could keep all that dead dinosaur oil to themselves." Miss Achambo walks through the classroom now, stopping at the desk of one of the older students, little Anna Bearheart.

"Miss Bearheart, can you tell us why our little tribe of monkey people is becoming so popular around the world right now?" the teacher asks. Anna is happy to share.

"Because you can only get *Ishkode* on our land and it's better than oil. We have what everyone wants, and it's better than burning dead dinosaurs," the mini Bearheart proposes.

"Good!" Miss Achambo says then spins back to address the class. "And does anyone remember what the rule of business is, that allows us to share our *Ishkode* with the world?" she asks, then points to a young boy.

"Supply and demand?" the proud fellow states with a tinge of question in his voice.

"You are correct, mister Lone Wolf," Achambo exclaims, while thrusting a pointed finger high into the air. "Supply and Demand! Never since the discovery of fossil fuels has a single resource promised to change so much for so many people," she insists. "Now, we have a choice, don't we? We can use gunpowder to defend our *supply* against enemies with more gunpowder, or we can satisfy the *demand* and make friends in the process," Miss Achambo proposes. She nearly runs back at the chalkboard. "When we satisfy demand, this is what we call, *TRADE*," she says, scribing the word across the board in large letters.

❖   ❖   ❖

"Where did you learn to cook like that?" Kate asks, while helping in the kitchen.

"You don't have to look beyond my dad's belly to know my mom's a rock star cook," Mary suggests as she pulls a tray from the oven.

"My dad raised my sister and I," Kate mentions. "He used to cook hot dogs in the toaster," Kate admits. "Three in each side, two for each of us – done!"

"That's a great idea! I never thought of that," Mary exclaims, sincerely appreciating the urban genius.

"Oh you say that now. Try that three days a week. That was unless my grandma stopped by with a vat of *cullen skink* and *clooties*," Kate recalls fondly. Lightfoot and Tyler filter through a box of old photos nearby while snacking on a bowl of peanuts.

"What's a 'clootie'?" Tyler asks from across the room.

"And, cullen sink?" Mary wonders while blowing on a hot spoon of something on the stove.

"Cullen *skink*. It's like a fish stew, with haddock

and potatoes," Kate replies. She turns to Tyler, who's still hung up on the 'clootie' concept. "Clootie is a dumpling with sugar and raisins. Total Scottish thing," Kate says. Mary regards Kate's wild mop of fire red hair.

"Scottish. That's where the beautiful hair comes from then," Mary says, causing Kate to blush again. Tyler lifts a dog-eared snapshot from the box and flips it over to read the back.

"No way?" Tyler blurts into the box of photos. "It says Papa Leo! This kid has to be no more than fifteen!" The photo shows a handsome Chippewa boy posing for the camera and staring with those familiar eyes, directly at the observer from behind years of yellowed resin.

"That's him all right," Lightfoot confirms. "He told me about that day. A lady from the Smithsonian was recording tribal history, Frances Densmore - she was pretty famous. She died about fifty years ago. She recorded ceremony songs and even dreams and visions by getting the clan leaders to talk and sing into this huge flower shaped phonograph."

"Check this out" Tyler says, holding the shot over the counter for Kate and Mary. Kate takes the picture and examines the inscription.

"Nineteen thirty-six?" Kate tries to finger count. "That's..."

"Eighty-one years ago," Tyler calculates instantly. Kate looks at him in awe.

"That was quick," she says as Tyler grins smugly.

"Math's my thing," Tyler boasts while cracking another peanut shell from the bowl. "Wait, if he's fifteen in that shot, how old is he?" Tyler asks.

"Pushing one-hundred, but no one knows for sure," Lightfoot says.

"Shiiiiiit!" Tyler mumbles, fixated on the photo. "Wow, I hope I'm in that good of shape when I'm that old."

"You're not in that good of shape now," Kate snorts. Tyler throws a peanut at her. Mary notices the affection forming between the two and looks to Lightfoot to share the thought, when she notices him stop cold while rummaging through the memento box. Slowly he lifts out a carved stone token, threaded with a long leather cord. He stares at it in his hand. Mary stops cooking to watch him, haunted by the small charm. Kate follows her gaze, to find Lightfoot lost quietly in thought.

"What's that?" Tyler asks laughingly, not always as keen to social cues.

"It was my mom's," Lightfoot says, without looking up from the stone in his hand. The medicine man placed it around her neck at her naming ceremony when she was born." He looks up to Mary in disbelief.

"This should have been buried with her remains." Lightfoot rolls the cord around the token and places it in his shirt pocket. Buttoning it closed, he pats the pocket to his heart. Suddenly sensitive to the heavy tone in the room, Lightfoot looks up and out of the daze. "You guys hungry?"

❖   ❖   ❖

Lightfoot splashes more wine into ancient ceramic cups as he circles the table. Most everyone has finished eating and are now leaning back into their chairs and toasting to another refill. Everyone except Tyler that is, who dives into a platter of second portions.

"This is great Mary. You're an amazing cook!" Tyler says through a full mouth.

"Where do you put it? You're so thin!" Mary claims, as everyone watches him eat.

"My mom used to say I had a hollow leg," he says.

"Go ahead Kate, sorry to interrupt," Lightfoot says, finally taking his seat again. Kate continues with her story, which she paused only to receive another refill of wine.

"I'm just saying, that it's not right for that Drummond jackass or the crooks he's in with, to get away with murder. I still think there's nothing wrong with winning," she says, as assertively as she can.

"I hear you Kate. But there's a difference between

winning and punishment," Lightfoot counters. "We will *win* our freedom and the right to better the lives of thousands of people. Now that we've cleared the Security Council, and the U.N. can finally vote for our membership. And if it's determined that his actions resulted in a tribe winning real nation status and slicing a section of land off of the United States, he will certainly be sidelined. The Corps will be ridiculed in the media, and the BIA might even lose their authority over the tribes. All because the civil case you built is powerful enough to force their hand and let us go. Justice over Drummond could very well become a by product of winning our freedom and sovereignty. That is real justice," Lightfoot insists.

"No, that's plea bargaining," she argues. "And what if this deal with the U.S. allows the vote to go to the General Assembly and it's ultimately rejected? Then you're left with no justice, and no freedom!" Kate takes a moment to sip her wine while the table considers the point. Then she decides to change strategy. "William, let me ask you a question. What do you think those Los Alamos scientists and the military want the element for?"

"Like everyone else, it's an unlimited fuel source, and frankly we haven't even tapped the gravity propulsion implications yet," Lightfoot states which for him seems obvious. "Its power surpasses anything on earth." But Kate isn't buying it and everyone in the room can feel something else coming.

"And that's it?" she asks rhetorically, preparing to venture into the next point without waiting for the answer. "You know as well as anyone, they want to weaponize it. That's the very reason we've added the clause, 'for peaceful purposes only' when we just allowed the U.S. to have access?" Kate sums it up, "You said it yourself, this is a 'total annihilation reaction', right? That's what makes it so powerful? So what if they make a bomb with it? That's all I'm saying. We need to take Drummond out of the mix. He needs to go to jail." Mary watches as he struggles between considering her point and weighing her argument against her burning desire to win the case. Tyler gulps back a swig of beer as he glances from side to side.

"Say something as big as a kilo of the stuff were to totally convert to energy, all at once," Tyler asks. "I mean, completely reacting with the matter surrounding it. Like a hydrogen gas or something. How big of a blast would that be anyway?" Lightfoot calculates this in his head, wondering as well if his struggle with Kate's argument includes the possibility of wrestling with his own conscience.

"Hypothetically, if a kilo of *Ishkode* were to fully react?" Lightfoot confirms, before adding the disclaimer. "Albeit an extremely difficult process and would require a wide particle bombardment. But okay, if all of it were to convert to antimatter at the same time - sure it could react with any matter surrounding it and produce the force of... a hundred maybe a hundred and fifty nuclear bombs, the size of Hiroshima," he admits.

"You're fucking kidding me?" Tyler gulps in total disbelief.

"But like I said," Lightfoot seeks to remind them. "It would take a collider the size of a city to do it," he says. Kate seems to settle into a quiet calm that only comes with the catharsis of being proven right.

"Don't you think that's exactly what they want it for?" She says softly, resting her case. Mary stands suddenly, with an expression of shock that quickly turns to awe, that serendipitous type of surprise that comes with knowing...

"It's time," Mary says calmly, gently grasping her belly. Kate and Tyler panic and spring up into action, but then freeze with wide, readied hands and not yet knowing what to do with them. Lightfoot on the other hand moves calmly to Mary's side and walks her out of the room. Kate and Tyler call to them from the dining room.

"Oh my God!" Kate exclaims. She looks to Tyler for some kind of support, but he's vapor-locked in the center of the dining room.

"What do we do?" he asks. "Do we drive somewhere, the hospital – how far is it?"

"Mid wives," Kate explains.

"What?" Tyler blurts.

"Mid wives, they do it here with members of the tribe," she says.

"That's insane, no way?" Tyler calls out. "They're not going to the hospital?" he yells, entirely unprepared for the concept of natural childbirth.

❖   ❖   ❖

Papa Leo rides his pony deep into the woods while shafts of late afternoon sunlight snap on and off between the birch trees. His horse stops at the edges of a fresh flowing stream and pauses to drink. The old man looks up river, enough of a gesture to prompt the mare to turn and follow his gaze upstream, along the water's edge. Her hooves splash in the shallow water, the flow of which increases as they get closer to the scent of smoldering sage. Papa Leo spies the smoke of a campfire through the slits of birch and maple trees ahead.

At the creek's edge the old medicine woman sits alone on a woven blanket. She faces a small but warming fire, surrounded by a day's worth of glowing embers. The old woman's eyes are closed and her back straight. She rests her arms on her knees and in her right hand she holds a tied bundle of smoking sage. She's wrapped in skins, furs and yes, her favorite MIT blanket, which Lightfoot gave her a couple years back. The old woman chants a series of names, first facing forward and then to each side. "Ayasha, Ayashe, Cholena, Kanti, Migisi, Namid." Over and over she repeats this string of names, each time lifting her hand to allow the smoldering bundle of sage to waft around her head and rise to the canopy of leaves above. The sharp but peaceful sound of a broken branch catches her ear, as the settle of a horse's hoof in the moist soil causes her to open her eyes gently. She smiles and greets the familiar visitor approaching from behind, while still facing forward.

"Nimishoomis, you were always good at arriving undetected, but your horse is limping," she says.

"Aren't we all, old woman," Papa Leo says as he slowly dismounts. He walks over and sits on the blanket next to her. Fondly, he inhales the scent of the smoke.

"I remember the first time I smelled sage," Papa Leo reminisces as the two elders face the trickling waters of the stream.

"I was there Nimishoomis, at your naming ceremony, but you were only a week old," she says before closing her eyes again.

"I still remember," Papa Leo says. "The older I

become and the further away from my childhood I travel, the more vivid it appears," he says before turning to watch his friend, sitting with her eyes closed. "Have you been given a name, old woman?" The healer turns to him and opens her eyes again.

"Migisi," she states affirmably.

"Eagle," Papa Leo confirms, nodding his head in approval, then once again letting the sound play to his ears. "Migisi." Papa Leo pulls himself up, these days with a little more effort. "The winds are coming soon, let's get you back to the village," he says, holding his strong wrinkled palm out, into which she places her even more aged and bony hand. Papa Leo looks at her silently for a moment, seeing as it were a life of friendship and memories of the many times she set his bones, and relieved the pain.

"What are you looking at?" the old healer barks affectionately.

"A lifetime, old woman. A beautiful life." He gathers her blankets and begins gently kicking out her fire as she walks to his horse.

"Old girl," she says to the pony, as she strokes the mare's nose. The pony nuzzles her neck, as if to say, 'back at you.'" Smiling slightly, the healer turns as Papa Leo approaches.

"What did she tell you?" he asks, nodding to his

mare. The old woman pats Papa Leo's tummy, which is starting to protrude lately.

"She said you're breaking her back and need to lay off the Moosehead." Papa Leo just breathes deeply and interlocks his palms into a stirrup for her foot, as he lifts her up and onto the pony's back.

❖   ❖   ❖

Gathered around a hearth of smoldering sage, members of the tribe watch as the healer performs the ritual of the Naming Ceremony. She burns tobacco while offering its smoke to the sky, and begins pronouncing the name she was given in her dream.

"Migisi," she says to the south then turning to the north, "Migisi," she pronounces the name again. She follows by offering the name two more times, once to the east, "Migisi" and finally to the west "Migisi," she calls until the spirit world accepts and can recognize the face of the child who Mary holds in her arms. Lightfoot stands at Mary's side, boldly observing the traditions of his ancestors, while viewing with fondness the rituals that for once, don't seem to conflict with his views as a scientist. "The spirit world and our ancestors recognize this child for the first time, and have begun to guard her through life, while preparing a place for her when her life shall end," the healer explains. She turns to the observers and opens both palms, revealing nine tokens – small stone carvings of an eagle in flight, each attached to a leather cord. Lightfoot steps forward and the old woman hands the tokens to him. He places one of the tokens across the bundle that swaddles the beautiful little girl in Mary's arms. He then steps to a line of four men and four women, including Kate, Tyler and Little Deer. Moving down the line, he places a token around the neck of each of the eight sponsors. Tyler lifts his token, examining the intricacies of the carving.

"Cool!" Tyler exclaims. Lightfoot pats his shoulder, then turns back to place his arm around Mary and face the entire group of sponsors.

"We ask you to guide our little Eagle through her life," he says, as he receives the nods of acceptance from each of them. With her head still facing down toward her daughter, Mary lifts her eyes to see Kate reach to the side to hold Tyler's hand.

❖   ❖   ❖

Concurrently and across the continent in Los Alamos, Doctor Drummond is unfurling his hideous wings once again, in a meeting of scientists and facility engineers.

"We need a containment chamber if we're going to pound this shit with the collider," a young scientist explains emphatically to Drummond, who half listens while studying some equations on a whiteboard.

"Huh?" Drummond turns, snapping out of his daze of calculations.

"Sir, I'm saying we can't just bombard this stuff in the existing containment apparatus if you want to hit it with such a wide beam," the young scientist presses further.

"So build a bigger containment chamber," Drummond says dismissively. But the scientist isn't accepting the doctor's flippant remarks with blind obedience.

"That's easily said. I'm serious about this, it would be more prudent to do this underground, at the test site in Nevada," the concerned fellow insists. But Drummond loses his patience with the underling's over-sensitive intrusion into his thought process.

"And how do you propose we expose it to acceleration underground?" Drummond snarls at the safety-conscious scientist, who at this point has had it with the the doctor's dismissals.

"Why not just tape the stuff to the side of a small nuke. You know the output you'd expect, you know the amount of protons that are emitted, we just measure the offset – safely!" Again Drummond brushes off the scientist's caution.

"You're over-thinking it," the maniacal doctor

protests. "Just build the containment chamber, make it ten feet thick if you want, and place it at the end of the collider. Done!"

"If there's any matter, any gas at all in that chamber this could go super critical," he retorts again, clearly not giving up. Except this time, it's Drummond who explodes with the force of a megaton bomb.

"Fucking stop! Are you not listening to me?" The young scientist stops, staring at the impulsive doctor with resigned indignation.

"Yes Sir, I am. That's the problem," he replies, then turns and leaves Doctor Drummond alone to fiddle with the whiteboard.

"Pussies," Drummond mumbles, while erasing a formula on the board and replacing it with another.

SEVENTEEN

"Dibendaagozi"

(Becoming a member)

Papa Leo nudges Harvey Bearheart in the ribs as a United Nations officer and an official escort, lead Lightfoot on stage near the podium of the General Assembly. The escort motions for him to have a seat next to the Secretary General. The General Assembly President stands at the podium, preparing to bring the session to order.

"Today the Assembly will hear an address by Professor William Lightfoot, of the newly declared Republic of Tribal Peoples," the General Assembly President announces to the full room of voting nations.

Mary, Tyler and Kate sit alongside the two elders in the mezzanine to the right of the platform, anxiously waiting for their champion to take the world stage.

"On behalf of the General Assembly," the Assembly President continues, "I have the honor to welcome to the United Nations, Professor William Lightfoot." The speaker motions to Lightfoot, "Professor, you have the podium."

In the back and along the mezzanine, people of all nations have come to observe what proves to be a most historic vote. Tonight, a star has risen as the leader of the most wealthy and influential *occupied nation*, appeals for sovereignty and world recognition. Lightfoot stands, feeling for a moment for his mother's token which hangs prominently over his suit and tie. He then takes his position at the podium and looks across the hall of nations, to the ambassadors and dignitaries, designated by a placard on each desk, stating their country's name.

"President of the General Assembly, Heads of State and delegations, Secretary General of the United Nations, distinguished guests, ladies and gentlemen," Lightfoot begins. He lifts his eyes to find Mary sitting next to Papa Leo who lifts his head higher, reminding his grandson to speak with boldness. "I am proud that my grandfather is here tonight," Lightfoot says, looking toward the mezzanine. "At ninety-seven years old, he remains the strongest, wisest and most kind man I have ever known. He is a proud man, ever aware of his heritage and the story of our people." Lightfoot turns to the assembly in a moment of silence to read the room. "My grandfather is born of a people that have been called by many names over the years. Some names I refuse to dignify, but there are those common terms we've all grown up with. Indians, Redskins, Alternative Etymology, Objections, First Peoples, Tribal People, and most recently, Native Americans. If you ask him, he will tell you that he is Ojibwa, more specifically of the Chippewa tribe, one tribal nation of many clans, the original inhabitants of the land that hosts this assembly today. As a child, I enjoyed his rich stories of hope and visions of a spirit world committed to guiding us through life. His stories also included the recollections of bold adventures, back breaking struggles and the glorious achievements of a people committed to learning. Then, there were those frightening tales, of nearly unspeakable atrocities committed by one breed of human against another. Yet even the most horrific of his stories were told to me as examples of the power of atonement over evil, triumphs over aggression by calling upon the strength of our better natures. Tonight, I'd like to highlight one such story, of a persecuted people who lived through the ravages of war and attempted genocide. This is a true story, of millions of innocent people, slaughtered in an attempt to eliminate them from the planet's surface. A story of an oppressed people who experienced massacres, torture, terror, sexual abuse, systematic military occupations, the removal of peoples from their ancestral territories, allotment, and a policy of termination." The young professor singles out various people in the assembly, speaking directly to each one after the other, instead of addressing the massive organism itself. "Imagine my horror. Why would he tell me this story at such a young age? Was it to militarize me, or instill hatred in my heart? Was he trying to indoctrinate my impressionable mind with some noble excuse for retribution? No. He was teaching me about the potential of love, about forgiveness and about the power of redemption. Yes, he was trying to teach me a lesson, of how a flower could grow from the ashes of a torched home. This was the very lesson that the descendants of the villains who perpetrated these crimes would learn as well. Where the sons and daughters of oppressors would grow to display remarkable courage to become the champions of the very human rights their parents ignored. A true story of frightful monsters who would bear better children, bravehearts of conscience, sickened by the concepts of hate and violence that permeated the generation before them. This was also a story of these descendants who proved that people are inherently good, and would instinctively display these qualities if not frightened into thinking they were better than another race. Yes, this was a true story of a nation who became a beacon of kindness, an example for all other nations. Descendants who today have sought to open their arms to the refugees of similar acts of violence throughout the world. The honorable, tolerant, inclusive, progressive descendants I speak of tonight, are the gracious and dignified people of modern Germany. The evolved children of a dark history of oppression committed against the twelve *tribes* of the Jewish people. Today, there is no greater example of fairness and inclusion than the nation of Germany."

From the reaction in the room, this was certainly not where they expected to be led when they followed Lightfoot along this tale. The hum and murmurs of epiphany reverberate across the audience like a distant rolling thunder off rock walls. Lightfoot singles out the German delegation, currently assigned by the rotating seating arrangement, to the desks near the front of the podium.

"This story was told to me, an eight-year-old Chippewa boy, not to toughen me up, but to strengthen my spirit. He knew the heritage of bitterness that consumed our people. Life on the reservation bore few examples of hope and faith in what our lives as 'Native Americans' could be. That story meant a lot to me as I grew up, and often when consumed with the fear and bitterness of reservation life, I would ask him to tell me that story again, the story of how I could too, join hands some day with the descendants of those who occupied our lands, and outlawed our way of life. It gave me hope in the progression of humanity, that history alone had no power over my will to succeed in life, to live with dignity, to excel and most importantly to move beyond my own sense of history, often crippled with resentment."

Lightfoot pauses to look up at the magnificent spherical ceiling, the dark center circle above the assembly floor, dotted with hundreds of spotlights, like eyes of the past, looking down on this profound moment in time. And in this arresting moment of pause, the audience shares his reflection, when soon a rolling and sober applause begins filling the chamber. He humbly lifts his hand to calm the room, while his eyes again find Papa Leo watching proudly from the wings. Lightfoot turns back to the assembly.

"In nineteen forty-eight, this body, this honorable experiment we call the United Nations chose to define the term genocide as an activity against a national, ethnic, racial, or religious group of people, to clear them from existence. In the year two thousand and six, the United Nations Permanent Forum on Indigenous Issues called upon western religious leaders to revoke and renounce the *Discovery Doctrine* that empowered European settlers of foreign lands with the pious destiny to inflict nearly five hundred years of slavery, *genocide* and a less than human identity on original peoples throughout the world. And in two-thousand and seven, this very body, the United Nations General Assembly voted to adopt the Declaration on the Rights of Indigenous Peoples. Article Three of that declaration states: 'All indigenous peoples have the right of self-determination. By virtue of that right they freely determine their political status and freely pursue their economic, social, and cultural development.'" Lightfoot stops to sink the next point into the record, by silently scanning the room for a long beat.

"And yet, the United States, Canada and Australia voted against it. Tonight however, we do not seek to condemn the history of the host nation. Instead, we seek an alliance with its descendants. We seek a real treaty, not one imposed upon the weak, or sold to the naïve, but a treaty between two sovereign nations, a treaty based on mutual respect and a treaty that promises to share in the blessings of the immense *resources* of each party, some of which just recently discovered - as many of you know."

Again, applause breaks out, more fervent and instantaneous than the previously rolling acknowledgement. This time, cheers rise from the assembly floor and even more surprising for the young professor, the audience begins to stand, first with the observers in the back rows and mezzanines, eventually flowing into the member area until the entire assembly is on their feet.

"We are the 'Republic of Tribal Peoples', " Lightfoot declares. "And tonight we seek your recognition, your support and the empowerment that only this body can give, by sending a clear and honorable message to our brothers and sisters to the north and south. The gracious and honorable descendants of a dark past, the recent majority of whom have shown us such kindness, friendship and dignity. We look forward to the honor of being a member of this great body and joining alongside our brothers and sisters in the effort to help improve this planet for all peoples. Thank you for the opportunity to address this great assembly," Lightfoot concludes, as diplomats, dignitaries continue standing and applaud the young professor. An applause that lasts nearly sixty seconds. During which the President of the General Assembly returns to the podium and shakes Lightfoot's hand.

"It appears you've made many friends tonight, Professor," he enthusiastically suggests. But was it enough? Lightfoot wonders.

❖   ❖   ❖

"*In a stunning vote tonight, the United Nations General Assembly welcomed the small Red Rock Chippewa nation of northern Minnesota as a permanent member nation,*" the news anchor announces, as the volume is turned up on the television screen. *"Tonight we have a panel of experts, gathered to discuss these historic events. Let's get to it. With me is Chief Political Analyst, Christen Mathers,"* the anchor states.

In his office, Senator Finkle smiles wittingly while watching the breaking news segment on screen.

"They did it! They really did it," Finkle exclaims while the segment continues on screen.

"So Christen – no one really thought this would happen, so how did it?"

❖　❖　❖

Mike Chambers and Deputy Director Smith aren't at all surprised as they watch the same report.

"Well that's exactly the question that everyone seems to be asking," Mathers says. *"For whatever reason, maybe due to intense international pressure, or impending lawsuits brought against the federal government by this now very wealthy Chippewa tribe, the U.S. decided to stand down in the Security Council and NOT veto the RTPs application for statehood."*

❖　❖　❖

Florian Mayer beams with satisfaction and pride as he watches the broadcast with his team at the lab in Darmstadt, Germany. Even Richter's hardened facial muscles struggle to pull into a wide, out-of-character grin, while entirely fixated on the news report.

"However, our sources tell us that the State Department never thought the vote would win in the main body, and felt that they had enough 'friends' among the other nations to make sure it didn't," the reporter continues.

❖　❖　❖

Amik joins a group of students around a laptop in the dorm, watching the same report streaming online. He holds his head up with both hands, his mouth hanging as he and the normally chatty group stare at the screen, entirely arrested by the implications.

"Basically, it was the impassioned plea, in the form of a magnificently crafted speech by Professor William Lightfoot, the leader of the tribe and former MIT Professor. The case was made that brilliantly supported the UN's continued efforts to promote the Indigenous Peoples Act passed nearly ten years ago, and designed to improve the lives of occupied tribes worldwide," Mathers claims.

❖　❖　❖

Papa Leo and Harvey Bearheart sit on the edge of the bed together, having gathered in Kate and Tyler's hotel room to watch the results.

"Where does that leave the United States then?" the news anchor asks.

"Uh oh, here it comes!" Tyler declares upon hearing the question of the century coming from the TV. He holds up a handful of small bottles that he's just retrieved from the mini-bar.

"*Ah, that's the rub,*" the reporter insists. "*They're stuck now. They've already tried to circumvent the law by force, and the public blow back 'forced' them into a hands-off situation. Now, it appears the Red Rock tribe will be able to actually secede from the Union, just like any State, theoretically can.*"

Lightfoot and Mary lean over the balcony, barely listening to the report coming from the room as Tyler and Kate joyously mix drinks in front of the television.

"Now what?" Mary asks, looking out over the balcony onto the Hudson river below.

"It won't be easy. Now I understand what Granddad was trying to tell me a while back about doing this for all the tribes, and not just our own. Navaho, Cherokee, Sioux, Cree, are all claiming precedent now for independence," Lightfoot says. Mary spins around to lean her back against the railing, watching Kate and Tyler toasting their plastic cups in the air while Papa Leo and Harvey Bearheart sit solemnly in front of the screen. She watches Tyler hand the two men a drink, which they take without removing their eyes from the broadcast.

"Can you imagine what's going through Papa Leo's

mind right now?" Mary asks. Lightfoot turns around to look into the room.

"Yeah, and your dad. I'm sure it hasn't sunk in yet," Lightfoot says.

"He never thought it would happen. He told me last night, not to get my hopes up," Mary says while chuckling at the sight of Kate and Tyler dancing around the two stoic elders.

"Did you?" Lightfoot asks.

"I was afraid to," Mary says, before considering her response. "Honestly, no... I didn't think they would really vote in our favor," Mary confesses, somewhat ashamed of her lack of faith. "You?" she asks, hoping he would share her surprise.

"I never thought I'd make it through the speech," he says. "I even had a dream I lost my voice in front of them. Like I opened my mouth and nothing came out while everyone was staring at me, Lightfoot admits."

"Were you nervous?" Mary asks.

"I was scared shitless," Lightfoot says. "My mom was there, though. Like when I was a kid, and too afraid to go to school because Lame Deer kept calling me a nerd.

"Wow, really. What did she tell you?" Mary asks.

"You mean, back then, in school?" he asks, to which she nods with that adorable grin. "She said, 'you are a nerd, *own it* and get your butt to school'."

Again, Lightfoot reaches for the token hanging from his neck. "And last night, she sort of said the same thing. I swear I could hear her tell me... when I looked out across all those nations, 'own it'." He turns back to Mary. "Weird huh?"

"No," Mary replies while spinning back to the Hudson. "You are a nerd." He wraps his arms around her while they watch a couple barges blare their horns and lumber together up the river.

❖　❖　❖

"No, no, no!" the headstrong lab official insists, while getting into Drummond's face. "All your bullying and pompous horseshit will not convince me to allow you to jeopardize the collider," the lab official says. Drummond rolls his eyes backwards into his skull and tilts his head up in petulant defiance. But the lab official continues to pound through his wall of ignorance. "If I catch you ordering my staff around again, I will report your ass to the Defense Secretary for censure". Drummond opens his eyes and slowly grins tauntingly.

"Are you done screaming at me?" he asks while playing the cool headed victim.

"Actually, no-I'm-not!" the official bellows. "You've already embarrassed this organization and I won't allow you or your reckless chums to compromise us any longer. You've been advised of the risks, and you still insist you can contain something you have no data on. Take your fucking marbles and go play at the test site and add to their craters if you want, but you're not doing it here," he says while well into stomping out the door. "You Jackass!" the lab official hollers, then slams the door so hard it fails to latch and swings back into the room. Drummond creases his lips and stretches his closed eyelids, a signature move of dismissal he's perfected with years of insisting he's right. Drummond dials a number on his cell and picks up one of the orange metal samples, examining it while he waits for an answer.

"Hey, ask Tamborro who's running the test site in Nevada these days. Call me back on my cell." CLICK.

❖   ❖   ❖

Papa Leo closes his eyes and breathes in the familiar afternoon updrafts off the water and wildflowers. With all that's changed over his lifetime, the scent of spring cuts through the years, transporting him to his childhood when he stood up here with his father, or when he brought his daughter to see the lake when she was only a child. He listens to the revelers below, celebrating their independence and statehood. But how could the joy of victory feel so disturbing and foreign? The old mare snorts and shakes her mane, causing him to open his eyes again. He looks to the festivities below. The huge fire at the shoreline burns like a nucleus, warming an orbit of dancing members.

"Okay," he whispers, signaling the pony to begin walking down toward the village.

Mary looks up to see Papa Leo disappear over the ridge line above them, while she nurses little Migisi. She and Kate sit together at one of the tables surrounding the fire.

"It's like a thousand years have passed since that day you first picked me up at the airport," Kate recalls as she admires the cherub in Mary's arms.

"What are your plans now?" Mary asks.

"Probably go back to New York, maybe even D.C. to start a practice," Kate says. Their eyes turn toward the yelps of children to find Lightfoot being chased by a band relentless kids, who manage to tackle him to the ground. "William offered to start a firm, I'm sure you know," Kate says. Mary nods her head, familiar with the offer. "I mean, that sounds really great and the idea of specializing in tribal law is really interesting," Kate continues before turning back to Mary with a lack of certainty in her eye. "I don't know," Kate admits. They turn to watch the band of kids grab at Lightfoot as he frees himself momentarily from their clutches, no sooner to be pulled back to the ground. They pile on him in maniacal laughter. Mary catches sight of Papa Leo riding back into the village.

"Good, he's back," Mary says. She slips her shirt back over her left shoulder. "Where's Tyler?" Mary asks. Kate points over Mary's shoulder toward the shore, where Tyler tries to learn a traditional dance from the three old Loon sisters. "Do me a favor, can you and he come to the ceremony circle in a couple minutes?" Mary asks.

"Uh, sure," Kate agrees as Mary stands with the child in her arms.

"I'll meet you there," Mary says, relishing the curiosity in Kate's eyes.

"Why, what's up?" Kate asks. But Mary just smiles and walks off to meet up with her dad. Kate shrugs and goes to extract Tyler from the sisters.

"Papa," Mary calls to her father.

"Ah, there's my little Eagle," he says.

"Papa Leo's back," Mary says. "Let's give out the names now." Harvey Bearheart wags a finger in the air, reminded of the schedule. He lumbers off to gather the medicine woman from her perch beside the fire.

"Old woman, it's time to honor our guests," Harvey Bearheart says, extending his hand to help her up. The partying members notice as well, having been prepped for tonight's event. He raises his arm in the air and motions for all the members to join him at the spot in the circle. The rest of the clan recognize the call to action and begin to gather their children and take their place around Harvey Bearheart and the medicine woman in the circle. Kate finally arrives with Tyler in tow, and now even more confused as everyone gathers around them.

"What's going on," Tyler asks but Kate tilts her head and pulls a thin smile in total confusion. Lightfoot looks up from under the pile of giggling children, catching sight of Mary motioning for him toward Kate and Tyler.

Papa Leo joins them at the circle when finally Lightfoot limps in, with a six-year old boy wrapped around his calf like a koala bear on a eucalyptus tree.

"Uh, Oh!" Kate says, as the old woman turns to face her and Tyler. Lightfoot starts the proceedings, with the six year old still clutching his leg and resting on his boot.

"Tonight, we take this time to honor our brother and sister who have honored us with their kindness and concern," Lightfoot says, smiling kindly at Kate and Tyler. "We've known them as our champions in battle and our neighbors in peace. Tonight, we welcome them as family, and offer this naming ceremony as our appreciation of all they've done." Lightfoot looks deep into Kate's eyes, "And all they've sacrificed on our behalf." Papa Leo nods to the old woman who has already started to burn tobacco and sage, waving her hand to waft her smoldering bundle around them. Kate and Tyler turn to each other, wondering where this is all headed. Stepping first to Kate, the old woman reaches for her hand and leads her to the center of the circle to stand beside her, facing the assembly. Lightfoot and Mary smile, savoring the surprise on Kate's face as the healer continues.

"Today, we give you a name," the medicine woman declares. "A name that our spirits from the four winds have given us, on your behalf." She holds up a small token in her hand, the leather cord dangling in a loop and then places the leather lanyard around Kate's neck. The stone token rests on her chest. "Misko-waagosh, misko-waagosh, misko-waagosh, misko-waagosh," the medicine woman says, while turning her head to each of the four directions, north, south, east and west. "Today you are named *Red Fox*, misko-waagosh," then places her palm over her chest, covering the charm.

"Misko-Waagosh!" Kate exclaims. "I can't believe this. This is so beautiful," she says, while offering a charmed grimace to Tyler. "I'm a Red Fox."

"You got that right, sister," Tyler asserts, causing the assembly to erupt into laughter. Next, the medicine woman moves to Tyler and repeats the procedure to all four directions.

"Agim-doonoo, agim-doonoo, agim-doonoo,

agim-doonoo," she utters to the four winds, again placing the token around his neck and cupping her palm on his chest, as if to sink the name into his heart. "Today you are named, *Counting Bull*." Tyler is so overwhelmed, he looks to Lightfoot in disbelief.

"Dude, that's so fucking cool," he says, before catching himself, but not before the medicine woman grits her teeth. "I mean that's so cool," Tyler corrects himself. This time the tribe roars to the old woman's chagrin.

"Hail, Professor Counting Bull!" Amik shouts with a launch of his fist in the air. Everyone applauds and again, the music resumes. Tyler turns to Kate and lifts his bull token and touches its nose to the red fox dangling on her chest. In a fit of the moment, he kisses Kate then again full tilt as she wraps her arms around him. Cheers rise soundly into the sky with the smoke from the raging fire and sage.

"I feel like I just got married," Kate says, when suddenly she realizes the weight of that statement. "Oh my god, did I just say that out loud?" Lightfoot steps to the center of the circle and places each arm around Kate and Tyler's shoulder, then turns to face the tribe.

"Our independence is now real. But we all need to remember that this doesn't set us apart from other tribes. We've been given a gift – but also an enormous responsibility lies ahead of us. One that soon will extend beyond our clan as we choose to share our blessings with all original peoples across this continent," Lightfoot declares. "We are the RTP, and this is how we roll," he says, removing Tyler's beer from his hand and lifting it into the air. But tonight... we party!" The entire tribe goes ape-shit crazy with glee and launches into a night of dancing, singing and celebration.

EIGHTEEN

"Ondizi"

(Inherits from a certain source)

Mary walks into the bedroom, stopping for a moment to absorb the comical sight of Lightfoot, fully dressed and passed out across the top of the bed. Outside, the occasional hoot from a partying straggler along the shoreline pulls a giggle from her throat. She listens to the rhythm of spring crickets as if for the first time, wondering how long they've been sounding off without her stopping long enough to notice. Mary sits on the end of the bed, loosens the laces of his boots and pulls them from his limp feet. She slides the bedspread over him and leaves the room.

Poking her head into the baby's room, Mary checks the little girl sleeping peacefully, cuddled in blankets and occasionally thrusting her mini fist in the air with a gentle coo. Mary straightens the child's eagle token which hangs over the headboard of her crib, protecting and guiding her little dreams. The little girl relaxes again into quiet slumber. With her family asleep, Mary takes her insomnia into the quiet living room, lit only by a receding fire. She cuddles into the cushions of the couch, turns on the TV and flips through channels to catch a glimpse of the complicated world. Mary stops at a news program when the segment tagline catches her eye.

On screen, the title *A NATION IS BORN*, banners across the screen, while one of those peripheral news readers allowed to host in the wee hours of the night anxiously delivers her report.

"The Red Rock Chippewa tribe, made famous from the discovery of a rare fuel element on reservation land, has now been recognized by the United Nations General Assembly as an independent member state. How such a ruling will play out in the top tiers of American government is yet to be seen?" the junior news woman says, segueing into controversy. *"But what does this say about Native American sovereignty in general? Already, the ruling is stirring protests by other, less fortunate tribes throughout North America. With us today is director of Indigenous Studies at Stanford University, Mark Carroll."* The anchor pivots to her guest. *"Professor, thank you for being here. Let me start by asking the simple question - why only this tribe?"* The professor barely forms a sound before he's quickly cut off by the bait casting host. *"I mean, what kind of message does this send – that only the*

384

rich and powerful have rights and less fortunate Indians, or Native Americans I should say, are left to suffer?" the news anchor adds.

Mary clicks the TV off and sits quietly, preferring to listen to the crickets.

❖   ❖   ❖

"I know Alex, but we banked on the GA following suit behind Australia and Canada in rejecting it," Baumgardener reminds her boss, Secretary of State, Alexander Biloxi. Alex rubs his eyes, avoiding the light of day for a brief moment. This emergency meeting has already gone on long enough to render everyone in the room weary and impatient and they are still waiting for the president to arrive. The secretary of state rotates toward a small pink man in his sixties sitting across the table.

"Where are we on this, Bob?" Alex asks Attorney General Robert Evans while still rubbing his closed eyelids.

"Dead to rights basically," the AG replies. "Red Rock won't acknowledge the Indian Affairs folks. The real problem is that every other tribe in the country is trying to do the same. Obviously Red Rock's legal team is well funded, the media is behind them and nearly every country on earth is relishing the opportunity to stick a finger in our eye over this."

The President of the United States enters with a couple nameless advisors in tow. He's a tall, exhausted looking man well into his second term. He sits down at the head of the table and places both palms on the desk. Without a word, he looks from one side of the table to the other. This is a tight-knit team, usually able to finish each other's statements or even answer a question long before it's asked. This morning, the communal silence speaks volumes. The president looks to the state department officials and flops his head into his palm while resting an elbow on the desk.

"Now what?" the president asks while exhaling across the table. Alex is the first to reply, his eyes reddened from lack of sleep and too much rubbing.

"Mr. President, I'm more concerned how our response will play with our allies – and our enemies, even more than how it plays here at home," Alex Biloxi says. "Red Rock is a done deal. They played this well, and frankly we didn't. And still, they've remained respectful and supportive of a continued alliance and we have millions of dollars in free fuel resource now. We need more. And whether we like it or not, we have to negotiate with them on a level with any other ally and possibly even craft a treaty commensurate with our other trading partners." But the president's impatience with stating the obvious is palpable.

"That pie is baked, I get it," the president confirms.

And there's a good chance we can craft the message to include a valued partnership with them, bla, bla, bla. Fine... but what bothers me is the floodgate now of every other tribe out there claiming their own independence and 'right' to ignore the BIA and try to negotiate new treaties directly with State," he says. The attorney general nods his head in complete agreement.

"We can never tolerate that!" the AG rapidly asserts. "The BIA was established for that very reason. Even if the U.N. never acknowledges another tribe, we can't allow the courts to be tied up with even moderately funded challenges even if only fueled by casino profits."

"You're just stating the problem again," the president says, while leaning back and looking at the ceiling. "I need ideas here!" the president laments. But, it's Baumgardener who seems to glow with insight at the moment. She leans forward, repeatedly lifting a couple fingers off the table as if she were tapping a backspace key.

"Mr. President, if I may?" Deputy Secretary Baumgardener asks.

"Hell yes Carolyn," the president exclaims.

"What if we ONLY negotiate with one entity?" Baumgardener asks. "What I mean is, we now have an official member state at the U.N. We also know that we have a hell of a lot more Security Council clout than we have *teeth* here at home." Baumgardener seems to be brewing the solution in real time. "What if we make all three-hundred-plus tribes in the U.S., the problem of the Red Rock *nation*?" The attorney general lights up as he hops on her train of thought.

"We call their bluff, yes," the AG says in epiphany. "You want independence, then join Red Rock. Let them fight your battles for you. Ohhh, I like it," he says. The president also grins that wide toothy smile that got him elected.

"Red Rock becomes the capitol, the arbitrator of all treaties," the president affirms, also running with the thread of thought. Even Alex is sitting a bit more upright, his eyes wildly washing the walls and ceiling with newly found insight.

"We essentially replace the Bureau of Indian Affairs, with the Red Rock nation. The weight alone of all that responsibility, both to the tribes and to the international body will trim any wild hairs", Alex declares.

"And you're right, we hold Red Rock - only one entity accountable for security, the president continues. "We look like human rights champions across the world, and hell... they're fucking rich as god... let them deal with the human welfare of all the tribes," the president says, while rising to pace the length of the room. "I like this. Baumgardener, great work!"

Alex proudly nudges Baumgardener in the arm, in a *kudos-to-you* gesture while the president continues to add the final touches to a policy he will eventually claim as his own.

"Yes, yes...YES!" the president shouts before stopping abruptly to sink some teeth into the implications. "But, we need a treaty that clearly defines what they can and can't do with their money. Just like any other nation we negotiate with. We guarantee their security and insist on a passive state," he insists.

"They're going to need a constitution too, that we can hold them to," the attorney general notes.

"Hell, we'll give them ours! Not like we've been using it lately," the president jokes while everyone's eyes in the room widen in horror at the bad taste.

"Let's pretend you didn't say that... Sir," Alex says, returning to the habit of rubbing his eyes, while this time hiding a chuckle.

❖　❖　❖

Tracking through binoculars, the stunning eagle-clad RTP jet touches down at Dulles airport.

"They're here," the aide says, lowering his field glasses. Deputy Secretary Baumgardener rubs her hands together warming her palms on this cold

D.C. morning, yet looking more like a mad scientist savoring the moment.

Eventually the RTP jet taxis to the private ramp near the reception spot, dignified with State limos and security.

From inside the plane, Kate watches the pomp assembled on the tarmac, as the plane settles before the delegation.

"Holy shit! They're really taking this seriously," she says. Papa Leo squints, not at all impressed with the reception outside.

"They want something," Papa Leo says instinctively. Kate notices the press corps nearby, their cameras tracking the plane to a stop.

"Well they sort of have to acknowledge us after the U.N. vote, I guess. If only from a P.R. standpoint," Kate says.

"No they're definitely are up to something," Papa Leo insists when he sees Baumgardener eagerly standing in the cold and blowing warm air into her cupped hands.

❖ ❖ ❖

Lightfoot, Kate and Papa Leo descend the flight stairs, to the greetings of the state department officials.

"Professor, and yes – Leo, it's a pleasure to see you, Sirs," Baumgardener gushes, while shaking their hands profusely. Papa Leo can't help from appearing dubious, allowing his hand to go for a ride of constant shaking by the toothy delegation.

"This is Kate Rose, our legal council," Lightfoot mentions.

"Yes, yes! Miss Rose, glad to meet you!" Baumgardener exclaims. "We have a lot to talk about," she says, now shaking Kate's hand and holding her elbow with the other. Papa Leo takes in the farce of such upper body aerobics.

❖   ❖   ❖

In contrast to their first 'unofficial' meeting in Baumgardener's office, this visit is being conducted in a grand conference room, on par with any visiting dignitary. Aides with notepads stand near the long conference table, well apportioned with refreshments along its length.

"On behalf of the State Department and the President of the United States, I'd like to congratulate you on your membership to the United Nations," Baumgardener says. Papa Leo's eyes pan the room dubiously. "Have a seat, please," she says with a motion of the hand to all in the room. She turns her focus to Lightfoot. "You look surprised," Baumgardener claims, while relishing the chance to set them off guard. "Let's be frank, Professor. It wasn't our first choice to have any territory, even a very small section of the border split off from the union. Essentially that's what's happened with U.N. recognition, you understand that I'm sure," the deputy secretary says, quickly leading into her rather meandering path of reasoning. "The United States appreciates your energy potential, and certainly your offer of cooperation in regards to the fuel element. God knows, the public relations mess we all found ourselves in was a nightmare, again - speaking frankly. But if full sovereignty is what you want, we feel compelled to agree with you," Baumgardener posits.

"Why?" Lightfoot asks as plainly as he can. Papa Leo prefers to study the room, considering with a single raised eyebrow, a tasteless historic painting on the wall of early white settlers.

"As allies, and now with established diplomatic relations, we do have our first official issue we need to address, between us," Baumgardener continues as Lightfoot simply nods for her to proceed. "Imagine the new position we find ourselves in. Here you, the Red Rock tribe, are the only ones who are fully independent of the United States' constitutional role as trustee of tribal lands." Baumgardener rises to her feet to walk the room as she presents her case. "Now imagine the blow back for both of us. That the only reason your plea has been heard is, if I may be so blunt

- is because you are wealthy. If we had a PR nightmare on our hands before you took your case to the U.N., you can imagine the appearance of hypocrisy we all face now, from the nation as a whole and from those bitter tribal members who can't 'buy their way' out of the current treaties?"

"What are you suggesting?" Kate asks. Baumgardener stops in her tracks and turns to the group in a dramatic pivot as if to say 'I thought you'd never ask'.

"Imagine this. We *essentially* abolish the Bureau of Indian Affairs and you, the Republic of Tribal Peoples become the capitol for all three hundred and ten recognized tribal nations." Papa Leo, lifts his head, if to catch the scent of an upwind fire. Kate flips a glance to Lightfoot, who himself looks as though he hadn't heard that correctly.

"The Capitol?", Lightfoot asks, hoping to confirm what certainly must've been stated as an allegory. Except Baumgardener sinks the concept into stone.

"Exactly! The Capitol! Of all the U.S. tribes who then become states as it were, of the RTP. We negotiate with one entity, directly through State and they, the tribes, obtain their oversight from your efforts as trustee of their wellbeing."

"What if our brothers and sisters refuse our 'oversight', as you call it?" Papa Leo asks.

"That's up to you," Baumgardener persists. "We're hoping you can frame it in such a way, to use your influence to win their, how do we say... *independence*. In fact, we'll play along to help sell that concept. Maybe fight back a little, to add a little drama and enhance the impression of your negotiating skills. You look like heroes and we, well... I think it's clear." Lightfoot looks at Papa Leo, thinking about the prophesy of Black Elk's vision now coming true before their eyes. Papa Leo tilts his head, not entirely surprised.

"Let's face it," the diplomat continues. "We're not the only ones with the PR headache here. Red Rock will only be resented if they don't share, and ignore the struggle of all indigenous people." But this time, the deputy secretary's presentation is clearly colored not by graciousness, but as any major superpower would muscle any other sovereign nation. This is a deal with no room for refusal. Baumgardener leans over to fiddle with a serving tray on the table and finds a pastry to her liking. She returns to her seat while relishing the sight of the pastry in her hand, as well as the strength of her position. "Mmmm, slightly bittersweet," she says while chomping down on the sugary treat. Papa Leo notes the irony with one of those tortured smiles that reflect good and bad at the same time. After all, when dealing with the white man, there will always be a demarcation.

NINETEEN

"Wayeshkad"

(Begin again)

The old horse stops at the edge of the ridge, while Papa Leo adjusts in the saddle, again settling into another morning of their ritual together. She plants her hooves at the cliff's edge into the same well-worn groves, like the familiar pair of slippers that have always waited for her there. She snorts two warm jets into the freezing air, punctuating their arrival at the lookout point. If she could speak, she still wouldn't bother. The old friends watch the coots peck at the shoreline below while a single loon pipes the same timeless note across the water.

Much has changed since Papa Leo began making this morning commute long ago. Today he sits firm in the saddle, adjusting in his stirrups and expanding his chest as the future fills his spirit like the chilled air entering his lungs. The mare follows his gaze as he focuses further down and past the shoreline. Lights are beginning to flicker off across the expanse of the college grounds and village center, while the old sun stretches its arms and pulls itself out of the water. The red hound barks at the roosters, and the belligerent ravens chase each other among a dozen massive cooling towers high above the trees.

Papa Leo exhales as he takes in the artistic sculpture of nature conscious architecture and technological advancements designed to honor mother earth, rather than challenge her sensibilities. He observes the terraced hillside and sparkling solar panels reflecting the low orange sun. He knows what independence means now. After all, he's old enough to remember losing it and has lived long enough to see it return.

❖ ❖ ❖

Papa Leo dismounts in front of a large but rustic cottage and ties off his horse at the hitching post out front. He slowly makes his way to the front porch.

From inside, a gentle knock on the door echoes off the roughhewn walls and hardwood floor.

"At least he's learned to knock," Lightfoot says before opening the door for his grandfather. The old man steps in and pulls his grandson into a quick hug, then makes a beeline for his great-granddaughter in Mary's arms. The little girl lights up and reaches out for her Papa Leo as he approaches, nearly jumping into his arms. Lightfoot pulls his favorite oiled cloth coat on and then places a wrap around Mary's shoulders.

"We'll be back by noon, Nimishoomis," Mary says, tenderly kissing the old man's cheek. But Papa Leo's interest is focused, his eyes fixated on the little girl's face as he taps her little nose gently with the tip of his leathered finger.

Migisi giggles at the sight of her big hero.

JON D. ANTHONY

EPILOGUE

"Fringe Elements"

"Enough already," Doctor Drummond bellows across the line of technicians in the underground test facility.

"We're just running the last checks," an exasperated lead engineer explains. But Drummond continues to complain.

"It's forty feet underground! Hell we were going to pound it from a collider in an office building before they chicken-shitted me here," he gripes. The lead engineer just looks forward, rather than entertain the futile act of responding to the grumbling old fart. The entry door buzzes and clicks open. The team at the consoles turn to acknowledge the test site director.

"Gentlemen, how we looking?" Director Tellis asks in a practiced voice that reverberates off the concrete walls. Drummond responds from over his shoulder.

"I thought you'd be observing from a 'safe distance' like, I don't know – Alaska?" Drummond jabs.

"Drummond, there's a reason for our procedures," Director Tellis expounds. "It's sure to react in a way we haven't seen yet." But Drummond wags his head as if to be saying 'yeah, yeah'.

"I'm months behind simply trying to obtain a low yield benchmark that can be used to approximate further tests," Drummond puts forth. "The sooner we get this done, the quicker we'll have the data to predict future yields. So, can we just get this going?" Drummond pleads mockingly. Director Tellis ignores the bully, instead focusing his attention on the technicians at the controls.

"You ready?" the director asks, deferring to his team and trying his best not to factor Drummond's badgering into the procedure.

"Yes sir," the lead engineer states affirmatively. Drummond sighs, nearly defeated with boredom. Director Tellis nods his approval to the lead engineer, who begins the countdown.

"Ten seconds to ignition, eight, seven, six," the lead engineer counts down, as the line of technicians monitor their screens. Drummond folds his arms, wishing they'd just press the damn button. "Five, four, three, two, one – ignition!"

With an explosive force exceeding any nuclear test this place has ever experienced, the entire facility is ripped to shreds, tearing all the occupants apart and consuming all matter in the cavernous underground facility.

Above ground, the surface formerly known as Area 51 and the Nuclear Test Site is completely and absolutely blasted off the face of the planet. A crater twenty miles in diameter is formed, as the surface of the desert crust is liquidated, imploding into the earth like a massive fallen cake. The blast is unimaginable, much too loud and fast to comprehend with our primitive senses. Ejecta scatters over a hundred square miles, followed by a growing darkness, broken only by the occasional reentry of glowing debris. Soon the entire scene is rendered in total darkness.

The End.

ACKNOWLEDGMENTS

The United Nations Permanent Forum on Indigenous Issues and specifically the *"Declaration on the Rights of Indigenous Peoples"* drafted in 2006 by the United Nations General Assembly.

Article 3 of that Declaration states:

"All indigenous peoples have the right of self-determination. By virtue of that right they freely determine their political status and freely pursue their economic, social, and cultural development."

W W W . L I G H T F O O T B O O K . C O M

For more information regarding various digital versions of this book, please visit the website above.

Special thanks to

Robert Scott Lazar
and
L. Wayne Alexander

Made in the USA
Columbia, SC
29 June 2017